FRACTURED

Journalist Peter Maguire has been kidnapped in Somalia's capital, Mogadishu. He does not know where he is or what is going to happen to him. As the days go by, his fear is shot through with remorse for the mistakes of his past . . . Peter's mother Nina comes to Somalia to wait for her son's release. His plight forces her to relive another trauma — the fatal shooting in Liberia of Shaun Ridge, a young photographer she once loved, and Peter's real father . . . Abdi, a Somali teenager working with Peter's captors, strikes up a tenuous friendship with the prisoner and decides to help him escape . . . Three people must journey into one of the world's most dangerous places, the human mind, to answer the question: are we ever truly free?

FRACTURED

CLÁR NÍ CHONGHAILE

LARGE
PRINT

First published in Great Britain 2016
by
Legend Press Ltd.

First Isis Edition
published 2016
by arrangement with
Legend Press Ltd.

A catalogue record for this book is available
from the British Library.

ISBN 978–1–78541–295–0 (hb)
ISBN 978–1–78541–301–8 (pb)

Published by
F. A. Thorpe (Publishing)
Anstey, Leicestershire

Set by Words & Graphics Ltd.
Anstey, Leicestershire
Printed and bound in Great Britain by
T. J. International Ltd., Padstow, Cornwall

This book is printed on acid-free paper

For David, Lucy and Rachel

CHAPTER
ONE

PETER

My name is Peter Maguire. That much I know. I don't know what day it is. Or where this room is. Or what time it is. I can hear those avian punks, the birds with the spiky tufts and long tails, yammering outside. It must be daytime. I can smell the outside; I can hear it; the low thrum of traffic and the shuffling of people overlain with the staccato rhythms of war. That other world that doesn't seem to notice I am no longer in it.

I don't know how long I've been here. The prickly mat beneath my cheek is black and green. My blanket is woven poverty, a brown-grey nothingness that says even colour is a luxury. These things I know because for the past few days, a thin teenager has brought me a bowl of greasy stew and a jug of tepid water. He comes in with a torch and waits for me to finish. He never speaks but he fills my mind. I need something to occupy my thoughts.

First, I hear his flip flops slapping towards me. Then a ten second pause when he puts the tin bowl and jug down and gets the keys. The clunk of the padlock being opened. Another pause. About five seconds this time. I imagine him bending down, picking up the bowl and jug, and then maybe shrugging his shoulders to nudge his AK-47 back into place. I spend a lot of time imagining what he does outside this room.

Once, a long time ago, or maybe not, I decided to run. I heard the flip flops and crouched down by the door. I waited until he lifted off the padlock, and then threw myself at the door. It gave and I thudded into the skinny teenager, my rage, desperation and throbbing fear acting like a force field. He collapsed, drops of spilt stew spattered around his screaming mouth, his torch rolling on the floor. I got about halfway up the corridor before they came. I think there were three. The memory is fractured like a Picasso painting: an out-of-place eye, a snarling mouth in a bearded face, a fist, the butt of a gun, blood on my T-shirt, a perfect drop falling and breaking.

The first blow was to the side of my head. I fell to my knees. Someone kicked me. They were screaming. I think I was too. I looked up. The skinny teenager was standing above me, his face still dripping. His hand shot out and he slapped me hard across the face.

They threw me back into the room. I woke to pain like passion. I don't know how long I lay on this mat. I could taste blood in my mouth. One eye wouldn't open. I wanted to stop breathing, just to stop the pain piercing my ribs. I tried to hold my breath. I thought I could kill myself by omission. They didn't feed me for two days. I didn't care. Despite my travels, my CV full of "danger zones", I had never been beaten like that. It broke me. And as I lay there, unable to move, I wondered what kind of man breaks after one beating.

2

A woman came to wash my wounds. She slipped into the room like a dream. A woman without footsteps tending a man without a shadow. Black eyes meeting mine over a breath-stirred veil as soft hands lifted a dirty cloth from a basin of cold water. This is a country of eyes. She bathed my face, stroked the cloth across my nose, let the cool water drip over the stubble on my chin. My tears ran into the dirty water. I shivered. When she was finished, she rose from her knees.

"Please, help me," I croaked.

I meant to whisper but I got the pitch wrong. It's strange how quickly you forget. In a film, she would have looked into my eyes, a potent connection would have been forged, defying convention and credence. But she didn't falter in her exit.

It's hard to say exactly when that happened. Time has lost its edges in here. What is an hour, a minute, even a day? I live by other measures. My life is determined by feeding, sleeping, the creak of a door, the thwack of a rubber sole on concrete. What does it matter when these things happen? They happen, and as long as they do, I am alive.

This tomb is made of rough bricks. They smell and taste dusty. I know because I licked them, just to do something new. There is no light here. I hear sounds, but from a distance, like shouts made unintelligible by a beachside breeze. Birds sometimes. Dogs barking. Raised voices, gruff and male. I have my blanket, the mat and a bucket to shit in. At first, I was on it for hours but my bowels have adjusted to this unlife. They have turned sluggish, like me.

In the early days or maybe hours, I shouted, banged the door, screamed and made that one attempt to escape. How long did that impulse, that ridiculous hope, last? Maybe a few days. My mother always said I had life too easy. I won't deny it. At least, I wouldn't have. Maybe all that good karma — the genes that gave me green eyes twinned with "Black Irish" cheekbones, those no-effort good grades, the shy smiles from fresh-skinned, naughty-eyed girls, the easy camaraderie with blustering boys — was being totted up and entered somewhere into life's ledger. Someone has decided my account is in the red and that it's time for me to pay the bill. It's as sensible a reason as any I can think of for winding up in a dark hut somewhere in Somalia.

Today was different. The teenager came with my stew and water. I was sleeping, although sleep is not really the right word for what happens in here. Out there, sleep is an option, a respite, a conscious act. Here it is none of those things. My dreams are more real than the nothingness around me. I have eaten butter chicken again with Michelle in that poky restaurant in Paris where the sweat-seared, hand-wringing manager served us lemony liquor in china thimbles with pornographic pictures inside. I have walked again from my apartment, along the stinky, silvered canal to Place de la République. I have swum again in the roiling waves off Monrovia. I have kissed, caressed, stroked, made love. Not just to Michelle. I have also felt Esther's shea-butter smoothness and watched her apple cheeks swelling as I entered her.

4

And all the girls before. Sometimes, they come into my dreams fully formed, their speech and habits perfect, as though my brain is reveling in this new, absolute power. Sometimes, they are composites and I wonder vaguely whose hair is sweeping over my face, making my whole body tingle.

The teenager must have been watching me for a while. I squinted into the torchlight, hauling myself onto my elbow and then pushing back to lean against the wall behind me. I like sleeping beside the wall, as far away as possible from the centre of the room. I always sleep on the edge of my bed. Always used to. Ready to flee, Michelle used to joke.

I ate my stew, burning my mouth. I welcomed the pain. The food isn't always hot and the blisters give me something to focus on between visits. I'm a casual eater, and have never been very good at identifying different meats, but this had the chewiness and mildly beefy taste of camel. I chewed rapidly and swallowed thankfully. My taste buds have also adapted to this new reality.

I used to wonder how the AMISOM peacekeepers posted here managed to stomach camel meat. Once, during a previous trip, I went to an AMISOM forward base on the road from Mogadishu to Afgoye, and three Burundian soldiers invited me to share their meal, offering a big tin bowl with wide smiles and frantic nods, as if they were afraid they might change their minds if I hesitated too long. I ate with them, crouched low in the meagre shade of a thorny bush, surrounded by yellow jerry cans, bat-sized cacti and bulging sandbags. Their khaki tents crouched low among the scrubs and bushes that stippled the sand.

On the way back to our armoured car, a Ugandan officer took me to a perfume factory that Al-Shabaab had been building before they were driven out a few months before. One room was full of sacks of dried limes, sharp-smelling brown balls that also covered the floor. I scooped one up, sniffed it, and put it in my pocket — Michelle would love it.

"They were building factories and markets," the urbane commander told me. "They were here to stay. Unfortunately, they were on the wrong side of history."

And now so am I.

The teenager watched me carefully, his almond-shaped eyes narrowed below arching eyebrows that seemed tasked with providing the perfect frame for the picture below. A thin beard perched uneasily on his chin. Can I get out? Not by the hairs on my chinny-chin-chin. Maybe I can huff and puff and blow this place down. Blow myself back to Paris, or Monrovia, or even just as far as Mogadishu. Assuming I am not actually there. Or that there is not here.

When I had licked my fingers with their black nails and red knuckles, fingers I don't even recognise anymore, I sat back, waiting for the teenager to leave. I did not expect him to speak. His head was still tilted as if he found me mildly amusing. He reached into the pocket of his shapeless black trousers and pulled out a packet of cigarettes and a lighter. He removed a cigarette, holding it the wrong way round for an instant before spinning it and placing it between his lips. The

6

lighter clicked and the acrid smell of cheap tobacco filled the room. I sucked his exhaled smoke through my nose, my eyes closed. I felt giddy already.

When I opened my eyes, the teenager was holding the packet towards me. I grabbed at it with both hands. He frowned, pulled it back and took one out, handing it to me with his long, bony fingers. The cigarette stuck to my dry lips as I dragged deep, tearing the skin when I removed it. I didn't care. I was as happy as I had been for days. Who cared where I was? What about the future? All I knew was that I had a cigarette. A silent teenager had given me a cigarette. Someone had noticed me.

They moved me the following day. Four men with black scarves tight around their heads and loose across their faces, came into my room and pulled me from the corner where I had crab-crawled when I heard them in the corridor. They hauled me to my feet and pushed me out the door. I was terrified, the trembling that had subsided a little came back. I wanted to say something. I felt it was important to say something but I was petrified. I didn't want to be beaten again. I didn't want to die.

They looked like men who shoot as others breathe. It's not as absurd as it sounds. I have seen many such men. And women, and children. The children are the worst. Before I started working in conflict zones, trying to interest an over-stimulated, addled readership in wars too complex to condense, I thought you could reason your way out of anything. I had a journalist's misplaced belief in the power of words. But I am wiser now having seen too many young-old faces at roadblocks, cold, bleary eyes staring above the barrel of a gun gripped in steady hands. You know you are in trouble when these kids laugh. It's a chilling sound — the insane giggle of a child high on drugs, with nothing to live for except the moment.

The guys propelling me down an uneven corridor towards a sliver of light were a little different though. Just as Somalia was different from almost anywhere I had ever been. The skinny teenager wasn't with them. I felt unreasonably bereft.

"Stop!" A hand grabbed the loose robe that flapped around my knees. Cold, hard fingers spun me and a scratchy sack stinking of garlic was pulled over my head. They turned me around again. I remembered playing blind's man bluff with my cousins on an arrow-shaped peninsula south of Kinsale in Ireland. I had hated the blindfold, but the worst part was being spun around and around, rough fingers on my shoulders and my waist, grassy tussocks making me stumble, my strangely accented whimperings tossed on the wind and jeered into pieces by the older, tougher boys.

Then I was outside. Light filtered through the tight weave hanging over my nose and being sucked into my mouth. I tried to breathe more carefully. After the dark of my tomb, even the filtered brightness hurt. I squeezed my eyes shut, grateful for the sack. I heard an engine, and below, like a baseline, feet on sand and other cars, seagulls and the faint sound of a muezzin, calling from a minaret.

I was lifted into the back of a truck. Someone shouted at me and I was pushed to the floor. I was on my knees, my head bowed, my stomach turning as I inhaled the chemical fumes of an ancient exhaust. Someone kicked me between the shoulders. I could feel boots on my back, on my legs. I tried to stay alert, to notice the smells and sounds as I had been taught in my hostile environment course. After the instructors "kidnapped" us as we drove down a gravel lane just yards from the ivy-covered manor where we ate curries, drank in a too-twee bar, and slept in four-poster beds, they praised me for behaving so calmly, describing me as "a cool customer". Pride before a hell of a fall.

Here, all I noticed was my breathing — stupidly fast despite my efforts to calm down — and the thudding in my head. I have no idea how far we travelled. I didn't notice any smells or any sounds beyond the thundering of the engine and the crunching of the wheels. I pushed into the steel floor, making myself as small as I could, trying to disappear, trying to forget the boots on my shoulders, ribs and the backs of my knees.

We stopped. My ears rang after lying on the floor for what seemed like hours but could have been as little as fifteen minutes. Everything has that dreamlike quality here. As if the regular rules of time, space and distance no longer apply. Welcome to Somalia, leave your measurements at the door. I felt sick and hoped I wouldn't throw up in the sack. It's odd how we cling to the little trappings of normalcy. What did it matter if I puked in the sack? I was probably about to be shot, or worse.

I was pulled out and thrown to the ground, a sack of bones, flesh and fear. I wondered if I should lie down again but no one kicked me. The sun hammered my head. Just as it battered Meursault in *L'Étranger*.

I have been thinking about that book a lot. I studied Camus in my pretentious, problem-riddled high school in Paris, and I was fascinated by Meursault's absurd "four short knocks on the door of misery". Meursault killed time in prison by listing everything in his apartment. He said a man who had only lived one day could live for hundred years in prison, passing time by reliving the surroundings and events of those twenty-four hours.

It was all about killing time. My fourteen-year-old self underlined that phrase, but I didn't really understand it. I thought it spoke to my boredom in class.

In this place, I have tried Meursault's prison survival plan, but I am not focused enough to pull it off. Or maybe it is the fear of dying. This dread, lying like a snake in my stomach, makes rational thought impossible. Or maybe the problem is that I don't want to spend too much time thinking about my life. Until I was taken, I excelled in avoiding self-reflection. My former girlfriends all agreed on that.

They weren't wrong about my failings. But they were wrong in attributing them to an inability to express my emotions. It has always been deliberate. I prefer to live life one day at a time, in the now. My personal self-help programme to avoid the past.

My captors pushed me into the shade. Someone snatched the sack off my head. Fresh air flooding my lungs, light exploding in front of my squeezed eyes. Nothing but sensation, overwhelming in its physicality.

When I finally opened my eyes, I found myself looking into another half-covered face, but these eyes were new. They looked at me for a long while. Then a hand came out from under a blue robe, and pulled back the red-checked scarf. A beaky nose over thin lips, hollow cheeks making me think of the fish faces my father used to pull to stop me crying when I was a child. *Don't think of that now.*

"Peter Maguire, this is your new home."

The voice was hoarse, the English halting but accurate, although he stumbled over my surname, giving it an Arabic cadence. Maquir, perhaps.

We were standing under a spindly acacia tree in a small compound. There were three houses, simple mud-plastered wood structures with corrugated iron roofs. A brick shed in a corner near the heavy iron gate looked new and raw. Chickens pecked the hard ground around a tilting blue truck, which was missing its headlamps, radiator and half the windscreen. I couldn't see beyond the high walls, which were topped with shards of coloured glass. The sky was flawlessly blue and unforgiving.

The four boot-men stood behind me, guns at their sides but hands on the barrels.

"I prefer my old home," I said, turning back to the head guy. My attempt at sarcasm sounded pathetic.

He smiled, an awkward slash that had little to do with mirth.

"You belong to us now," he said. "This will be your home until we decide otherwise."

A glimmer of hope flared in my brain, so strong I feared they might see a cartoon lightbulb flashing above my head. I struggled to stifle it. This guy did not sound like an Al-Shabaab leader. Besides, I was still alive. I was not being beaten or tortured. If he belonged to Al-Shabaab, he would not be talking politely to an infidel, a *kaffir*, a Western journalist. Al-Shabaab would drag me to a dank room, seat me in front of a cheap video camera and film me begging the powers that be to free their brothers, withdraw African troops from Somalia, and let them turn this land into a country-sized, Taliban-style prison. I had seen these videos from Somalia and elsewhere. I wanted to look away, to turn from this humiliation, but the desperate eyes always seem to beg the viewer to stay. As if witnesses, even virtual, could somehow prevent the worst.

"I'm at a disadvantage here," I said slowly, savouring this opportunity to speak. "You know me, but who are you?"

Brown, khat-stained teeth flashed again as his face split into what passed for his smile.

"You are not a journalist now. No more questions," he said. "That part of your time here in Somalia is over."

He nodded his head to one of the yes-men and I was prodded across the dusty yard to the brick shed, scattering the chickens. My guard pushed me inside, as though I had any resistance left, or anywhere else to go. I almost laughed at this clichéd gesture. Sometimes, I think we have all watched so many movies that we have no originality left. We mimic the screen, while we think it mimics us. He locked the door and left me to my trivial thoughts.

In this new room, I have a little light from a small, square hole high up in the back wall, a glassless, barred window on the shrunken world. At night, when moonlight shines through the thick bars, this hole looks like the mouth of a fiendish spirit. It leers at me, filling my dreams with horror until I wake, drenched in sweat but shivering in the night chill. For a moment, I am terrified, until I realise it was a dream, then I remember reality, and I am terrified again.

I have a mattress now. Thin, stained and itchy. The same blanket. Another bucket. And another mat on a bare concrete floor in front of a wooden door shot through with rusty studs. The dust and the mosquitoes torment me but it is a small price to pay for the light.

I am trying to structure my days. If I cannot control my fate, I can at least put my mark on what happens inside these four walls. When the sun sends its delicious rays through my devil's mouth, I turn to the light and lie on my bed for a while. This is my time to think of my parents, of Paris, my school friends, my cousins. I actively recreate each person, quizzing myself on exact hair colour, shape of eyes. I pretend I have to write a character sketch of each individual. I think of good times and bad times. I tally my findings.

And I think of Michelle. Of what she must be feeling now. I am putting her through so much, and this is only the tip of the iceberg. If I am killed, it will be but the beginning of my betrayal. I do not, I cannot dwell on this. When I think of Michelle, I must acknowledge what she does not know, all of it, and these thoughts flay my mind. When I can no longer stand it — and this is another betrayal, I know — I move to the red mat and sit cross-legged.

This is where I think of my situation. In my mind, it's really My Situation. I prefer to think of it in capitals, like a crosshead, one of those partial headlines that journalists use ostensibly to keep our readers going beyond the first four paragraphs, but mainly to help our editors get through the article. If what is happening is but a crosshead, then surely it must end so that we can progress to the next section. My Release? My Recovery? Or, in my more gloomy moments, I think, My Death.

After sitting on the mat for a while, I do some exercises. Push-ups, squats and some jogging on the spot. I have always hated exercise, and I am too floppy for a 30-year-old, although my height makes me look slender. It's another optical illusion. You see a handsome man and you think he is an interesting man, a man with something to say. Isn't it what we do all the time? Don't good-looking people always benefit from a beauty handicap when they speak? Their every utterance sounds more weighty, more captivating. We mistake our eyes for our ears. Like I said, an optical illusion.

These daily exercises take a long time. But time is the one thing I have a lot of right now. That's the irony. I have hour after hour of inactivity and endless thought until I feel like I am going mad. But always the fear, the fear that someone, somewhere, has a pair of scissors poised over the fabric of my existence.

A little later, my food comes. The skinny teenager brings it. He is back, like a guardian angel. Or a talisman. Now we talk a little. It happened on my second day here. I finished my stew, mopping the greasy dregs with hard, mouldy bread, and he offered me a cigarette again. I didn't speak while I smoked. I needed to feel each puff. My daily smoke makes me high now. The way your first cigarette makes you wonderfully sick to your stomach and delightfully giddy. A guilt-and-nicotine rush.

Maybe it was the nicotine racing through my blood that dared me to speak after I had crushed the miniscule butt on the concrete floor.

"Thank you," I said. "*Mahadsanid.*"

His eyes remained fixed on mine. He shifted his feet, large and knobbly and coated with dust. He wore cheap red flip flops. He was sitting on the mattress, his gun across his legs.

"What is your name, friend?" I asked. I didn't really expect him to answer. He probably didn't speak English.

"Abdi, my name is Abdi."

He picked up the tin bowl and the spoon and left.

Abdi? Many of the men I met over the years in Somalia called themselves Abdi. If I were Somali, and brave or foolhardy enough to talk to a foreign journalist, I would probably call myself Abdi.

Last time I visited, I asked Guled about this. He had been my paper's fixer and occasional stringer for three years, and at fifty-five was a tough, cautious survivor, who found humour in the blackest of situations.

Guled smiled. He always smiled, whatever I asked him. A smile did not necessarily mean he knew the answer. Neither did it necessarily mean he was amused.

"Abdi means servant. It is a very common name here, very common," he said, chuckling and flicking ash from his cigarette out of the car window as he drove at breakneck speed through Mogadishu's "green zone", the few blocks of deconstructed buildings held by the transitional government and the AMISOM peacekeepers at the time. I was on my way to interview the minister for information and was hunkered low in the back seat.

I could see Guled's eyes in the rear-view mirror. One cloudy, one clear. He had cataracts and could barely see out of his right eye.

"But do you think it's always the person's real name?" I persisted.

He laughed uproariously, tipping his head back so that all I saw was the henna-orange beard covering his chin and the wrinkles on his neck.

"Ah, Peter. What do I always tell you? Never trust a Somali. We cannot be trusted."

His shoulders shook.

"And what is a name, my friend? I would still be your friend whether my name was Guled or Abdi. Maybe my name is Omar. What do you care? If I am your friend, I am your friend. At least as long as I want to be. If I am not your friend, the question of my name is irrelevant."

I laughed with him.

Guled was my friend. He trusted me as much as he trusted anyone. He didn't see that I was a human vortex, sucking lives and hopes and dreams into my own personal void. What does it mean to be the friend of a man who cannot care, or who will not care? One day I will ask the others. For Guled, I will never know, but I bet he would have answered with a laugh.

CHAPTER
TWO

PETER

This is what happened. This is my mind-movie and it plays on a loop in this dark, cinema cell. I came to Somalia on July 23rd. A lot of journalists don't travel here — it's too dangerous, too expensive, and really who cares? But the *International Post* is based in Washington, and Somalia was hot then because of the links between Al-Shabaab and Al-Qaeda. Congress was about to hold another hearing on the radicalisation of American Muslims, and Somalia was hovering near the top of the domestic policy agenda. A rarity.

"I want a solid piece on what this is about, today. Why are these young guys going? Where exactly are they going? And who is paying them?" Don Struddle, the *Post*'s foreign editor, barked down the phone from the paper's offices in a dour brown-and-cream building overlooking McPherson Square on 15th Street.

Don is a thirty-year veteran of the news-today-fishwrapper-tomorrow world. He is spherical, balding, bearded and red-faced from his whiskey nipping. His fuse is as short as his sentences.

"The Homeland Security Committee is going to zero in on Al-Shabaab at the end of the month. I want a solid piece before that. No expense spared."

He permitted himself a chuckle.

"I say that, but remember this is a dying industry."

"It's not going to be easy, Don," I said, thinking mournfully of the hassle involved in getting into Mogadishu. It's not that I didn't want to go on another trip, but this was no walk-in-the-park assignment, and I wanted to be sure my editor understood that. I've found that diminishing expectations is key to delivering acceptable results.

"I get it," he said rapidly, like a man running out of time, or more likely patience.

"I'm not asking for the moon. Do your best. Be careful. But get me something meaty. And play up the terrorism angle. If Al-Shabaab wasn't chopping off hands and feet, banning football, bras and samosas shaped like the Holy Trinity, plus threatening global jihad, this would just be another African basket case. I need you to tell us why we care."

"It's going to be pretty complicated for your average reader," I cautioned.

"There's way more going on than just bad guys versus good guys. You've got your warlords, your venal politicians and your aid-swiping militias. Somalia is a witch's cauldron — think of anything that can complicate life in a country, throw it in, and stir it around."

I paused because I could see Michelle chopping tomatoes. I could tell she was listening, and not happily. I shrugged my shoulders apologetically in the general direction of her furrowed brow, and left our "bijou" kitchen. For Don, the pause was as good as an invitation.

"I may be old but I'm not stupid, Peter. I know it's your patch but I read the wires too. I get all that. But the paper cares today because of domestic politics. Keep that in mind."

From across the Atlantic, I could hear his heavy breathing. I knew he wasn't worked up. That was just how Don always breathed, as if he was offended that he had to, as if it was an imposition on his precious time.

"And give me some solutions. I don't want another whiny piece about how desperate it is. I know the food situation is dire. They're even starting to mention the F-word. But get me some answers on what needs to be done. Throw it forward."

"Forwards or backwards, it's always about money, Don," I said. Now that I was out of range of Michelle's silent rage, I was getting into my stride and enjoying the chance to pontificate on a subject I had studied for months.

"Why are so many young kids joining Al-Shabaab, both locals and foreigners? Yes, some of them are kidnapped or coerced, but that's not the whole story. The name Al-Shabaab might mean 'the youth' but the hard core's perverted version of Islam has nothing to do with the joy of youth. It's all about control, power and money. Always money."

Don laughed.

"Preaching to the converted, Peter. Save it for the paper. I know you get it. Now go get me the story. Good lad."

Don hung up, leaving me fired up and smiling. He's a clever operator. No wonder my mother liked him. She had known him in the field. I could only imagine what Don's passion was like then, when he took on stories face-to-face before he was promoted to long-distance nannying.

Michelle *was* furious. We were supposed to go away the following weekend to the Loire Valley. She had spent weeks searching for the perfect hotel, finally booking an overpriced, over-chintzed room with an elaborate four-poster bed.

She had taken the Friday off work and I had agreed reluctantly. Sure, it would be fun, and the Loire Valley is stunning in an over-the-top, Louis XIVth way, but it seemed like a lot of hard work, and hard cash, essentially for something I could get at home.

"I'm sorry," I said, reaching out to hug her. She stepped back, shaking her head.

"You know how it is. I can't say no. This is my job, Michelle."

She didn't bother answering, and she didn't speak much over the next few days. There was nothing to say. When the taxi hooted in the pre-dawn dark on the day I left Paris, her kiss was closed, dry and abrupt. I didn't blame her, but neither did I blame myself.

By the time I got to Charles de Gaulle airport, slaloming through a freakishly heavy summer downpour, I was already gone from her, or rather she had been swirled down a time tunnel to the limbo-land where I store my erratic personal life while on assignment. She was no longer on my mind. I boarded the flight to London where I would catch a connection to Nairobi. My biggest worry was that the rain might delay the plane.

Sitting here now, I don't blame Don. I knew the risks. Most journalists travel into Somalia with the African Union peacekeepers. There's a misnomer. There's no peace to keep, and the underpaid, ill-equipped Burundians and Ugandans who make up most of the force would not be the ones to keep it if there were. Instead, they hole up at the airport and around the presidential palace, trying to keep the transitional government safe, lobbing the occasional mortar towards Al-Shabaab and obliterating civilians along the way. Collateral damage is a whole class of people in Mogadishu, a ghost town where young, red-eyed, angry zombies spook the streets.

As I stood smoking outside Heathrow's Terminal Four, I remembered my first visit to Somalia two years ago. Then I sped through the streets in a Casspir, one of the armoured personnel carriers used by the peacekeepers. The plastic seat coverings were ripped and the felt on the underside of the ceiling was coming off, but there was a dried yellow flower hanging beside the windscreen. Behind me, two red-eyed jittery gunners stood on the seats, their heads and shoulders rising out of the roof hatch as they swept the streets with machine guns.

We rushed to the frontline between the Al-Shabaab-controlled south of the city and the government-run mini-state. We ran along abandoned trenches, occasionally spotting the covered heads of the rebel fighters just yards away. We ducked behind walls peppered with bullet holes.

When they called my flight, I picked up my computer bag with a sigh. I was anxious, but also eager to be back in that *Boy's Own* world where every emotion was heightened, where even boredom had an edge.

This time I didn't want to have anything to do with AMISOM. I don't like people looking over my shoulder and I don't like going where I'm told, even in Somalia. It might smack of arrogance, and maybe there is a bit of that, but I prefer to call it being professionally savvy. I couldn't do this story with a babysitter. It wasn't my first time in Mogadishu and I felt like I knew the city, or the bits of it that I had been permitted to see. Guled would see me safe and I knew too that he, like all Somalis, had friends with guns. As long as I was willing to pay, it should all be fine. As I headed to the gate, I nervously tapped the bundle of dollars inside my jacket.

It was dark when we landed in Nairobi, a schizophrenic city locked in an erratic orbit between the gutter and the stars. I lived in the Kenyan capital for six months after getting my journalism degree from City University in 2002. I scraped a living from small-fry freelancing and kept hunger at bay by drinking a lot of Tusker, my beer of choice. I lived in a seedy hostel that reeked of cooked cabbage and mould, smoked cheap *bhang* on the roof, and had uncomplicated sex with curvy Kenyans who knew what they were doing, and earnest aid workers who didn't, in bed or out.

I still knew a few people from those iridescent days, and from more sober work trips since, and I decided to risk rush-hour mayhem to see them. Over mojitos at the Havana bar in brassy, sassy Westlands, we distilled the years into snappy stories, and then spilled onto the throbbing street to smoke and watch the city's beautiful people: girls in preposterously high heels and sequined, low-cut tops, stepping delicately around taxis and puddles, shouting in sheng to men swaggering in chinos and untied trainers, mobile phones at the ready.

Next day, I drove through the city before the sun's rays brought the daily gridlock to life, and caught a small plane from Wilson Airport to Mogadishu. We flew in over the limpid, deceitful Indian Ocean, and dived sharply onto the pitted tarmac. Outside, the air remoulded our features, sheening them with sweat as the wind cheekily tugged at the scarves the women on my flight had hastily pulled over their hair.

The crashing of the waves filled my ears, making thought impossible. The squat airport building sat low in the heat, as if reluctant to be here. Clustered outside were men in loud shirts and louder sunglasses. There was backslapping, handshakes and loud bellows of laughter. You'll find the same characters everywhere, but in Mogadishu, there is something extra. Inside the terminal, AMISOM troops in full battle gear watched the doors, the stone in their faces reflected in the way they held their sub-machine guns.

24

Guled was leaning against the hood of his brown Toyota Corolla outside the terminal's main gate. When he saw me, he straightened slowly, threw down his cigarette, and came forward, arms outstretched. A laugh ran before him like an unruly page boy.

"*Salaam alaikum*, Peter. You can't stay away. Good to see you, man!"

"*Salaam alaikum*, Guled. How are you? How is the family?"

"They are well, surviving," he said, taking my bag and throwing it into the boot. He laughed again.

"Come on, let's not talk here."

I got into the back of the car. Guled had hired some armed men for the journey to his home. We would travel down Maka al Mukarama, an uneasy trip along a stretch of fragmented tarmac. The road ran from the airport to the presidential palace and it was the government's lifeline, its link to the planes that could get the elite out of Somalia and into the relative safety and sanity of Nairobi.

One of the guards, a pockmarked teenager with bird-like hands, sat in the back with me. The other sat beside Guled. They put their guns between their knees and hunched forward, eyes glued to the road. The teenager had a mole on his neck and a pistol in his belt. He nodded at me, but did not speak. The older one muttered a few words in Somali to Guled, who raised his eyebrows skeptically. I was nervous and alert, but not scared. I trusted Guled, and I knew he would have hired reliable men from his clan.

Everything in Somalia revolves around the clans. It's the most intractable element of the seemingly endless conflict, and the one that is most inaccessible to me. I simply cannot understand these ties that go back generations, that are revered above and beyond the realities of today. What does clan matter when the whole country is burning? I know that's simplistic. I know that question doesn't do me, or the story, justice. But deep down, when the more sensitive quotes are written up, and my articles have been finely balanced and subbed for political correctness, deep down this is what I think.

Guled lived in a government-controlled area close to the presidential palace. His house was a quiet place of dusty carpets, a few pieces of life-laden furniture, and the comforting aromas that said a woman was around. When Michelle moved into my flat in Paris two years ago, she brought those smells with her. A faint whiff of perfume, a hint of unknowable creams with mysterious functions, soft scents, the essence of woman.

Guled's wife, Aisha, came from the kitchen to greet us, wiping her hands on her robe before adjusting her yellow headscarf to hide, momentarily, the girlish smile that sat amid the crow's feet and wrinkles. It was khat time, and Guled sank to the floor, with his back to the wall in the dining room. I joined him. I like khat. It is the perfect drug for a new arrival in Somalia. At first, you feel euphoric, you delight in your crystal-clear mind, even the conflict seems logical. But later, this joy evaporates and depression sets in. You get cranky. Fantasy with a reality-check kicker.

We chewed and spat the streams of brown juice into Guled's silver spittoon.

"It's much worse than the last time you came," he said, finally.

"Nobody expects the government to last much longer. Not that that's all bad. They've been useless. But then, what's the alternative?"

He closed his eyes and shook his head.

"AMISOM?" I asked.

Guled smiled and shrugged.

"Same problems as before and the extra troops haven't really helped. They are attacked. They shell the market. People die. They are attacked. They shell the market. They are not helping. But there is talk of an offensive to clear the city. It will be difficult," he said, with the deadpan understatement that characterises many Somalis.

"And Al-Shabaab, where are they at these days?"

"They are strong," Guled said, with a hint of admiration. He spat, smoothly.

"They still control parts of the city, and down south, it's all theirs. They killed the interior minister last month. His niece blew him up. She was one of them. They are everywhere. And new fighters keep arriving. From Pakistan, Britain, America, Sweden, Germany and many from Yemen."

He nodded his head slowly.

"But there are splits too. Some of the Somalis don't like the way the foreign fighters are climbing the ranks. They are angered by the power they are given, their fame. So there is something to exploit."

We chewed silently for a while. We both knew that nobody was ready yet to make the kind of commitment that any exploitation of internal splits would require. The AMISOM troops didn't have the training, or subtlety, to do it.

"And you, and Aisha? You are managing?"

He sniffed, as if the question was offensive, which in a way, of course, it was. But how else could I phrase it? Perhaps I could have done it more sensitively in Somali but my knowledge of Guled's language was shamefully limited; I knew little beyond *mahadsanid*, the "thank you" so little used in this brusque land.

"We are struggling, friend, but what do you want?" Guled said. "This is Somalia. We are alive, we eat today, we pray for tomorrow."

It happened three days later. We were driving along the seafront, passing buildings so battered they looked like medieval ruins. Windows like gouged-out eyes, roofs like caved-in skulls.

But in some places, in the old city by the cathedral, if I squeezed my eyes into slits, blurred my vision, I could almost glimpse the past: instead of a fragile stack of bricks reaching beseechingly to the clouds, I could imagine the two towers of the cathedral rising above yellow taxis in the square below; I could see swaying palm trees fringing sandy pavements; I could hear the low thrum of Vespas. If I closed my eyes completely, and listened to the scream of the gulls, and tasted the salt on my lips, and maybe had the good luck to catch the guns asleep, I could go deeper into the past. Until Guled swerved to avoid another cavernous pothole and

I smashed my head into the doorframe. That's what you get for dreaming here.

Guled was driving like a maniac, or like anyone in Mogadishu, and humming along tunelessly to an Arabic song on the radio. I can't remember what the song was. I only caught snatches above the judder of the Toyota's old engine, the breaking waves and the occasional *pop-pop* of gunfire behind the crippled buildings. I feel now that I *should* remember the song. It's an important detail.

I *do* remember I was trying to imagine what the port was like centuries ago, before Somalia became a byword for hell, or chaos, or whatever the latest nut graph of choice is for us journalists. Mogadishu, the "Seat of the Shah", a city with clout and custom, where frankincense, myrrh and beautiful cloths were traded. I was thinking of how catastrophic the fall from grace had been.

And then it started, with a squeal of tires. They came like children, heard before they were seen. We had no armed men this time. This was supposed to be a fifteen-minute trip through government-held territory. I just had time to find Guled's misty right eye in the rear-view mirror before they were upon us.

Their technical — a pickup with a machine gun bolted to the floor behind the cabin — came roaring out of a side street, jolting to a stop in front of us. Five, six, maybe eight men, armed with sub-machine guns and pistols leapt out, screaming, firing into the air. Some wore aviator-type sunglasses, some wore boots, some flip flops, all were strapped with bandoliers of ammunition.

Guled stood on the brakes and they came running. I don't remember if he said anything to me in those few seconds. I didn't hear him if he did.

They pulled me out. Hands everywhere, ripping off my hat, pulling my hair, slapping my head. They threw me in the road. I gashed my knee when I fell. I grunted. I was new to pain then. I looked to the car. Guled was still sitting in his seat, his hands raised. He was talking in rapid-fire Somali. I had never heard that tone before. His voice was an octave higher. I don't know what he said. I suspect it didn't matter. I tell myself this because to even entertain the idea that there was something to be done, or said, or given, or bargained for, is too awful.

A skinny man in a red-checked scarf and sunglasses, a cartoon mobster, was screaming at Guled, gesturing to me. Guled was shaking his head, never taking his good eye off the yelling man.

"Leave him alone. He doesn't know me. He's just a driver," I yelled. "He's just a fucking driver!"

The butt of a gun slammed into the side of my head, catching the delicate skin just above my eyebrow. The blow knocked me to the ground. Dust and blood in my eyes, gulls screaming overhead. I dared to look again.

The guy with the sunglasses was looking at me. Guled was looking at me, all eyes above that big nose and trembling lips. He looked like a frightened old man and I realised, suddenly, how wrong it was that he was here. Casually, the guy turned away from me, and shot Guled in the left side of the head. My friend's eyes didn't leave mine until his head jerked sideways, blood and brain spraying onto the windscreen. I screamed, a raw, animal cry, as my brain struggled to catch up with my eyes.

I was terrified, but not for myself. It was the magnitude of what had just happened. And the speed. I didn't expect death to be so sudden. It was too abrupt to be real. And then it was gone, Guled's lolling, shattered head was gone. Someone had stuffed a sack over my head, over my burning, wet eyes. I was dragged across the ground, my legs useless to me now. They threw me into the back of their technical and kicked me into a ball. I welcomed the blows. I wanted oblivion. I embraced it gratefully.

I know now that those first guys weren't anyone. They were just bandits, war opportunists. They might have joined in the fighting sometimes, on one side or the other, but basically they were guns for hire. On that day, July 26, they were working for themselves. A few dark, dread-filled days later, they sold me to Abdi's group. I call it Abdi's group although he is the most insignificant player in this farce.

The original group, Guled's murderers, didn't have the ability to hold me. That was not their thing. Somalia's war is an industry, and like any other industry, there are specific functions that are carried out by specific people. The first guys were the grunts, Guled was a statistic and I am, or was for a while, the story. Was I also the catalyst?

I don't know how they knew where we were. Maybe one of Guled's neighbours informed on us. Perhaps the shopkeeper in Guled's street where I bought two bottles of lukewarm Coke that morning. Maybe one of Guled's relatives, jealous that he was working for a foreigner and getting a salary.

The trickier question is why. Why did Guled have to die? They could have beaten him and left him. Or maybe he recognised the pickup, or one of the men. Maybe that is what that high-pitched, panicked conversation was about. The fact that I don't know infuriates me. I put Guled in that situation. I should know exactly what happened, I should not be lamely speculating because I don't have enough local knowledge to understand.

Not that I forced Guled to work for me, or for the paper. It wasn't like that. And it wasn't just about money. Guled had worked with the Somali National Media Agency for years, and then with Radio Mogadishu. But reporting became too dangerous when Al-Shabaab started killing journalists. He became an undercover fixer, perhaps believing that working for an international newspaper would offer better protection, as well as more money.

I asked him once why he did not leave Somalia, why he kept working here?

"Will your paper fly me and my family to Washington? Will they give us all visas, find us a small house, help us set up a business?" he had asked.

I met his smile with my own, not mocking him, mocking myself and my world and the stupidity inherent in my question.

"Of course not. And where else would you have me go? Nairobi? Yes, I could live in Nairobi. I could live with my people in Eastleigh, and go to the mosque, and chew some good khat. But then I am just another Somali living in Nairobi. What is that? And my son, and his daughter? They would come too. And what then are they? Somalis living in Nairobi. Somalis paying bribes to the police so they don't arrest them for being Somalis. And so it goes on."

He paused. Ahmed, a rake-thin, intense twenty-five-year-old with his father's laugh but not much reason to use it, lived in Guled's house with his timid wife, Ubah, and daughter, Lila, a two-year-old with seen-too-much eyes. Ahmed had been studying to be a teacher until Al-Shabaab closed his college. He now worked in Bakara market, doing odd jobs or selling fruit bought from relatives who had farms upcountry. Ahmed was hunched like a man who felt all struggle was futile, but something about his eyes suggested there might be something else smouldering inside.

"And if your paper would not give me the money to fly my whole family to Nairobi, do you suggest I walk across the border to one of those camps? You would have me live in Dadaab, that sweating fleapit? You would have Lila grow up there? You've seen it. She deserves more," Guled said, smoothing the girl's soft, black hair as she sat on his lap.

Lila tilted her head, turning her serious eyes up to her grandfather. She was a quiet toddler, restrained already by the chaos outside her home. Not for her the mad, dashing whoops and shrieks of other children. It was as if, knowing her life could be short, she had decided to grow up fast.

"You know, Peter, I am no idealist. Maybe the opposite. But if we all leave, who will save Somalia? Not your lot, for sure," Guled said, spitting out another mirthless chuckle.

Guled Adan didn't die because he was a hero. He died because he did a job — a lot for money, a little for professional pride, a little because it was fun, and maybe a lot because I happened to be there that July 26th. In Somalia. In the back of his car. Or maybe because I bought those Cokes.

If I survive this, that thought is waiting for me. Godwin is waiting for me, and Esther and Michelle. Because this, this unbearable hiatus, is just part of my story. And maybe not even the most interesting part.

CHAPTER
THREE

ABDI

I don't know why I gave him the cigarette. I suppose I felt sorry for him. I will not tell the Sheikh. He would not approve and I don't want to make him angry. He is a silent man, but like a scorpion: when he strikes, he will be fast and fierce. And then, this job is important. It will not be for long. I still think I was right to leave Mogadishu. Especially after Nadif. It is good that we brought the prisoner here. It was not right to keep a man like a rat in the dark. It reminded me of how we used to hide in the cellar during the heavy fighting when I was a boy. But at least I had *hooyo*'s arms around me, the shield of a mother's love. Or Nadif holding my hand.

Here at least the prisoner has some light. Not that I feel any real sympathy for him. But it is a question of dignity. I know what they say about us. They say we love war. They say we cannot be helped, we are bloodthirsty, we care for no one, we are ruled by our clans. These things and more I read on the Internet when I visited cyber cafés with Nadif, in the time before. They are wrong. We don't love killing. Ask me, ask my friends. Why would we not want to live? What kind of person does not want to live? But *we* live here, at war, so what do you want?

I was born in Mogadishu in 1993. The year of the Battle for Mogadishu, but in our house, the year of my birth. Nadif was two then. He was a child of the world after leader Siad Barre, a baby born in the chaos of that afterlife. My mother says he hated me at first. He used to try to push me off her breast. I can imagine her husky, deep laugh as she tried to keep him off her knees. *Hooyo* would have called my father. "Omar, take him please. What an angry one we have!"

The day the American helicopters were shot down, the day we call *Ma-alinti Rangers*, my father ran into the house and bundled us downstairs to the basement. We lived just a few streets north of where the first helicopter crashed. My mother had heard the noise and was peering through the bullet holes in the gate when my father banged on it. He rushed in, his 6ft 2in burly frame making her feel unreasonably safe. I don't remember this, of course. My mother told me later. Even Nadif didn't remember that day, though he used to talk about it a lot, after he joined them.

"The infidels were afraid to come back after that," he would say as we sat under the mango tree on the edge of a patch of waste ground between our house and Bakara market. He would laugh and punch me on the shoulder, knowing I did not like it when he talked like that. Many of the boys from our neighbourhood came to that tree. Maybe we thought its thick branches and wide, rubbery leaves would protect us when the mortars started to fall.

Sometimes we played football on the sandy, barren lot nearby. But we didn't go into the open ground so often after Abdirakim and his brothers were killed when a shell landed on them. But that makes it sound too simple. They were blown to bits. The littlest one was only three. He was never found. He just disappeared. Everyone said the shell was fired by AMISOM. I don't know. I wasn't there that day. And anyway, what does it matter who did it?

Nadif was my hero. When I was a child, he looked out for me when others made fun of my stutter. But time does not stand still, and by last year he had become a warrior for a cause I could not share. He was still my hero, my handsome brother with his curly hair and thick beard. But it was not just a beard anymore. It started as a fad, then it became a way of avoiding trouble, and after he joined them, it was a political statement.

As the beard grew, so the words coming from inside it became louder, fiercer. But for a while, even when he was ranting about the infidel, even when he was carrying his gun and shouting at wide-eyed, diminished people at roadblocks, his eyes were warm. To me, he still looked as though he was about to burst into laughter and punch me on the shoulder. Then, he was still my brother, but I wonder if that was still true at the end.

When we were younger, he taught me about football. He supported Manchester United, like many of our friends. Before Al-Shabaab came, we would watch matches at an iron-and-wood bar near the market, standing outside and straining to see the tiny screen inside. Nadif worshipped Ryan Giggs. I liked Gunnar Solskjaer, though I could never say his name right. I liked his face. He looked kind, almost like a child. Nadif told me they called him the baby-faced assassin. I liked that too. The bar owner didn't like us being there, but as long as we didn't come in, he let us gather like flies in the rain. If we became too rowdy, he would waddle out, swinging a broom, gently clipping bottoms and shins. It was a game. The beautiful game.

When Al-Shabaab came, they put an end to football. They put an end to so many things.

Our house was by the market, on the edge of Al-Shabaab territory. It is clear to me now that Nadif was always going to end up with them. It was because of my father, but also because of the way Nadif was.

My father was killed near a bread stall at the market during a three-hour battle between government soldiers and their Ethiopian friends, and Al-Shabaab. I don't know who fired the mortar that chopped my father into pieces so that we never found his left leg. He was buried without it. That was my leg. When Nadif and I fought about sitting on his lap, he would lift us onto his knees, saying, "Boys, I have two beautiful knees. I have two beautiful sons. Where is the problem?"

But that was four years ago now. Nothing was ever the same again. Mother almost never went out afterwards. Maybe she was still grieving, or maybe she was too terrified of the shooting, the mortars, the death dropping like soft rain from the sky, and later of the

Al-Shabaab fighters screaming through the streets in their technicals.

I know many of them, and I am still terrified. Some are Nadif's friends, some are my friends, but I don't know if you are allowed to be a friend when you are in Al-Shabaab. Nadif, I think, was always my friend, but he changed last year.

He wanted me to join too. I said I was too young. In truth, I was afraid and I didn't understand them, I didn't understand the point of it all. They seemed fierce and their beliefs were so harsh. Of course, I never said this to Nadif. He disappeared for two weeks a year after my father was killed. When he came back, he was thinner, dirtier, harder. The warmth had left his eyes, except when he spoke to me. I think he still loved me. I don't think they managed to take that from him. But my mother was frightened of this seventeen-year-old who no longer hugged her, but wore his anger on his sleeve and a gun on his shoulder. Then they had the row.

He had returned for lunch. His gun was leaning against the wall. I picked it up, put the strap over my shoulder and held it across my body as I had seen Nadif do when he was manning one of the roadblocks around Bakara. It was heavier than I expected. I felt strong holding it. I felt like a man.

"Abdi!"

My mother had come in carrying plates of rice and vegetables, her face steaming.

"Put that evil thing down. Now!" she hissed.

Nadif was sitting at the table, resting his head on his arms. He was often out all night now. We didn't ask what he did but sometimes his clothes were muddy and torn. Once I caught him washing his shirt in a bucket in the yard. Red drops dripped from his fingers as he waved me away, silently, wearily.

"*Hooyo*, do not speak like that," Nadif said, his voice serrated with a new authoritarian edge. I put the gun back against the wall and sat down quickly, opposite Nadif.

"I ask you again, do not bring that thing into your father's house," my mother retorted, a soft spray of spittle sheathing her words as she bent with the plates to the table. She dared not look him straight in the eye, squinting at an unseen demon above his right shoulder instead.

"I cannot leave it outside. Besides, why do you care if Abdi touches it? He needs to learn. It is his destiny, as it is mine, to drive the Crusaders and their apostate African servants from this country."

Nadif was almost shouting now.

"Abdi will not join you," my mother yelled back, her voice shaky but unyielding.

She straightened her back and turned towards Nadif.

"I have lost a husband, I have a son crazed with anger and bewitched by the foolish teachings of thugs with guns . . ."

Within a second Nadif had leapt from his seat and slapped our mother across the face.

"Do not speak of the Mujahideen and martyrs in that way!"

My mother fell back. I could see the marks of Nadif's fingers already forming on her cheek. I wanted to crawl under the table, crawl under the floor, crawl into the very heart of the earth where it is warm and quiet. I wanted to cry.

"Out!" was all she said.

I looked at Nadif. In that moment I thought his face was about to crumble, that he was going to weep as well. I saw it for the last time, his child's face. I wanted to say something to comfort him, to stem the rage swelling behind his high forehead, but I was also scared. I used to know the why of what was in his head. But a part of his mind was closed off to me now.

I knew he was lost to me for ever. He waited, his hand held at the ready, tense and dangerous, hovering near his hip. I thought he might hit her again. But Nadif just grabbed his gun and walked out. He gave me a strange look as he passed. It was as though he blamed me. When he was gone, my mother sat at the table and cried for a long time. I went to hug her and pulled her head to my chest, but after a few moments, she drew away. I had never seen her cry like that. Not even when my father was killed.

Then, when they came to tell her, she fainted. Afterwards, she was silent for days. But she never cried. Not like this. Not these sobs that seemed about to consume her, to pull her limb from limb.

Nadif did not come home again. Until his last day that is. They found his body in the street. Like my father's. He had been setting up a roadside bomb near the presidential palace. It went off, leaving a huge crater

41

in the road and taking Nadif. He was never very good with his fingers. His fingers are, were, like mine: thin and awkward. He used to tickle me with those fingers, ants on my stomach and my feet, making me squirm and squeal in pained delight.

I wonder if the best bomb makers all have short fingers. Nadif's body had no fingers and no arms when he was buried. His face was a bloody mess. The face of a martyr, they said. My mother refused to see the body.

"No more," she muttered when they carried him through the gate.

She went to her room and only came out after the funeral. He was buried by his brothers, his other brothers. They fired their guns in the air, waved their black-and-white banners, and gave me an envelope.

"Your brother was a martyr. He is with Allah. *Allahu Akbar*," said Cabdulle.

He and Nadif used to play football together, in the time before. Cabdulle has another name now. He is Sheikh Cabdulle. Another sheikh. We have become a country of sheikhs. Cabdulle, who had lost the teenage twitches and awkwardness I remembered, said I should come and talk with him.

"You will want to avenge your brother's death. We will find a way. You can continue his work."

"I . . . I . . . I don't know," I eventually said.

My stutter, which I had conquered by the age of ten, came back when Nadif was killed. It only lasted a few days this time. I said very little for those first days anyway. I hid in the dark corners of the house. I did not want to go outside. They were outside. They were

42

waiting for me to feel anger, to demand revenge. But I did not know who to blame.

I told my mother what Cabdulle had said. It roused her from the apathy that had become her shield.

"You will not join them. As Allah is my witness, if you do that, I will kill myself. I will kill myself in front of you," she hissed.

We were sitting outside, in the small garden behind our house. It was a beautiful morning, a soft breeze, the sun like a kiss and the smell of the frangipani perfuming the air. Mogadishu can be beautiful if you can sit still in a quiet place with someone you love. On days like this, the pain of Nadif's death was all around us.

I lowered my head.

"Maybe it is the right thing to do," I muttered. "I cannot let Nadif's death go unavenged. Father is not here but he would not let it pass. He would act."

My mother lifted my chin, her henna-stained fingernails digging into my skin.

"Your father was a man of life. A man of integrity. He would never have allowed Nadif to join those bandits who are ruining our country. Look what they have done to this town."

She opened her arms wide, taking in the frangipani, the broken wall we were sitting on, the half-empty buildings nearby, the devastated market, the mango tree and the waste land where Abdirakim and his brothers had died. Her dramatic, defiant gesture took in all the unseen horror beyond the walls of our garden of secrets.

The shuttered bars, the blood stains on the stunted grass in the football stadium, the mutilated bodies found in the street at first light, the gunfire that had become the theme tune of our lives, the whoosh of the mortars, the slapping sound of bare feet running another casualty to looted hospitals that were little more than places to die.

"I swear to you, Abdi, I swear, on the graves of your father and brother, that if you go near Al-Shabaab, I will turn this robe into a short skirt, and I will walk up to the first Al-Shabaab roadblock I can find and I will wait for them to kill me. And if they do not kill me for that, I shall take off the rest of my clothes. And I will dance and swing my hips. And I will sing and loosen my hair, and I will swing it in their faces."

By now, she was giggling and I was smiling. Soon we were laughing. My mother's face was light. She cupped my cheeks in her hands and laughed in my face. And we were happy. And so sad. How is it possible to laugh and be sad? I don't know. But here it is possible.

"Okay, okay," I said when we had stopped.

"I will not join them. But you know they will want me. You know they are taking children. Even younger than me."

She nodded.

"I saw Mariam last week. You know, they took Mohammed. From the beach. He was looking for firewood. A lovely boy. Bright, decent, respectful. Mariam is going crazy," she said.

Mariam and my mother had grown up together in Mogadishu, attending the same school and then training as secretaries. When they met at our house, the kitchen rang with laughter. Mariam was taller than my mother, but thin and dainty like a gerenuk. Mohammed was her only son. Her husband had worked at the Ministry of Education. He was killed at a graduation ceremony. He was setting out plates of tuna sandwiches, and was blown away by a teenage suicide bomber.

We went to their house when we heard. My mother walked straight up to Mariam, her face rigid. They embraced and then my mother led Mariam away from the guests, from the shrouded corpse. She took her to a back room where they stayed for a long time. When they came out, their eyes were dry, their faces like masks, proud, aloof, powerful in their unity. They were magnificent.

"You must leave Mogadishu. We must leave Mogadishu," my mother said.

"We will go to Kenya. My brother is already at the Hagadera camp in Dadaab. If we can slip across the border, we can find him. We will go and live with him. He will get us one of those ration cards you need to get food. And when we make some money, we will try to get to Nairobi. It is not allowed but many have done it. I have heard of people who can help. You are a strong boy, and I can still work. We will make it happen."

As she spoke, her eyes flashed. She started believing her own story. She sketched an impossible future, waving her arms and nodding her head. We would need money. She would go to her family. She would raise what she could. She would sell the carpets, my father's gramophone, Nadif's clothes. She would sell everything.

"Then, we can go. You and I. I will ask around for the best way. Maybe we can get a ride with someone. There are people who go to the border at Dhobley every week. But we will need money to get across to Liboi on the Kenyan side. We can bribe the Kenyans. They ask a lot, but we can find it."

She paused, took a breath.

"Abdi, we can start again."

Tears were now rolling down her cheeks and in that moment, I saw my mother as a young woman. She was only thirty-seven and she wanted to live again. I saw the teenager who had studied typing and shorthand only to get married straight out of training college to a tall man who promised to keep her safe. And in that world he did. But then the world changed, and Somalia changed, and now that young woman was a middle-aged widow, the lowest of the low in her own country. Ryan Giggs was still playing for Manchester United when he was thirty-six. It isn't that old. For my mother, thirty-seven was too young to give up.

We decided I would go to Wanlaweyn while my mother tried to raise the money to go to Kenya. She was afraid of Al-Shabaab, afraid they would come for me too. Her cousin, Yusuf could take me in, and maybe I could even find a small job to help us on our way.

I travelled by bus. It was ninety kilometres to Wanlaweyn along the road, but we veered into the bush a few times to avoid roadblocks. I think I slept despite the bucking and weaving, despite the smell of hot, unwashed bodies, the stink from the sputtering exhaust. My mother had given me a phone with some credit. She promised to call when she was ready to join me. Then we would make our way to the border with Kenya.

That was in early July. Her last call to me was five days ago. She said she was finding it hard to get out to sell our goods. Government soldiers had joined with AMISOM and launched an attack on Al-Shabaab, a push to reclaim the city, they said.

"But nothing is changing," my mother said, her voice crackly and weak.

I pressed the phone harder to my ear.

"Nothing is changing. Al-Shabaab are still in the neighbourhood. But now it is so dangerous to go out, my son. I have not been outside for four days. I have very little food. I must go to the market soon or things will be desperate for me."

"Take care, *Hooyo*," I said. Then louder in case she did not hear me, "Take care."

"I will. How are things with you?"

I hesitated. By now, I was back in Wanlaweyn, but the week before I had been in Mogadishu, barely two kilometres from our house. Carrying food to a white prisoner in a black room. Because that is the job Yusuf offered me. I didn't want to have anything to do with it at first. I didn't want to be involved with kidnapping. This man had never done anything to me. Why should we imprison him? Weren't we all prisoners here anyway? Why add to the misery?

"My mother will kill me. She does not want me mixed up in that," I said when Yusuf suggested I help out.

"What? Now you are not Somali? Whether you like it or not, you are already mixed up in *that*, as you call it. We all are, because we live in this hellhole."

My cousin laughed.

"Might as well make some money. And this is easy money. They have him already. They took him yesterday. But now they don't know what to do. We just need to go there, hold him, and then move him here to Wanlaweyn when it is safe. You are just the help. We do not expect you to do the dirty work, Abdi. You are a boy. But if you want to make some money to help your mother, this is what I am offering you."

And so it began. My relationship with the white man with the scared, green eyes, the battered face that I slapped when he tried to escape, the stubbly beard and the dirty fingernails. I fed him in that dungeon in Mogadishu, then I came back here on another battered, stinking bus and waited for my cousin's gang to turn up. Now I am feeding him again.

This I did not tell my mother. I told her I was well, and that I was working as a trader's assistant. I would have money for her when she came.

"It's going well. Your cousin is a good man," I said, feeling sick.

She said she hoped to join me in two weeks. That should be enough time to finish this job. Then I will have money to take us across the border. Out of this.

But I have heard stories from these camps in Kenya. Poor, dry, dangerous places where thousands live too close together, sitting prey for bandits and Al-Shabaab. Because they are there too. Borders mean nothing to them. I want my mother's dream of a new life to come true. I don't want more of the same. I don't know if I can bear that. But I don't know if I can bear *this*.

It is time to go. The Sheikh will be making the phone call now. He has asked me to be there. I think Yusuf told him about Nadif. They think I am connected. Later, the white man will need his food. I will give him another cigarette. He can do nothing now but smoke.

CHAPTER
FOUR

PETER

Today, I spoke to my mother. She was in her apartment above the Tunisian restaurant where sometimes the owners park a camel outside the door to coax in finicky Parisian diners. I used to feel sorry for that camel, sitting grumpily on the cobblestones, feeling like a fool in a tasselled red saddle.

The man with the beaky nose — I call him The Eagle — sauntered in, ahead of Abdi and two muscle men who held their guns at the ready, like boys playing soldiers. I stood. Not out of respect. I didn't want to die sitting down, and I didn't want to be looking up at them. A pathetic gesture of defiance, I know.

"It's time for business," The Eagle said, almost cheerily.

"We have informed your employers that we are holding you. We have demanded a ransom. If they do not pay, we will kill you."

It was almost a relief to hear the words. At last, the worst was out in the open. They were prepared to kill me, but there was a chance. It wasn't just about ideology. They wanted money. I knew others had paid to have their people released, despite all the official rhetoric about not engaging with terrorists. And I didn't think Don Struddle would enjoy being in the middle of a media shit-storm about whether or not he should have allowed me to go to Somalia. Especially not if I was dead.

The Eagle grunted something at Abdi. He stepped forward with a Thuraya, the satellite phone of choice for rebels and bandits everywhere in Africa.

"They want proof that we are holding you. You will speak to your mother. You will tell her you are fine and that you are being treated well. Let's see if that is enough. If not, maybe she'd like to listen in to hear what it is like when you are not being treated well."

He paused. He didn't need to. I got it.

"Tell her to get them to pay the money. This is your chance to do something to save yourself. Take it."

His voice was not unkind, just emotionless. In a way, the flat tone was more frightening.

Abdi gave me the phone. He didn't look at my face and I was glad. I dialled the apartment where my mother has lived since we returned from Ivory Coast. The apartment where we lived as a family until my parents couldn't hold it together anymore.

"Allo?"

She sounded her full sixty today.

"Mum, it's me."

"Peter? Oh my God, where are you? Darling, where are you? Are you okay?"

"I'm fine. I've been . . . taken, kidnapped. They want money. They've contacted the *Post*."

I paused. What do you say to your mother when you are being held hostage? What you feel? What you want? What you need? What she needs?

The Eagle was watching me, his eyes narrow, his face pinched. Suddenly, he lunged forward, grabbed the phone from my white-knuckled hand, and struck me hard across the face. I cried out and immediately regretted it. But I didn't see it coming. In my head, I was in the apartment in Paris, standing in the red-tiled entrance hall, looking through the kitchen into the courtyard, listening to the noisy city outside.

His ring had cut my lip. The physical sting was a pinprick compared to the pain of losing the phone, losing that crackly lifeline.

"Tell her you are being treated well and to pay the ransom," he growled.

He handed me the phone again. I could hear my mother's breath, short and ragged.

"Mum?"

"Peter, what are they doing? What's going on?"

"It's okay, Mum, I'm okay. They are treating me well."

The Eagle nodded and granted me a patronising smile. I wanted to smash those stained teeth into the back of his throat. I had never felt so powerful an urge to break a man, to pound him into nothingness. It felt good to yield to my anger. I closed my eyes, letting the wave roll over me.

"I love you, Mum. Please talk to Don, and the others. Tell them to do what these men want. I want to come home."

And then I was crying. Like a child. My mother's child. Abdi grabbed the phone, clicked it off and they were gone. I slumped to the floor and slowly curled into a ball on the mat.

Later, Abdi came back, alone. He had my food. I ate, noisily, gracelessly, ignoring the pain in my burst lip. I had cried myself empty.

Abdi offered me a cigarette. He joined me, and the smoke spiralled above our heads, silver sylphs gyrating as shy sunrays peeked through the bars high up on the wall. He smoked loosely, languidly. Not so much a man who didn't have a care, as a boy-man who didn't care. I wondered why. And then he spoke.

"Your mother is alone?"

His voice was soft, barely a whisper. The English was heavily accented but good, a little self-conscious perhaps.

"Yes, she lives alone in Paris."

"Where is your father?"

"He lives in Ireland."

Abdi looked puzzled.

"They are divorced."

"And your brothers and sisters?"

"I have none. I am an only child."

"And your wife? Where does she live?"

"I am not married."

Thirty years in a nutshell. The bare details I give up when people ask me about myself after I have interviewed them, when the tables turn and they justifiably seek to know something about the reporter

53

who has just mined their lives, their feelings, for his own glory.

Maybe people need an observer, a listener, someone to make what is happening real by putting it on paper. Otherwise, everything might just be taking place in our heads. It's the only explanation I have found for why so many people have opened their hearts to me over the years.

Now, I am the one who needs someone to record what I say — a stenographer of my soul — to convince myself that I am not dreaming this.

"I have a son," I offered, and immediately felt ashamed.

You are not supposed to give any information to your captors. We learnt that on the hostile environment course. Don't give anything up. It made sense at the time, but they didn't tell us how lonely it would be. How everyone needs to share, everyone wants to give their lives meaning and shape through narration. Especially when time's frame has been smashed, and dreams meld into nightmares. I spoke to remind myself that I existed beyond these four walls. My shame was in my weakness, and in the impure use of a boy I had neglected for so long to define my humanity.

"He is with your mother?" Abdi asked.

"No, Godwin is with his mother. They live in Liberia. Do you know Liberia?"

For a moment, I thought he wouldn't answer. Maybe this conversation was just an interrogation. I felt like a fool for falling for it. Angrily, I stubbed out my cigarette. It had burnt low and singed my fingers.

"I have read of it. That place is fucked up."

He uttered the expletive delicately, as if unsure of its exact import, and shook his head, his face solemn. I couldn't help it. I laughed, a little too loudly, a little hysterically. The new sensation hurt. Abdi stiffened.

"You are laughing at me? Don't laugh at me, infidel!"

He picked up the plate and turned to leave.

"I'm sorry, Abdi. I didn't mean to offend you. It's just funny. You, a Somali, talking to a kidnapped journalist in a shed in God knows where, in a country shot to hell, saying Liberia is fucked up. I'm not laughing *at* you. It's just funny."

I hoped his face would crack into a smile. I needed to know he wasn't so far gone that he couldn't see the humour in this. I craved Abdi's approval. Not because of any fanciful dream of escape. He was just a teenager. No match for the men around him. I just needed someone in this timeless underworld to react to me so that I could still believe I existed.

He walked out, slamming the door behind him.

The next day, he spoke again, but this time it was to hurt me. To avenge his teenage humiliation.

"We are going to sell you. To Al-Shabaab. You will die. Even if they pay the money, you will die."

He twisted his lips into a grimace, a half-smile so bleak it scared me more than his words.

"Yes, it is also fucked up here." He lit a cigarette and put the packet back in his pocket.

I was quiet. I did not want him to go yet, and I was digesting the new information. If I were sold to Al-Shabaab, all hope would be gone. A British journalist working for a US paper would be a massive coup. They could get the ransom and still cut off my head. And then post the pictures on the Internet.

I thought of the videos I had watched on assignment in Baghdad. How long it had taken that aid worker to die. The screams turning to gurgles as they hacked a toothless, monster-mouth into her neck.

That video haunted me for years. I still dream of it, the images distorted and reconfigured by my malevolent subconscious. I am being cut. I am hacking. It is my mother. It is my father. Sometimes, I dream of Esther's arm. Even though that was not on any video.

When they chopped off Esther's right arm in the forests outside Freetown, there was no need for cameras. The young boys with the stained, blunt machetes were not trying to frighten anyone outside Sierra Leone. Their only targets were the people locked inside the killing fields. The people who could not escape, including sixteen-year-old Esther, whose arm was sawed off below the elbow, and who became the mother of my son, Godwin.

"My son is five." I'd spoken before I realised it. The atmosphere in the room shifted.

Abdi swatted a fly from his nose. When he spoke, it was reluctantly.

"So, you live in Liberia?"

"No, I live in Paris. I do not see my son. It's complicated."

I waited for another question. I thought I could sense curiosity, but Abdi finished his cigarette in silence and left.

Complicated. Three decades on this planet and that is the best I can come up with to describe what has happened. Complicated does not come close to explaining why I have a girlfriend in Paris who wants me to marry her, a son in Liberia born to a one-armed beauty with eyes of coal and a gift of silence, and one father on a farm of fat cows in Cork.

Of course, Michelle does not know of Esther, or Godwin. Michelle, who said, as we sat in front of the television watching a report on the release of a British contractor who had been held in Baghdad for three months, "God, I would hate to be kidnapped. All that fuss when you come out. Photographers everywhere. My eyebrows would be out of control, I'd have a moustache. Can you even imagine?"

That makes her sound superficial. She isn't really. No more so than any of us are when we live safe lives in safe places where our horrors are drawn from daily life. If we want more, we simply go see a scary movie. Or become firefighter journalists, hopping on a plane whenever the dull dreads of daily life become too much to bear.

I was fleeing again when I met Esther in 2005. Michelle and I had just started seeing each other, somewhat regularly and almost exclusively, and I needed to be gone for a while. I *did* like her. It wasn't that.

We were having fun. Climbing onto the wide ledge outside my eighth-floor apartment to look over bejeweled, brash Paris. Sunday brunches in dim bars built to hold secrets, where we drank tart Bloody Marys and sent smoke-wraiths twirling to the ceiling. Kir royals at sunset. Ice cream by the Notre Dame. These were good times, but I'm not good with good.

I was sent to Liberia to cover the presidential election. I met Esther at a rehabilitation camp for former child soldiers. She had moved to Liberia with her family after the rebels took over Freetown in 1999. Frying pan to the fire. But they had relatives next door and Charles Taylor was in power and it seemed a little more stable. That was a few months before rebels started to creep out of the north, heading towards Monrovia. And so began Liberia's second civil war. It would end in 2003 when Taylor finally left the country, boarding a plane in a white suit, looking for a moment like a bewildered old man as security officers prodded him up the steps, past supporters crying into comic-book-sized cloths on the tarmac.

For most of that second war, Esther and her family lived in the bush around Sanniquellie. After Taylor left for exile, Esther came to Monrovia and got a job serving food in a camp for former child soldiers. When I came to interview the tiny Italian nun who ran the compound, Esther served me a bowl of rice and bitterleaf sauce, carrying the chipped blue china bowl carefully in her one hand and setting it down on a wooden table speckled with flowers that had fallen from a purple bougainvillea bush overhead. I asked Sister Maria about the girl with the smile.

"Oh, she is not one of our charges," the elderly nun said in a faint, fluttering voice that sat uneasily with her no-nonsense muscled arms and solid, can-do face.

"She came from Sierra Leone. She was not a child soldier but, as you can see, she suffered. She has been here a year now. She says her family crossed over in 1999. They have relatives in Nimba. After what happened to her, they could not stay near Freetown."

I asked if I could interview her. Even now, I don't know why I wanted to speak to her. It didn't fit my story. Of course, the wars in Sierra Leone and Liberia were linked, and of course, people crossed borders into countries more fucked than their own, but those realities did not fit the linear narrative I needed to construct to explain the story to my readers in New York and Omaha. Liberia was doing well, about to elect a new president, a new day was dawning. I would never be able to find room in my piece for the woman who had lost her arm in a separate war that nonetheless sprang from the same hunger for wealth and was directed by the same big men.

Maybe I just wanted her to like me, maybe it was as simple as a smile, her smile. I wanted to see her face light up, and feel that flush of warmth that meant I had snared another soul. Maybe I just wanted to prove, now that I was seeing Michelle regularly, that I could still attract a woman. Maybe I was trying to prove to myself that, at twenty-four, I was not tied down to one woman, one colour, one class, one definition of beauty. Or maybe it was simple lust.

Esther did smile. She did not say much during the interview, but she agreed to meet me for a drink later. She didn't waste words, she didn't look for affirmation of herself, or myself in chatter. She fascinated me. We made love in my mildewed hotel room under a fan that caressed the soupy air that clung to our bodies.

I stroked the stump of her arm, filled with hot anger and pity for the girl she had been then. For her and all the others. I kissed the hard, bumpy flesh. Her eyes widened but she did not say anything.

And that is how my son Godwin came about. That night, or one of the other fragrant, flesh-filled nights during those few intense election weeks. Some would call my son a mistake. And yes, there was a condom that split. Such banalities lie behind life's transitions.

But I think the real mistake is everything I have done since then. Or rather everything I have not done. Even here, as I lie under the bared teeth of the window-monster in this outer space of reality, my face is hot, and my shame clings to me like a shroud.

"Why did you go to Liberia?"

Abdi was back, lounging on the mattress, his gun leaning against the wall beside him. Without the weapon, his body was again an ordinary teenager's, all legs and arms. I sat on the mat, my back curved, my head lowered to suck up any cool air I could.

I knew I shouldn't talk to Abdi but I didn't feel like making a stand on privacy when I might only have a few days left. Abdi might be the last person I would have a relationship with. These might be my last conversations. Maybe if I kept talking, I wouldn't die. I was Scheherazade to Abdi's Shahryar. The servant is king but I am still the storyteller.

"I'm a journalist. I go where there is news. I have been to Liberia many times but my son was born after

I went in 2005, to cover the elections. You know, the people voted for Ellen Johnson-Sirleaf. She is the first woman to be elected president in Africa."

"Why did they choose a woman?"

"She's a clever politician, she promised the voters what they wanted to be promised. Reform, change, peace and money. After so much killing I think the people were tired of men and boys running things. There had been too much suffering. They thought maybe a woman could do better."

"Women can be strong, but they cannot be leaders."

It was not offered for debate and the words had the dull ring of rote.

Abdi took out another cigarette and offered me one. He threw me the matches. I threw them back. He fumbled the catch, his fingers shooting out awkwardly, flicking the box down. He grabbed the packet off the mattress and stuffed them in his pocket. I pretended not to notice.

"Your son's mother, she is black?"

"Yes. She's from Sierra Leone. She was living in Monrovia when I met her."

"Why did you go with a black woman? You have a white woman too? You can marry many women in your country?"

Morality lessons from a teenage kidnapper. I could hear my father's voice, with its faint Cork sing-song, "Naught as strange as life, Pete."

"No, you cannot have many wives. I have a white woman in Paris but I am not married."

"She would not make a good wife?"

"I don't know. She's nice. She's smart. She's very pretty. But I am still young. There's time enough for marriage."

Or maybe not. That's the problem. We always think there is time enough for everything, even when we are complaining about the days being too short. We believe tomorrow will always come. Even people like me, who should know better.

"And the black woman? She would make a good wife?"

"She might. She too is beautiful. But I don't think I can live that life. It wasn't the plan, you know. It wasn't my plan to have a baby there. It just happened."

"Why didn't you try to live there? You can go wherever you like with your passport."

I didn't know what to say, and after a while, Abdi peeled himself from the thin mattress and pushed open the heavy door. For a second I glimpsed the outside; the dusty courtyard, a scraggy thorn bush in the middle distance, a sky bleached white by the heat. When the door closed, the over-bright flash of outside stuck on my retina, growing fainter and fainter. I closed my eyes.

The next day we talked some more. I had not seen The Eagle again. I assumed he was busy negotiating with Al-Shabaab. Abdi seemed less reticent. Maybe he too needed to have some last conversations. This time I asked the questions.

"You are not married?"

"No."

"You have family here, I mean, in Somalia?"

"My mother. My father was killed. My brother also."

"I'm sorry."

"No, you are not. Why should you be? I don't need your pity. I have suffered. Now it is your turn. It comes to everyone. It's just a question of when."

I paused, taken aback by the brutality of his words.

"What was your father like?"

"He was a strong man," Abdi said curtly.

I worried I had assumed too much intimacy. Maybe I was not allowed to ask questions. I thought we were becoming friends. Or at least fellows. Fellow inmates.

These chats kept me going. Not because of what we said but because they stopped my mind from torturing itself with its endless focus on me. Other words. Other ideas. Not these same damn thoughts going round and round until I thought I would collapse from the sheer, terrifying monotony of my own company.

Meursault was wrong. A day was not enough of a life to make imprisonment bearable. It was either insubstantial, or too substantial.

"My father was a teacher, but he was killed by a mortar. Four years ago. My brother died in June. They say he was a martyr. He blew himself up. Now, it is just me and my mother."

The information came in a rush, as though Abdi had made a decision. The words streaked out before he could change his mind. I didn't say anything for a while. I felt as though this rush of personal information had embarrassed him.

"Your English is very good. Where did you learn?"

"At school, before the fighting became too bad. And from the television, before it was banned. I used to watch a lot of football at the kiosks and bars. I am a Manchester United fan. So was my brother."

"I'm a City man myself. You know, Manchester City."

"I am sorry for *you*, my friend."

And finally, Abdi smiled. His sterile handsome features bent into something less perfect, but more beautiful.

The sight of my boy-man jailer smiling was like a knife in my gut. Something wonderful and terrible was happening. I was seeing Abdi. And he was seeing me. In my work, I rarely managed to break through meaningfully into another person's world. Often, it was unnecessary for the stories I was writing. But also I think there has always been something frivolously selfish about me. I want to be liked but I don't want to invest too much. Then, there is always the next story.

Here, now, I had done it. I was investing. Around Abdi and I, the world was wrong. Everything was distorted. But in this room, in the few metres that encompassed us both, normalcy was fighting back.

The next day, Abdi came in earlier than usual. He had no food this time.

"They are coming for you. Tomorrow, they will take you."

And then he was gone.

CHAPTER
FIVE

ABDI

This is nearly over. Yusuf will pay me. I will join my mother in Mogadishu and we will leave. The prisoner will probably be killed. I don't know what is happening with the ransom, but that will now be their problem. The Sheikh told me they are sending a Somali-born *mujahid* who came here recently from Britain. He will be in charge of the operation. Maybe the prisoner can talk to *him*.

The Sheikh would not be pleased if he knew we were talking. I am curious though. I don't understand why the prisoner came to Somalia. But I like to hear him talk. I am learning. I feel more at ease with him than with Yusuf or his men. I do not want any extra contact with them. They are dangerous, or maybe just bad, they are men like those who stole Nadif from me. I want to be out of here. The prisoner is not dangerous. And he will not be here long. It is like talking to a ghost. A dead man. I can talk to him because the words he hears will die with him.

My mother must call today. She should have called earlier this week but there has been heavy fighting in Mogadishu. They say Al-Shabaab is retreating. Maybe she hasn't been able to buy credit. She does not keep her phone on because there is often no power. I must wait for her to ring me. I will go outside and sit under the acacia tree, and then she will call.

I sit on a flat stone in the shade and close my eyes. I almost sleep. I do this easily now. This job is all about waiting. My life is about waiting. I wait for it to restart.

"Abdi, come!"

Yusuf is calling. I get up and walk past the scrawny chickens pecking in the dust, through the dazzling sunshine. He is standing in the door of the main house. His face is in shadow. He walks in before me, turning his back too quickly. He takes me to the main room. Some of his men are sprawled by the walls, chewing khat. I have never joined them. I am saving my money for our journey.

"Please Abdi, sit down."

Something is wrong. Yusuf is agitated. His fingers fumble with his scarf. He is not looking at me. I remember this happening before.

"What's wrong? What has happened?"

I don't really want to know but I recognise, once again, that I am not in control of this part of my story.

"It's Faduma. She is dead."

I hear the words. They mean everything, and nothing.

"Abdi, have you heard me? Faduma has gone to Allah."

There are moments in life when time does stand still. This is the third time for me. Maybe this time, it will not start again. I would like that. Yusuf's words echo in

66

my head. I am silent because they are screaming. Let them roar out their evil inside my head. Let me keep those words inside, on repeat. Let us not speak them again, and if we do not say them, they cannot exist.

"I am sorry, Abdi. I have just been told. She has been dead for some days."

I sink to the ground, crouching at the feet of the dead-eyed men along the wall.

Yusuf said my mother had got cholera. She couldn't leave the house because Al-Shabaab had tightened its hold on the neighbourhood. When a friend found her, she was dying.

Neighbours took her to the hospital, but there was nothing they could do.

I felt like screaming at him to stop. Stop making it real with your words, Yusuf! Be silent! Be silent and this will slip away. As though it was never here.

I walked back outside and sat again under the spiky, stunted tree. I watched those dinosaur chickens and the sun falling in the sky, dropping lower through air that shimmered like steam above a cooking pot.

Eventually I closed my eyes. There was nothing behind them except the sun shadows burnt onto my retina. I looked at them too, filling my mind with their forms. I opened my eyes, looked at the main house, at its tin roof and mud walls. They needed redoing in places. Yusuf's Land Cruiser was parked in a corner. I looked at the prisoner's shack. Nothing to see but bricks and a closed door.

It is quiet here. A dirt track leads to our compound from the main road two kilometres away. There is nothing around. Bare, hard earth, hills that are really just mounds of dust waiting for a giant to blow them away. This place looks like nothing and nowhere. It is a good place for me now.

Later, I took the prisoner's meal to him. He was lying on his mattress and did not sit up immediately, but he was not asleep. I placed the food on the mat and sat there.

The stew was cold. I was late to collect it but nobody said anything. The prisoner rose and sat in front of me.

"I'm not hungry," he said. "But please, may I have a cigarette?"

He has lost hope, I thought. I know that voice. The voice of someone who does not now, or ever, expect things to get better. The voice of someone who has lost too much, seen too much, heard too much and smelt too much. It is my voice.

"Thank you," he said when I gave him the cigarette. I smoked with him.

"I want to ask a favour."

He spoke without looking at me. He was tracing the mat's woven pattern with a dirty fingernail.

"You said they are coming tomorrow. I need to write a letter to my mother. I have things to say, and not the things they will make me say. You know what I mean. Can you get me paper and a pen? Can I leave the letter with you?"

He looked at me then. I saw a broken man, a condemned man, and I saw that he knew all these things. He wanted me to help him. But I, too, am those things. And who will help me? Who will send my letter? Who will say goodbye to my mother for me?

"I cannot help you."

"Please, Abdi. You know how this will go. They will make me say things I do not believe. They will film me. I don't want that to be my last message. I have other things to say to my mother. Please, Abdi. It is all I ask."

"Why should I help you?"

The prisoner put his head in his hands. He began to rock back and forth. He was muttering.

"Just one more fucking story. Give me one more story to write myself, please. One more."

He looked up, eyes like broken windows in an abandoned house.

"I don't have anyone else to ask. What do you have to lose? I'll be gone tomorrow."

He would be gone tomorrow. I would be gone tomorrow. This room, these talks would belong in the past. Like my parents, my brother, my home, my life. We would leave this compound and nothing would remain.

If I were to vanish tonight, to be plucked out of my bed by a *djinn* and turned to air, what difference would it make? None to me. I feel I could disappear. I feel I am fading away. Whatever holds us on this earth is letting go of me. I am dead already. I am a dead prisoner. Just like this man.

I bring him the paper and pen and promise to come back in an hour to get the letter. Nobody bothers me. I am protected today by grief. I am unlucky, maybe even contagious. The prisoner grabs my hand but I shake him off. Nobody will touch me now.

"Thank you," he says.

His voice is cracking. I feel tired. I go outside to sit in the shade again and watch the chickens.

It is dark now. Yusuf came and sat with me for a while. He told me to eat. He said I could stay here with him, or head for the border. It makes no difference to me. I don't want to do anything.

It is cool now. There are stars and a half-moon. The moon is the malicious grin of a malicious god, leering at me, at all of us stuck here in this hot land. The stars do not banish the dark. They just let us see exactly how black the sky is.

The prisoner gave me his letter. He said nothing, just handed me the four pages I tore from a school exercise book I found in the main house. His writing is untidy, but I could read it. I read it here in my bed in this outhouse where I have slept for weeks. Reading by torchlight like we used to do, lying on our stomachs on a mattress in the basement. Nadif would read, I would whine that I could not see the pictures, and then he would turn the book around. Down there, you could hear the distant pounding of the mortars. It was hot, and sticky, and dark, but it was safe. We should have stayed in that basement.

Mum,
All that writing and I can't find the words that matter now. I don't know when you will get this,

70

or even if you will get this. This letter has no context, no place in time.

I am sorry. I am sorry for putting you through this. They say Al-Shabaab is coming to take me tomorrow. So, I doubt I will be able to write again. There is a young guy taking care of me here. His name is Abdi. He feeds me and gives me cigarettes. He is going to take the letter. I hope it gets to you somehow.

I'm sorry too for everything before this. I am sorry for cutting you out of my life for so long. I just didn't know how to deal with it. I knew you and Dad had problems, but even with the divorce, you were still my parents. Until you told me what happened in Liberia.

I don't want to overanalyse or make excuses, but when you told me that Dad was not my father, I was angry. I was lost too. Maybe, it shouldn't matter. It doesn't change anything about the love I feel for Dad, it doesn't take away the things he did for me. But it changes everything. I am not who I thought I was. And I never had a good grip on myself anyway. You know that better than anyone. I have never committed to being me. I have been the job, or the man my woman wanted, or your son, or Dad's son. I have been what other people wanted me to be.

I'm not trying to make you feel guilty. I don't want to start all that up again. I wish I had asked you more questions. You said his name was Shaun Ridge. He was a journalist. I wish I had found out more. If you were here now, in this small room, sitting on this mat with me, I would ask you: Why did you do it? Didn't you love Dad anymore? What was Shaun like? Would you have left Dad if he had lived? Did it make you feel any different about me? Did this ruin your life? Did it ruin Dad's?

These are rhetorical questions now, and maybe they were always irrelevant. Or maybe they are the wrong ones. I try not to think about dying. In a way, I don't even mind dying. I feel I might have died already. Remember that ghost story you read to me when I was about eight? It was in that book Aunt Bernadette gave us? It was about a woman who died, but didn't notice. She went about her day and then, there was that awful moment when she realised she was dead. I can't remember what triggered her realisation. Was it a story in a newspaper? Anyway, I feel a bit like that now. I don't want to suffer though. That scares me. That makes me want to curl up now, stop breathing and go. Just so I don't have to live this. I wish I didn't have to live this.

I'm running out of paper. Please Mum, can you look out for Godwin and Esther? They are still in Monrovia. I didn't mean for that to happen like it did. I tried to do right. I have given Esther money every month. You'll find the Western Union details in the drawer of the desk in my office at home. The key is in the carved box you brought me from Iraq. Maybe you could go and see them one day? Godwin is your grandson.

Maybe you can be a better grandmother than I have been a father.

I should give you a message for Esther. I should say something to Godwin. You can tell them I am sorry. For failing to be there. For leaving them. For being a bastard. I didn't know how to start loving them. I didn't give myself a chance. I was afraid. Afraid of not loving them enough, afraid of leaving Michelle, afraid of changing. Please look out for them, Mum. Tell Michelle I love her. I do, I'm just not sure if my love is enough. I'm not sure I am capable of loving anyone enough, or maybe I just don't know what it means.

And Dad, tell him I miss him. I want him to make this right like he did so many times in the past. I want him to put me on his knee and tell me it's all going to be all right. He is a wonderful father.

If the worst happens, know that I will have you all in my heart even at that time. I will keep you with me. I love you,

Peter

This is a sad letter. I do not understand all of it but I understand the pain. I wish I had had time to write to my mother. I would also have said sorry. For leaving, for not protecting her, for not knowing how to save Nadif. Sorry for this life, this country.

It is too late. For her, for me, for this place. I will not stay here with Yusuf. I will leave tomorrow. I will leave once the prisoner is gone. Our story can end together. For me, at least, there will be no other story. I have lived. What happens next is just how I die.

CHAPTER
SIX

NINA

I've taken the phone off the hook and switched off my mobile. Just for half an hour, to give me a bit of a break. They haven't stopped ringing since he was taken. Everyone wants to know how I feel, or how I am coping. That is the word they use. Coping. As if I have a bad cold or a sore back. But then, there probably isn't a tactful way of asking a mother how she is dealing with having her only son kidnapped in Somalia. My friends are at sea. I feel as though I am putting them out by making them face things they don't want to. And then there is the irony of being at the receiving end of calls from the press after so many years in the business.

In the silence, I question myself. Did Peter become a journalist because I was one? Does he have some sort of personality defect, a thirst for danger, for risk, because of me? How deep does my responsibility lie? These thoughts have tormented me every night since I heard. My face is grey with fatigue, even though I didn't sleep much before. It's one of the ironies of old age that just when it's so hard to fill the hours with anything useful or interesting, the days get longer as sleep gives up on you too.

Don Struddle called earlier today. He said the kidnappers had contacted the *Post*, and asked for a ransom of one million dollars. My Peter, the million-dollar man.

"So, what next?" I asked, grateful that my friend had the good grace not to ask me how I was doing.

"We've hired a kidnap response expert. He's based in London and his firm works for a bunch of shipping companies. They've had a fair bit of experience dealing with Somali pirates. He is going to fly to Mogadishu for us on Thursday. We're hoping he'll be able to set up a handover on the ground."

Don paused. I could sense his frustration. How helpless my feisty, never-say-die friend must be feeling. I had seen it before. Don had been with me in Liberia in 1980, covering Samuel Doe's coup and the killings that followed. Baby Liberia's first steps into madness. Don is one of a handful of people who know what happened there. He was among the first to realise. Tim found out later, but Don saw it all, and guessed even more.

"Is this expert confident the kidnappers will release Peter?"

I was struggling to keep my voice steady. I knew Don wouldn't hold it against me if I cried — we had been through a lot together and I wasn't afraid of appearing weak before him — but I guessed he was also trying to hold it together for my sake. He and Peter were close.

"Yes," Don said, his voice blowing on the wrong side of bluster.

"He reckons the men who have taken Peter are just bandits. They don't seem like ideologues. So that's a good thing. If they just want money, that's a lot easier to deal with. Of course, this has to be kept quiet. The British government will not sanction talks with terrorists, nor will the US authorities. Officially. But the paper is ready to put up the money. That's what insurance is for."

"Will the kidnappers sell him on?"

I had to ask. I might be retired now but I still follow the news. Whenever Peter is away, I embark on my own little home-study course to keep up with whatever's happening where he is. I have little else to do since I stopped working a few years ago. Now, at least, I don't have to search for his by line to find out where he is. He tells me.

I used to do the same kind of research to track Tim when we were first married and he was travelling. I suppose I was trying to feel closer to him. That unrelenting need you have in those first months. I can just about remember it. It comes to me like a faint fragrance on a country lane that yanks your brain into reverse. In those days, there was no Internet, no Google Maps with their see-all satellites. Now, I lap up everything that technology offers, sitting here at my computer with the high-pitched chatter of Parisians slinking through my open windows, and my stern Senufo masks staring down from the walls, daring me to forget.

"Frankly, Nina, I don't know. And the expert doesn't know either," Don said. "We'll just have to play it by ear. Even if Peter does get handed on to Al-Shabaab, they have never publicly killed a Western hostage in Somalia before. African soldiers yes, but never a foreign civilian. My hunch is it's all about the money."

He hesitated.

"But, things are changing fast. There are hundreds of foreign fighters in Somalia now, and with the internal splits in Al-Shabaab, and the threat of a new offensive by AMISOM . . . I don't want to be morbid but it is a tricky situation. And I know you know that, Nina."

"Where is the expert flying from?" I asked.

"London to Nairobi and then onto Mog. I know what you are thinking, Nina, and it's a bad idea. What will you be able to do in Mogadishu? You'll just be putting yourself in danger, you might make things worse."

"I can't sit here, Don. I just can't."

Don sighed again. I could imagine him running his big, hairy hands over his egg-like head. I remember him doing the same thing with his hands that awful day in Monrovia, thirty years ago, when he came to my room to comfort me.

"Let me talk to our local stringer in Nairobi. I'll get her to contact AMISOM to see if we can get you onto their base at the airport in Mogadishu. But I'm not promising anything, Nina. You can't just go dashing off like we did before. We are the old ones now. The ones who wait. That's our role."

"I know, I know."

Now, it was my turn to sigh.

"And I've been doing really well with that until now, Don. But not this time. Peter is there, and I'm damned if I am not going to be there for him when he gets out. I owe him that."

And so much more, I thought. And now the tears came, filling my eyes so that I had to move the phone to wipe them away.

Don said he would get back to me by the end of the day. He would talk to the kidnap expert, a guy called Edward Chadwick. It would be better if I went with him.

"Maybe I can actually help," I said, hating the pathetic need in my old lady's voice.

Don's sharp, angry breaths told me he was holding back.

"Maybe," was all he said. He always knew when to keep quiet. A man of few words and no waste. He spoke as he wrote. I have always liked that.

I made myself a cup of tea, staring blankly across the concrete inner courtyard three floors below as the kettle boiled. The scrawny black cat was back, lurking in the shadows, lifting its paws delicately as if stepping across a minefield. I had never realised how naturally wild cats were until I went on safari in South Africa with Peter, before we fell out. It was five, maybe six years ago, and it was our last real holiday together.

He was all grown up but his face flared like a child's when we came across some cheetahs by the road. They were sleek, thinner than I had expected, and deliciously aloof. We watched them for an hour as they sat in the dry, brittle grass, licked their fur, swished their tails and clambered onto a fallen tree to survey the surrounding area.

"They really don't care that we are here," Peter whispered, letting the camera drop to his knees for a moment. "So dignified, so remote. They seem to need so little. It's the perfect existence."

I took my tea through the red-tiled hallway, past the open cupboard where Peter's dinner jacket was still hanging. He left it here after the Foreign Correspondents' dinner last month. He stayed that night. I thought maybe he had had a row with Michelle, but he said it was just easier, closer to the restaurant. Knowing Peter that was probably true. He isn't the man for a dramatic walkout on a girlfriend, and he left happily the next morning.

Michelle. That had to be dealt with before I left.

I slumped on the couch and turned up the volume. I had been watching the news obsessively since Don called me to say he had lost touch with Peter. His name was out there now, but few other details. The paper, of course, was saying little, just that they were in contact with the relevant authorities. No photo of him yet. No confirmation of who had taken him.

A French journalist from AFP had called me, but I said nothing. That's what the young man from the Foreign Office advised when I spoke to him. In his plummy voice he told me they were doing their best to find out where Peter was being held, but he was vague on the details, prefacing every tricky answer with an awkward, guilty-sounding cough. He said they knew about the ransom demand but insisted Britain could not be involved in direct negotiations with terrorists. I said little. I didn't expect answers from Whitehall. This would have to be resolved at some other level.

The sun poured in my long, thin windows. We bought this flat when we returned from Ivory Coast in 1983. It's probably worth a lot now, although the 13th is still not Paris' most fashionable district. At that time, I suppose Tim and I had imagined we would grow old here together. Despite our problems, and the distance that had been growing between us in Abidjan, we had still not given up all hope.

Now, I am here, an old lady in a young city. A city made for lovers, for new lives, for dreams and fresh hopes. Sometimes, I enjoy walking along the Seine, especially when it's sunny but cool, looking at the paintings and posters, and the youngsters cuddling, rollerblading or holding hands. But sometimes, it makes me so sad I hurry home and hole up for a few days, preferring to be invisible in private rather than invisible in public.

Tim was devastated when he heard about Peter. I hated having to tell him over the phone. I imagined him sitting in that navy armchair in his little cottage not far from Cork city, looking out at pine trees being tickled and teased by the cheeky sea breeze. The feather-fingered branches would have kept dancing as I spoke, as if nothing was happening, as if the bottom wasn't dropping out of his world.

He didn't say much. He asked if he should come. I wasn't sure if he meant to Paris or to Mogadishu.

"Sit tight for now," I said.

I wasn't planning to go myself at that stage, but in any case, age has been kinder to me. Tim suffers from arthritis and finds it hard to move around. He can still walk and lives by himself but when I saw him last year, I was shocked by how long it took him to sit down.

"Damn rugby," he grimaced, half angrily, half foolishly as he lowered himself inch-by-inch into the chair, clinging to a part of his youth if only through his injuries.

I said nothing. We are all falling apart. It is only something to joke about before you realise what it really means, and what it feels like.

"I'll let you know as soon as I hear anything," I told him.

"Okay, okay. He'll be all right, Ninny, won't he?"

I couldn't answer. Tim hadn't called me Ninny in years. We were already too far gone for nicknames by the time we left Abidjan. The secret of staying together is to never imagine being apart. We had started to imagine it. And, of course, it was my fault.

After we split up in 1985, Tim stayed in Paris, working with a French relief agency. He still travelled, often to West Africa or to the French overseas territories like Guadeloupe, Martinique or Reunion. He moved to Cork when he retired two years ago. I had never really believed he would end up back in Cork, just a few winding miles from the house where he grew up.

We used to joke about it when we were first married, when the future was hard and certain.

"So, how about a little house in Crewe, near the railway. A nice, wee place with net curtains and a tidy, miniature garden and maybe some gnomes?" he would ask, picking on the things he found strangest about England, and about my hometown.

"Over my dead body," I laughed. "Maybe a little thatched cottage in Cork, with fat-arsed Friesians in the fields and the sea twinkling Irishly behind the rolling hills."

He laughed. I loved to make him laugh then.

"You could wear a flat cap and ride your black bicycle slowly up the boreen, and stop to chat to the neighbours about the weather, or the price of hay."

"I don't think so," he had said, shaking his head, chuckling.

But so it came to pass. Life is what happens when you're making other plans, as they say. It is cruel like that. Surely, some of our plans should count for something. I never planned on being divorced, I never planned to finish my days alone in Paris, and I never, ever dreamed, my son, the son I loved and feared and betrayed and then loved again, would be sitting somewhere in a tent or a hut in a hot land, thinking of death and home and God knows what else.

I felt so helpless. I sipped my tea and cried. For Peter now, for Peter then, for Tim and me, and me alone, and again, yes again, after all these years, I cried for Shaun. Is this all life offers? Mistakes and the time to rue them?

I had to see Michelle. I walked slowly along the canal, past lunchtime strollers staring into the dirty waters, letting the soft sway of the water slough away their workday worries. It was a beautiful day, a day without compassion. No mood-matching dark clouds or rain for me. Just a blue sky, soft sun and a light breeze. A group of school children in bright red T-shirts stood on a green metal bridge that arched over the water, looking at their perfect reflections, an almost indecent symphony of colour and symmetry.

I was nearly there. I knew Michelle would be home. She had been waiting by the phone since news of Peter's kidnapping broke. I wondered if the press had bothered her. Peter's colleagues here knew about her, of course, but they were being tight-lipped, honouring him with their silence. And Michelle did not want to be part of the story. Would that change after what I had to tell her now?

I had thought for hours about what I was about to do. I was still not sure but I thought Peter would approve. It's all bound to come out if the worst happens. And then I will not be here to try to explain. And even if the worst doesn't, something will leak. Peter will be famous. It will be less than fifteen minutes, of course. He's not a woman, he's being held in Somalia, a place few lay people know very much about at all, and he's not going to be communicative, or engaging, or dramatic when he is freed. If he is freed. But people know about Esther and Godwin. I know, Don knows and I'm sure some of Peter's friends and colleagues in the field must know too. And Esther is part of the story, even if Peter hasn't figured out yet where to place her and his son.

After he told me about his son, and I foolishly shared my own secret, Peter pulled away. His silence was my fault but I was still hurt by how easily he had banished me from his life.

He stayed close to Tim, and that rankled, of course. I'm not saying Tim did anything wrong, he was an innocent victim as well. But maybe not entirely blameless. I can't be the only one responsible for the collapse of our marriage, can I?

Michelle opened the door so quickly she might have been waiting with her hand on the handle.

"Have you heard anything?" she said. "Couldn't you tell me on the phone?"

Her voice was heavy, drenched in the tears she had already cried. I had a sudden urge to hug her, but we have never been close. She just looked so frail standing in the dim hall.

Suddenly, I didn't want to do it. I didn't want to demolish another certainty. Enough. But maybe this was my punishment. Redemption through suffering. I was too tired and too old to work it out so I followed my original plan.

"No news, well not anything really new," I said as I followed her down the narrow hallway into the sitting room. A room that we all, even Michelle, call the *seomra suite*. That's Tim's influence, a few Irish words from his childhood, echoing down the decades to this tidy apartment.

I sat on a plump armchair and she leant against the grand, fireless fireplace, an absurdity in a room so small. Peter's face beamed at me from the mantelpiece.

He looked dashing, his smile wide, crinkling the edges of his cheeks, but his eyes were hidden behind his sunglasses, which showed only a faint reflection of Michelle behind a small camera.

Perched awkwardly on the edge of the obese chair, I felt shabby and ancient in my high-waisted, badly cut jeans. My hair is still blonde, but the shade is a touch softer than my natural colour, and my curls are gone, cut short in deference to my age. Michelle is lithe and curvy. But I have known that grace, that confidence. We stared at each other, future and past.

"I need to tell you something, Michelle. In case it comes out, later. I'm sorry. There's no nice way to do this. Peter has a son in Liberia. He's five."

I stopped. I was not sure what to say next. I had rehearsed this speech, but even then I couldn't get beyond these words. I was not sure I had much to add. I know the mother's name, and where she is from, and how Peter met her, and that he supports his child, but that's it. I guess our relationship is still not wholly repaired. I should know more, but then Peter is not an easy man to know. He's an easy man to think you know.

Michelle took a breath, straightened, changed her mind and sat down on the sofa opposite me. At first, her face didn't change, and then it was as if someone stuck a pin into her neck, letting the air hiss out. She shrank, her shoulders sagging. She stopped fingering the wooden bangle that Peter brought her from his last trip to Africa. Her hands fell into her lap, like birds shot from the sky.

I wondered if I should leave. Not yet, I needed to get this done properly before leaving for Mogadishu. She needed to know everything she wanted to know. Everything or nothing. Slowly, she shook her head, raised her face and beneath her slowly smudging eyes, she smiled.

"I think I always knew this day would come," she said, speaking slowly as if she wanted to get the words exactly right. Maybe she had been rehearsing as well, I thought.

"I'm surprised that he has a son. I'm not surprised that he has another woman."

"I don't think that's how it is," I said carefully. I took a breath.

"Her name is Esther, she's from Sierra Leone. I think it was just one night."

I couldn't say "one-night stand". It seemed too flippant, too much of a cliché, and somehow disrespectful to Peter. To Esther and to Godwin.

"I don't think he's seen her again. He . . . he has a photo of the baby, of Godwin, but as a very small baby. I don't think he has been back since 2005. He doesn't have a relationship with Esther, apart from a financial one. He sends her money every month to take care of the boy, of Godwin."

Michelle listened, watching my face closely as if she was a human lie detector. I blushed as I spoke. I wasn't exactly ashamed of my son, but I felt sorry and sad for him, for them all, and for this tense, hopeful and now angry woman sitting in front of me, her legs in an expensive velour tracksuit crossed at the ankles, like a woman playing a role, a role she had long suspected she would be given.

"I'm sorry."

I didn't know what else to say. I wanted to ask her what she was going to do, but I imagined she didn't know yet. I eased myself up from the chair.

"I should go. I'm flying to Nairobi on Thursday and then on to Mogadishu."

I had to ask.

"Do you want to come? I'm going with a kidnap-and-rescue expert hired by the *Post*. I know it's a bit silly but I can't sit here."

I waited. Michelle was looking at the ground. I picked up my bag and turned to go.

"I can't go," she said, her voice steady now.

"I can't go *now*. To be honest, I'm not sure I would have wanted to anyway. But I don't want to see him, straightaway, if he . . . if he is released. It wouldn't be fair on me or on him. I wish you hadn't told me."

Her voice choked on the last words and she slammed her mouth shut, twisting her lips.

"You've poisoned this, everything. I mean, he has. Peter has. I could deal with the worry, but now, what am I feeling now? And how can I be angry when he is in danger? And yet I am. This isn't fair."

"No, it's not," I said. "Of course, it's not."

I didn't have anything else to say. I felt I should be more sympathetic but I didn't know how to be. I lost faith in life a long time ago, on a sloping street in Monrovia and I don't have what it takes to empathise with those who have yet to lose theirs. I slowly walked out and shut the door softly behind me.

I flew to London two days later, arriving with the sun in Heathrow. I had a three-hour wait before the flight to Nairobi, and I had arranged to meet Edward Chadwick at the information desk in the departures hall. I was rummaging in my handbag for my phone when I felt a tap on my arm. I turned to face an imposing man with short, brown hair and an easy-going, open face.

"Mrs Walters?"

He had a deep voice, shot through with the cadences of a soldier. Something about the lie of his hair made me think it wanted to be cut even shorter, and there was something about his eyes that gave him a somewhat sinister, capable air. A tattoo, possibly of the end of a dagger, peeked out from his shirt cuff when he stretched out his hand to shake mine.

"You must be tired. Would you like a coffee? We can get up to speed then."

He ushered me to a table in a nearby coffee shop. He went to order, taking his expensive-looking briefcase with him. I watched him in the queue. Was Edward Chadwick the man to get my son back? Don had emailed me a backgrounder on him. He'd been doing this job for three years, and had been involved in last year's headline-grabbing release of a Saudi oil tanker, which had been held by Somali pirates for fourteen months. He was the one on the ground, negotiating with the pirates' middle-men, and he organised for the money to be parachuted onto the deck as the massive ship lay at anchor off the pirate town of Hobyo, north of Mogadishu. The pirates then boarded small, rickety boats to make their escape. One boat capsized in a sudden storm and the two pirates drowned. A body was found a few days later, washed up on a beach with wet clumps of ransom dollars floating around it like the seaweed of the damned.

"So, what do you need to know from me?"

He leant back in the chair, studying me, keeping his voice low. I suddenly felt out of my depth. I had not expected to leap into details so quickly. I don't get a lot of blunt speaking these days. The few friends who have stuck with me in Paris are my age. We don't have much occasion to quiz each other. We know everything already so our conversations usually revolve around daily oddities, or anecdotes: we spin our meager story-webs elaborately to cover up the emptiness that lies beneath.

"What will you do when we get there?" I asked.

"I'll have to go and see the authorities first, a courtesy call really. They don't have any real sway in this matter, as far as we ... eh ... I understand. Obviously, I'll be talking to AMISOM commanders. But again I am not expecting much there. There are others in Mogadishu who are more ... informed, military men, of course. I can't really say any more. So far, we think ... there seems to be a consensus that Peter is not in Mogadishu. He might be somewhere just outside the city, probably not in Al-Shabaab territory for now. If these kidnappers are bandits, then they will be in neutral terrain. I've been in touch with our chaps as well. They believe, and I'm sorry I can't tell you why or how, they believe he is being held in Wanlaweyn, it's about ninety kilometres north of Mogadishu."

"Do they know anything about the people holding him?"

"To be honest, I don't think so. I'll be meeting someone in Nairobi. I can't tell you any more than that, but this person could help clarify some of these points. The British government obviously will not be officially involved in this extraction, but they are aware that we are working on it, and have ordered a media blackout on the case."

"Can they do that? Some of the details are already out there."

"Yes, I can't guarantee that nobody will break the terms — and it can't affect what's already been reported — but it's a legal ban ordered by the courts that should stop any new stuff coming out. The idea is that reporting details of the case could scupper our attempts to get Peter back."

"Did the British have any information about how he is? I know Don told you I spoke to him, and he sounded okay, I mean he sounded . . ."

I struggled to find the right word. Did I mean calm? Nervous? I actually couldn't remember exactly what Peter sounded like during that brief call. Did he sound scared or is that just what I think he must be? Like that time I tried to teach him to ride a bike in the Bois de Boulogne. We had taken his stabilisers off and he was so eager to get going. His friends were already riding up and down the street everyday, doing wheelies in the cobblestoned square near our apartment. But he was so scared. A delicate, heartbreaking mixture of determination and pure fear. I held onto the back of the seat, as he pedalled carefully, his knuckles white on the handlebars, his legs wobbly, his head bent, his eyes focused on the road, as if he feared it would suddenly rear up and attack him.

"Are you there, Mum? Are you there, Mum? Don't let go!"

I ran after him, holding the seat. Then as he gathered speed, I gave him a push.

"There you go, see, you are doing it!"

He wobbled away from me.

"Mum, are you still holding on?"

"No, but you're fine, you're fine. Good boy!"

He turned his head to look at me and I caught a glimpse of terrified eyes before he crashed to the ground. He wasn't hurt, but his eyes were hard.

"You let go!"

Maybe I always expected too much of him.

Edward was staring at me. I flipped a tear away with the tip of my finger. I have less shame now.

"No, I have no definite information on his condition. My contacts in Whitehall say they have confirmation from a reliable source that he is still alive. Who knows who that source is. Maybe someone who knows the bandits, or someone who works for us in Somalia. They may not be officially present, but you can be sure MI6 have people working around there, especially with all the young Brits heading over to join up with Al-Shabaab and the other foreign fighters from Al-Qaeda."

Edward spoke calmly. He clearly knew his subject.

"Have you been to Mogadishu before?" I asked.

"Yes, a couple of times."

He paused, the kind of pause that acts as a full stop.

"How about you?"

"No, I've never been. I lived in West Africa in the late seventies and eighties, and I've been to Nairobi a few times, but never Mogadishu. It wasn't really a very big story when I was in my prime. By the time the US soldiers were killed in 1993, I was already doing travel pieces in Europe. By then, I had my eye on a slow, steady drift to retirement. My last big assignment was Iraq in 1991. Not much call for women over the age of forty in journalism firefighting."

He smiled. How could he imagine not being useful? *It will come to you*, I thought with a hint of malice. It comes to us all.

The plane was on time. Edward helped me lift my bag into the overhead bin, and then pointedly buried his nose in a book. I didn't mind. I don't like talking on planes. I have always thought that it is best to rein in any desire to chat until the plane is on its way down. At least then you won't run out of things to say, or get trapped for too long in a soulless conversation about plumbing or cars.

I looked out the window at the baggage-handlers hefting suitcases onto the conveyor belt that would carry them into the plane. I closed my eyes. I always liked long plane journeys, except when Peter was small, of course. Before, when I travelled alone, across West Africa or back to England, I welcomed the vacuum created by being suspended in the air, caught between worlds in the ether, able to think but not able to do anything. Reflection without the need for action.

Sometimes I fantasised that the plane wasn't actually going anywhere, that it was all some kind of optical illusion and that hundreds of little men were moving the scenery around outside us, while the plane's engines hummed meaninglessly, and the air circulated loudly, and we sat, watching movies we didn't want to see, reading books, and avoiding our neighbours' eyes.

Mogadishu was hot. Hot is hotter when you're older. Everything is more when you get past sixty. More wet, more slippery, more bothersome, more steep. A Ugandan soldier, a green giant in combat gear and armed with a heavy sub-machine gun and a toothy smile, met us in the airport's basic VIP lounge — all massive armchairs with delicate, inappropriate lace back covers.

"Welcome to Mogadishu," he said jauntily.

Then, as if only just remembering that we were not relief workers on a donor trip or diplomats on a whistle-stop, credential-boosting fly-through, he stopped smiling. He shook my hand gravely.

"We are praying for your son. I had the pleasure of talking to him before his capture. He came to the base when he arrived, just to let us know he was here."

I grasped the big, toothy man's hand hard. At last, a tangible link to my son as he was, is, in Somalia. I had to stop myself from taking his hand in both of mine.

"I am Colonel Francis Mugweri. I will take you to the base now and you will speak to the AMISOM force

94

commander. He will tell you what we know and what we can do."

Later, I sat alone in the shipping container-cum-bedroom they had assigned me. Edward had left the base. He didn't say why or where he was going but I didn't really want to know. I sat on the bed and started to unlace my boots. I had stepped in a puddle by a newly washed truck on my way across the yard outside, and my soles left footprints on the bare lino floor. Footprints that led straight to the past.

I lay on the bed and drifted back to Monrovia, back to 1980, to the place where my life came off its tracks, back to the start of Peter's story, the beginning of the journey that led him and me to Somalia thirty years later. Back to the footprints that promised so much, and led nowhere.

CHAPTER
SEVEN

NINA

I met Shaun Ridge in Monrovia in the crazy April days following Samuel Doe's coup. I was living in Abidjan at the time, covering West Africa for an American newspaper, the *Chronicle*. Tim and I had moved to Ivory Coast in 1978. It was our Big Adventure. We had married in Paris the year before and we wanted to get out of Europe.

When Tim got a job as regional director for a Canadian NGO based in Abidjan, it seemed like a godsend. We packed two suitcases each and moved to that sweaty, lush, smelly city on the lagoon. We lived in a low, cool house not far from the landmark Hotel Ivoire, watched bright lizards do push-ups on the rim of our pool and waited with childish excitement for the bananas to grow on our only banana tree. They grew, we admired them for a few days and then, one night, they were stolen.

Our new life was everything we had dreamed of, and we were happy. Maybe that was the last time I was really happy. Not delirious, but excited, and untroubled by the complications that would come to be such a part of my life. Later, I would have to look for happiness, and grasp it firmly.

We both travelled a lot in those days. It was an exciting time to be a young journalist in West Africa and although my editors only had a limited attention span, especially for news from French-speaking countries, I found enough good stories to keep me busy. I flew into a febrile Accra after a young air force officer, Lieutenant Jerry John Rawlings, was broken out of jail by his friends and seized power. I travelled to Freetown to report on a new one-party state. I reported on the end of the Paris-Dakar rally in the bougainvillea-scented Senegalese capital. Years filled with one-room airports that shook when planes took off, rickety aircrafts carrying nervously fluttering fowl, bone-crushing journeys in low-slung cars on roads that barely deserved the name. Sweet coffees on wooden stools under corrugated iron roofs, blessedly cool Cokes after hours riding in the dust, cold bucket showers in shabby, closet-sized hotel rooms, and beers in lean-tos on the edge of vast, chittering forests. I loved it all.

Tim was dealing with the fallout from the perennial droughts and floods that ravaged the region. After years working as a press officer for a pharmaceutical company in Paris, he had found his life's calling. We were apart a lot and when we met on the road, in run-down, dirty hotels halfway between nowhere and the back-of-beyond, we were usually so exhausted by what we had seen or done that we just lay side by side on our vaguely itching beds, holding hands and silently sipping giant, lukewarm beers.

Liberia was always the big story for me. The country was set up as a haven for freed American slaves in 1822 and became independent just over two decades later. So, for my editors, this was a little bit of America in Africa. There was something romantic about the country, about the very concept behind its creation, about its name and the name of its capital, which honoured James Monroe, one of the founding fathers of the United States. These words were round, substantial and full of potential. They conjured up elevated dreams that might one day become reality: Liberia, Monrovia, Utopia. Liberia was also an important Cold War ally in those paranoid decades.

The first big shock came in 1980 when Doe, a bulky, thick-lipped, almost illiterate master sergeant, seized power in a rush of blood and brutality. The coup marked the end of the political and economic dominance of descendants of the American slaves, who had ruled the country as their own personal cotton ranch since independence. Doe was a Krahn, a member of one of Liberia's largest native tribes, and now, it was his people's turn at the trough.

I flew in on April 14th, sweeping low over the forbidding mangrove swamps and rigid rubber trees, two days after Doe, who had been trained by US Special Forces, burst into the presidential palace. One of his men stuck a bayonet into the terrified, sleep-addled president, William R. Tolbert Jnr, spilling his guts onto a plush, purple carpet at the door to his bedroom.

The killing was still going on when I arrived. Doe had captured around a dozen of Tolbert's cabinet, including the dead president's elder brother. The execution of these men on a beach in Monrovia marks the beginning of Peter's story, and the start of a new chapter in my life. As I watched their bodies jerk and slump forward, the wires used to tie them to the wooden stakes cutting into suddenly lifeless flesh, I caught Shaun's eye and, in that terrible moment, all the suggestions, hints and doubts of the past week hardened into the certainty that we would be together. And that night we were.

I won't use this as an excuse. I wanted Shaun. But I was also probably in some kind of shock. The executions on the beach beside the army barracks were messy and cruel. Four of the condemned were forced to watch the others die as there were only nine stakes. The executioners were lousy shots, it took a long time for some of the men to die. Some of them trembled, urine staining the legs of their crinkled trousers. Some tried to preserve a little dignity, raising their eyes away from the dancing, jubilant crowd. An unspeakable fear blazed from some of the men's eyes as the killers cocked their rifles. Seagulls wheeled overhead and the waves crashed, and all these sounds were so normal, such an affront to the extraordinary horror taking place.

Shaun and I were in the crowd, but then he moved forward, crouching and bending so that he seemed almost to be dancing himself. I still have some of his photos — years later I found them online and printed them out — but I don't need them. I will never forget that scene, those eyes, that terror. Today, as I lie here on this cot bed in Mogadishu, those eyes burn inside my closed lids. But now they are Peter's eyes.

I met Shaun a week earlier at a beachside hotel, just hours after I had arrived, flustered and agitated, from the maelstrom that was Robertsfield Airport. Crowds of people desperate to leave a country turned on its head, tense soldiers with guns held like shields, grasping hands, and rising above the cacophony, the peremptory screeching of officials.

I had stayed at this same hotel during the rice riots the previous year, when Tolbert ordered his soldiers to shoot at crowds protesting a new tax on their staple food, an order that led directly through time to the bayonet that eviscerated him. This was the journalists' hotel — every African city has a place like this, with fixers, sporadic water, belching generators, and a bar that is open for the asking.

Sylvia, the receptionist with the hooded eyes and long neck, welcomed me warmly.

"Miss Nina, you have come back. Ah dese times, dey are strange."

"They are, Sylvia, for sure," I said, dropping my duffel bag on the floor and slowing my speech, adjusting to the rhythms of the place.

"But, at least, they give me a chance to come visit again. Are there any rooms?"

"But, Miss Nina, as soon as we knew you was coming, we kept your room. Certainly. You can go straight. You need anytin'?"

"No, no, thanks, Sylvia. Is there water?"

"Water there be, Miss Nina. Of course, now it is not hot. Now is late."

I smiled, picked up my bag and headed up the dark stairs. The lights were out, but since it was daytime, they had not put on the generator.

In my dank, dark room, I sat on my bed, catching my breath after the rush. It was starting to rain, big, slug-like drops slapping onto the broad leaves of the trees in the courtyard below. I stood on the balcony, filling my lungs with the rich, rotten smell of soil at the start of a downpour. I have always loved that smell. So full of promise but with a sinister whiff of things unseen, buried in the soon-to-be-swirling mud.

"Nina!"

The shout came from the other side of the balcony that ran around the second floor of the building, circling the pitter-pattering courtyard of oversized plants and obscenely bright flowers. Through the curtain of rain, I saw Don Struddle.

He was heading towards me with the hunched-over, hopping walk of a man who is sensitive about his height. He folded me in a bear hug. I had met Don in Paris, just weeks after I moved there to take a job as a junior reporter at UPI, a once-mighty newswire. He was working for Reuters, and also looking for his big break. After journalism school in the States, he had spent a year in the south of France, working in bars and picking grapes to improve his French. He was already losing his hair, and had a great line in terse put-me-downs, as well as a much older hack's disrespect for hierarchy and the bullshit of getting ahead by pleasing your superiors. I was a little in awe of his easy confidence, his writing, his professionalism. In those early days, I wondered if something else might happen between us, but then I met Tim, and Don faded a little from my life as I immersed myself in my new relationship, barely able to believe that I had found love in the city of lights. I was twenty-five and still believed in a fairytale ending.

"So good to see a friendly face," Don said, wiping a thin sheen of sweat off his forehead. He had already grown the scratchy beard that would become as much a part of the man as his staccato sentences.

"Did you just get in?"

"Yes, when did you arrive?" I said.

"This morning. I was in Sierra Leone. You know that story on the diamond mines that I told you about? Well, they finally sent me last week. So when this shit blew up, I hopped on the first plane — mind you, that's a bit of a misnomer for the crate I came in."

"So, what's the latest?" I said, lighting a cigarette and offering Don the packet. He lit up, took a drag and sighed.

"It's crazy, Nina. This is such a fucked-up place. Doe's like a cartoon character, he's too bloody colourful to be real. You couldn't make him up. Mad of course, evil. But some seem to like him. Guess the others weren't much better, although they didn't wear their craziness on their sleeves. The killing hasn't stopped. More bodies on the streets every day. God knows when it will end."

102

"What have you got on this afternoon?" I asked.

"Going to head out to the centre of town, try to get some colour. Maybe cruise past the presidential palace, see what's going on."

"How is Doe with the press?" I asked.

"Okay, well, so far he hasn't caused us any trouble, but it's a bit dicey out there. The boys on the roadblocks are high on booze, power and blood. Best to travel in numbers. Do you want to come?"

I agreed to meet Don a few hours later. He strode off after asking about Tim and giving my arm a tight squeeze. I went back to my room to call my husband.

The line was crackly, and an irate woman kept breaking into our conversation. I could just about make out Tim's voice. I imagined him slouched on our battered sofa, looking out at the pool and the lizards.

I filled him in on the journey, the roadblocks, the state of the hotel, and then started to talk about meeting Don, but the repeated interjections of the woman and the disconcerting two-second gap between what I said and when he heard it rendered the whole effort ridiculous.

Frustrated by another delay, I snapped. "Never mind, it doesn't matter. I'll tell you later."

I felt bad immediately and could only hope the static had swallowed my senseless rebuke.

"I miss you," I said, overcome suddenly with tiredness, sapped by the thought of the work ahead.

"What? Oh yes, I miss you too. Do you know yet how long you are staying?"

I told him no. It would depend on the story. It always did and Tim always understood.

After a few more minutes of interference-ridden, mistimed endearments, we hung up. I lit a cigarette. So often, these phone calls left me wanting more. A side effect of the unrealistic expectation that a phone call could somehow make up for solitude, that it could effectively transmit the level of your longing, that simple words could convey the almost physical sensation of missing someone.

And maybe even then, there was something else.

I *do* remember vaguely worrying at that time if our travelling was a tribute to our individual independence, or just a way of obscuring cracks in our relationship, fissures that would otherwise have demanded treatment. I don't know why I felt so morose sitting in that hotel room. Maybe it was the rain, or the chaos outside on the streets. Maybe I was just tired. Sometimes, the big changes in life demand little more.

I decided to get a coffee and headed down to the bar. Three Lebanese men were hunched over a plastic table, whispering like spies in a bad movie. Two Liberian teenagers were perched like dolls on wobbly bar stools, their hair laboriously straightened and dyed red and blue. Their skirts were short, skimming plump buttocks, their tops tightly stretched over full breasts, their heels high, their eyes empty as they scanned the bar's few occupants.

"Excuse me, are you a journalist?"

I looked up, annoyed at the interruption, a frown ready to repel the idly curious or seedily opportunistic, and saw a dark-haired man, his pallor startling in the tropical heat, smiling down at me. He had a camera around his neck and another slung over his shoulder.

"Good guess. Can I help you?" My tone was frosty.

"Well, I've just arrived and I'm basically looking for a little information."

He paused, eyebrows raised expectantly.

I hated this: foreign journalists parachuting into Africa and seeking me out to poach my local knowledge before heading off self-importantly to cover stories I considered mine. But there was something engaging about the way the gangly stranger had asked, straight up with no pretence. And his smile was disarming.

"You'd better join me then," I said.

That's how it happens. A gesture, an open palm motioning towards an empty chair.

He sat down gratefully, placing one heavy camera carefully on the table.

"Shaun Ridge."

He stretched his hand across the grimy, fly-speckled table.

"I'm a freelance photographer from London. I mean, I'm not from London. Obviously. I'm from Colorado but I live in London."

The smile again. I couldn't help smiling back.

I introduced myself, told him I lived in Abidjan. At least he knew where that was.

"Ah, a real Africa hand. My lucky day," he said. "Well, I know you are probably thinking how presumptuous of me to just waltz in here and badger you for information, but would it help if I bought you a beer?"

My face lit up at his accurate strike, but I accepted the beer. By the time the waiter returned and laboriously opened two large, almost-cool bottles, Shaun had told me a lot about himself, speaking quickly as if to justify his request for help, to prove his credentials.

He was a regular visitor to Africa and had worked in Ghana, Sierra Leone, Ethiopia and Angola, but never in Liberia. He had spent time in Nairobi, and Johannesburg, but was now based in London.

"You've been here before obviously," he said, sipping his beer and fixing big green eyes on me. I felt uncomfortable under those eyes. They seemed to miss nothing. They were smarter than his face, which was a little too pretty, perhaps.

"Yes, a couple of times. Last year, during the rice riots, of course. Mind you, it doesn't mean I have much more of a grip on what's happening now. It's a little crazy, and Doe is something of an unknown quantity. I mean, his character is obvious. A typical bully with a massive chip on his shoulder. But he's not just a buffoon. He's way too dangerous for that."

I liked the way he listened. Actively, with those eyes never moving from my face. I tried to look at his lips instead, but that didn't help. I was unsettled, but I wasn't sure I disliked the feeling.

"I wonder where's a good place to get some street pictures, you know, people going about their lives, shopping at the market maybe?"

He tucked his too-long brown hair behind his ears. They were small, I was surprised.

"I'm not too sure yet. I'm meeting up with a friend soon, Don Struddle from Reuters in Paris. Do you know him?"

He shook his head.

"He happened to be in Sierra Leone, working on a story, and flew here when Doe took over. I'm meeting him in about half an hour, then we'll go out, drive around, try to find out what's going on today."

I hesitated. Don would not be thrilled to have an out-of-town stranger tagging along. But then again, like he said, it was safer to travel in a group.

"Do you want to come?"

Five little words. That's all it took.

Shaun headed off to his room to get ready. *Safety in numbers*, I thought as I went to get my stuff too. Even then, I had a foreboding, or no, not even that. Just a vague sense that Shaun Ridge would not just be an on-the-road acquaintance.

I spent a lot of time with Shaun over the next few days. Don was wary, terser than usual when he joined us that first day, but he relented. You couldn't dislike Shaun. That sounds a little dismissive, like saying he was "nice", but it was true. He had an innate charm, an ease of being and a sincerity that just melted resistance because it was clearly not put on.

We worked hard, tearing around Monrovia in a battered Ford with a garrulous driver called Stephen, who kept us up to date with the latest rumours. And there were many. People were disappearing every day, mutilated bodies were turning up overnight, as though some mysterious plague was scything through this shabby city by the sea. People were terrified but Stephen was not one of them. He belonged to Doe's tribe, the Krahn.

"We have suffered for too long, eh. My brother will do good by us," he would say, even as he swerved to avoid another decomposing corpse.

One day, we attended a hastily convened press conference in the executive mansion. Convened is the wrong word. We were summoned. The big man strode in, almost bursting out of his grand uniform with its fake medals and stolen stripes. His speech was nearly unintelligible, like trying to catch bubbles and put them in your pocket.

I listened to Doe expound on the future of a country he was bleeding of its people. Spit showered from his fat lips, his hands flashed gold and silver. I tried to note down a few full quotes but the bubbles floated away, crazy ideas that would survive only as long as this crazed bubble-master lived to breathe them out. I didn't think he would live long. As it turned out, I was very wrong.

That evening, we sat in the hotel bar, bantering the day away over beers and greasy samosas. After a while, Don excused himself. He had to check in with his editors. I was done for the day. Shaun had managed to find a driver to take his film to the airport in time for the evening flight to Freetown. He had a man there who would send the rolls of film on to London. With luck, his pictures would be in his newspaper's office in four or five days. Maybe because of this, he was happy, despite the stultifying heat that would soon liquify into rain, the mosquitoes buzzing around us, and the almost inedible samosas.

"Do you enjoy living in West Africa?"

I liked the way he spoke. Not a drawl but not a rush. As though every sentence was perfectly thought out and he had no doubt about it. Or about anything else.

"I think so." The way he talked made me want to take my time too. With Tim, we tripped over each other's sentences, rushing to find the right words, or better jokes, or smarter asides. Ironic really when we had all the time in the world.

"It can be tough sometimes. Everything seems to take longer, to be more complicated, and then there are the bugs and the illnesses, the heat. But it beats living in Crewe."

"Is that where you're from?" I nodded, taking a sip of beer, swallowing some jokes, some put-me-downs. I wanted to be careful here and I was trying very hard not to wonder why.

He talked a little about his hometown in Colorado but it seemed so far away from Monrovia. So we talked about common ground in London. He had moved there with his wife but they were divorced three years ago. I was curious to hear more about this failed marriage, but I didn't want to presume too much intimacy. And maybe I didn't want to talk about Tim. I remember how guilty I felt already. Not because of what I had done, not then. But because of what I wanted to do and because I wanted to do it despite

Tim. And what did that say about me, about him, about us?

I can't remember everything we talked about that night. I remember when it started to rain, he moved his chair around the table so that we sat side by side watching the rain waterfall off the thatched roof of the bar. We could barely hear each other, so we bent closer. I remember marvelling at his long lashes.

Finally, too late and too soon, it was time to go to bed. We walked upstairs together. His room was around the other side of the courtyard. I fumbled to get my key from the pocket of my jeans. I finally tugged it free and turned to say goodnight. He was leaning against the railing, smiling slightly. I could just see his mouth in the feeble light thrown from the lamp above my door. The rest of his face was in shadow. He stepped forward. Slowly, he ran his finger down my cheek, lightly brushing away my damp hair.

"You're a lovely woman. Goodnight, Nina."

Then he walked away.

They executed the politicians three days later. That night Shaun and I slept together. I had filed my story from the restaurant downstairs, unhappy with my inability to reproduce what I had seen, what I had felt. All my words were not enough. Shaun had disappeared to send his film. I climbed slowly up the dim steps to the second floor, the images I had failed to convey flashing in the dark corners of my mind. He was standing outside my door. We didn't say a word, but as soon as I turned the key, he pushed past me, slammed the door and pulled me to him. We kissed feverishly. I

110

remember finding the soft hair at the back of his neck and clutching him to me. By then, I had stopped thinking. I had stopped wondering why, and what if, and why not, and what next. I was just a mouth and hands and skin. Everything was touch.

Of course, it was lust and desperation. This happens all the time in places where death is all around, making the body ache to live, to affirm life in the most basic way. Maybe it *was* just a one-night stand. Maybe it could have been more. Those "maybes" have tormented me ever since.

We didn't talk much afterwards. There was nothing to say, and everything to say, and no way to say it.

I woke to a soft knocking. The bed was empty. I shuffled across the damp boards to the door. Shaun was standing there, dripping in the relentless rain.

"Hi," he said, sounding a little uncertain. "I've brought you some coffee."

I wanted to stroke the drops that were sliding down his cheeks. He put two blue-and-white china cups with tepid coffee on the bedside table, and then stood awkwardly facing me.

"I don't know what to say," I finally murmured.

"Me neither," he said. "I'm not sorry. I'm happy, but . . ."

He smiled now but his eyes seemed troubled. He had lost that easy composure, and looked younger.

"I'm not sorry either," I said finally. "Well, I don't think I am. I don't know what to think. I'm not sure what happened here."

He didn't answer. Outside, we could hear the irregular thud of distant gunfire. Another day for Monrovia. He came to me and hugged me. I buried my head in his chest, breathing in his mix of chemical-smelling hotel soap and dank rain. Even today, I can remember that precise smell. We stood together for a long time, listening to the drops drumming on the roof, the whistling birds and the distant bullets. When he walked out, his heavy boots left muddy footprints on the wooden floor.

When I was younger, my cousin was killed while driving his motorbike along a road lined with fields and placid cows near Crewe. He wasn't speeding, he wasn't drunk, he wasn't high. He came to a corner and a woman in a small car came the other way, and she cut the corner a little too much, and hit him. He was thrown off the bike over a stone wall and hit the soft part of the back of his head on a rock when he landed. That was it.

If the car had been an inch to the other side of the line, if a more conscientious farmer had chucked the stone to the edge of the field while wandering around, if my cousin had been five minutes late that morning. I have always been fascinated by how random our lives are. I like stories about the almosts, the "what ifs", the "might haves" of history. If Halifax had not gone to the dentist, Churchill might not have been prime minister. What if John F. Kennedy had decided not to travel in an open-top car? What if I had not gone to the hotel bar that first day, what if Shaun had found someone else to question? But what Lord Random giveth, he taketh away. I, of all people, should have known that.

Shaun, Don and I went out later that day to see what was going on in town. We decided to go to the Masonic Lodge, an imposing white building that stood on a hill, frowning down on the sea and the city through long windows protected by self-important columns. Tolbert had been the Grand Master of the Lodge, and it was dominated by Americo-Liberians. Most of the men shot on the beach were Freemasons. Stephen drove as usual, swerving dangerously and stepping on the brakes so hard that we slammed our heads into each other and into the car doors.

Shaun sat in the front and I was glad. I didn't want to deal with our new intimacy in a tiny car in front of Don, who was part of my other life. I did not want to let that in yet. There was no place for the real world in this sinister otherworld of goons, and villains, and lust, and maybe love. But I felt that Don sensed something anyway.

He gave me one of his sharp looks soon after I joined him and Shaun in the lobby. I greeted them both casually but I was probably blushing. I have always blushed. And maybe my questions about where we were going were too quick to be casual. Or maybe I just looked different. I did try to avoid looking at Shaun. Maybe that was it. Now, I wish I had feasted my eyes on him.

It happened so fast. We were outside the Lodge, which seemed quiet and subdued, suddenly too visible and too vulnerable behind its white stone outer wall.

We scanned the street for soldiers, armed men and beggars, anyone who could target or trouble us. Don was saying something about how the Lodge looked like it had been plucked from America's deep south, when Shaun fell. We didn't even hear the shot. Of course not.

I found out afterwards that it had been fired almost a kilometre away, somewhere on a nearby hill where two soldiers I would never know, or ever meet, were arguing over a stolen car. Shaun fell without a word.

He died instantly, they said, the bullet tearing a hole into his skull just above one of those shell-like ears, ears that only hours earlier I had been kissing. I didn't realise he was dead. Don and I dropped to our knees, yelling his name. Stephen started the engine, screaming at us to get in.

We pulled Shaun's lifeless body into the backseat. I jumped in beside him. At some point, I thought I heard someone screaming. It took me a while to realise it was me. I rested Shaun's head on my lap. His beautiful green eyes were closed, his lashes still. His blood was on my fingers as I stroked his soft hair.

I sobbed his name over and over like a prayer. But Lord Random has no time for prayers. We took him to JFK Hospital, but I don't remember much about that. There was nothing to do. Later, Don took me back to the hotel, I closed the door on him and lay on my bed, eyes dry from crying. It was then that I saw Shaun's footprints on the floor. The mud had dried but the imprint was clear. I crawled from the bed and traced the outline with my hand. I slid down until I was resting my cheek on those marks. In that awful, dark, endless moment, they were all I had left. But of course, there was also Peter.

It is late now. I came out of the container to get some fresh air, to stare at the bobbing lights out on the softly seething Indian Ocean. The moon is up, and the city beyond the base's sandbagged walls is quiet. I return to the container, turn on the air conditioner and crawl under the thin covers. The bed is too small and the slender mattress is going to wreak havoc on my back. But I am tired. I don't know where Edward has gone. I will find him tomorrow. Maybe he has learnt something about my son. About our lost, lonely son, our Liberian love child.

CHAPTER
EIGHT

PETER

Footsteps. They are coming. I am lying on my mattress, face to the wall and I do not turn around, not even when the door bursts open. The footsteps are in my cell now, along with heavy breathing, and the offensive, threatening smell of unwashed men. Someone clicks off a safety. They don't need to threaten me. Something broke inside me when Abdi told me Al-Shabaab were coming. Hope has no place in here now.

"Get up."

It is a new voice and the familiar accent catapults me into the past. I am in Soho on a rare, real summer day, sitting at a metal table perched precariously on the narrow pavement, outside one of those tiny cafés that cherish continental aspirations, dreams that have been thwarted by the British climate.

"I said, get up!"

The voice is harsher now but still very London. I stand slowly and turn around. The Englishman is shorter than me, and that is the first surprise. Dark, lazy eyes assess me through rimless glasses. He tilts his head and his eyes disappear as the sunlight catches his lenses, making him look like a sci-fi villain. He is dressed like the others but his foreignness cannot be contained by the black-and-white chequered scarf or the khaki fatigues. He is wearing expensive hiking boots, while the four men next to him have flip flops or sandals hemming in knobbly, poor-man toes. Abdi stands by the door, his gun in his hands. He looks different, somehow lost, or maybe I am just imagining this. It is the least of the hallucinations that have tormented me these last few hours. Beside him is an older man in a striped shirt and red-and-orange *macawis*, bony ankles peeking from the bottom of his sarong-like skirt. He is smirking. He whispers something to Abdi, but despite the self-satisfaction on the older man's face, they are clearly on the fringe of this event.

The Eagle is in the room too, his big nose covered by his scarf, his eyes restless. He is standing behind the Englishman, another almost-irrelevant watcher. He is only a minor character after all. This is a new story, and it belongs to this slender youth with the glasses and the boots. I realise he is younger than me too, and that this is not necessarily a good thing. Youth can distinguish itself by its cruelty, a kind of unfettered, irresponsible excess of energy.

"You will come with us today," the Englishman says. "You are now in the hands of Al-Shabaab, *Allahu Akbar*."

The others echo the final words, and I begin to shake. I am adrift between this accent, its provenance, and these words. I am losing the fragile grip I had on this new sub-life.

I do not answer. There is nothing to say. I have said all I am going to say in my letter, and I can only hope that Abdi will somehow get it to Mogadishu and to the African Union forces there. They will know what to do with it. By then, my name might be known, if it is not already now. My face will be known — a bloody image hopefully hidden deep in the Dark Web where only the initiated will find it. Or a black-and-white dated photo in the bottom right-hand corner of a British broadsheet with seven paragraphs about what happened to me. The what, the where, the when, the how, but never, the why. No one will ever know the why, because the real whys are always too big to include.

The Englishman is staring at me. I stare back, not defiantly, but I want to meet his gaze with something. I will not hang my head in front of him. I have nothing to be ashamed of. At least not here.

"They told me you have spoken to your mother. They say she lives in Paris. It is a beautiful city. I have been a few times. You have come a long way, Peter Maguire. And it wasn't the wisest of journeys."

He pauses, waiting for a reaction. I will not respond to his fake familiarity, even if his accent, his very nature is stirring faint hopes. This man is like me. He speaks like me. He has seen what I have seen. Maybe I could talk to him?

"But you know that now," he smiles. "You are obviously a man of courage. I have read about you. I like to do my research and, in fact, I almost became a journalist myself. I have read your stories from Africa, Iraq and elsewhere. You write well."

We could've been outside that café in Soho. I feel dizzy. I need to be alone again.

One of the fighters coughs. Another shuffles his feet. The Englishman smiles, almost apologetically.

"They are right. It is time for me to go. We will take you this evening. It is better at night. This has just been a staging post, Peter. It is time now for you to come with us. I think you know what's coming. You are a British spy in Somalia. Our Somalia. I won't insult you with the usual diatribe. You know how this works but don't worry, it won't last much longer."

He leaves quickly, his rapid step a throwback to life in a jam-packed city with dodgem-style pavements and colliding umbrellas. His pace marks him out from the others too. They walk slowly, silently with their heads down. Abdi leaves last and I can hear him locking the door. I try to catch his eye before he turns, for no other reason than to make a connection. But he does not look at me. Something has happened to him. And again, I think that Abdi may be as much a prisoner as I am.

The Englishman came back a few hours later. It was mid-afternoon. Abdi had left my food earlier in the day, but he did not speak to me. Maybe there is nothing left to say. The Englishman had removed his headscarf and opened the top buttons of his shirt. He looked even younger, like a teenager going through a military, camo phase.

He held out his hand.

"My name is Burhan."

And with those few words, I began to hope again. Here was a name, not just an institution or an ideology.

My fate was no longer on some cosmic roulette table where my job, colour and nationality had decided the outcome before I even spun the wheel. Here was an individual. I could work with that. Maybe.

Burhan didn't seem to have a gun. I felt slightly offended by his nonchalance and I did not offer my hand. He shrugged and eased gracefully onto the mattress, his back to the wall. I sat on the mat, my fingers nervously pulling at loose strands. My hands looked thinner, the veins more prominent. My body was sloughing me off, getting ready for the next phase.

As I twisted the prickly red threads, I thought of a Frida Kahlo painting I had seen years ago in the Petit Palais in Paris. *The Two Fridas* showed her holding hands with herself, blood ribbons connecting to two figures, their two hearts. One Frida had cut the end of the scarlet filament with a scissors. Red drops stained her white dress. I held a red strand over my dirty white robe. If only I had scissors.

"Why did you come to Somalia?" Burhan asked.

Fury washed over me, heating my face. My rage had nothing to do with his innocuous question, and everything to do with the answer. Because the answer was never going to be enough. Not for me, not for Guled, not for Michelle, not for my mother, not for Esther, and not for Godwin.

"Why did you?" I retorted. "I'll be damned if I'm going to be a field study for some wannabe journalist-turned-*jihadi*."

The Englishman smiled.

"A reporter to the end."

He stressed the last words, laughing again to see me flinch.

He began tracing shapes with his slim fingers on the mattress. Squares and circles, and circles within squares.

"But let me humour you. I guess you have a right to know a little about your executioner. You will not understand because you cannot. I can give you the facts and you will make assumptions as all media do, and you will think you know my story. I was born in Mogadishu in 1985. My father was an academic but we fled when Siad Barre fell in 1991. He may have been a dictator but my parents could see that what would replace him would be worse. They made their way to the camp at Dadaab in Kenya. I don't remember much of that time, but my father told me he paid for a ride to the border, and then bribed his way across. We were not your typical refugees, Peter. You wouldn't have written about us then."

A mocking smile.

"Eventually, we were offered asylum in the UK. My father was a mathematician, a good one. He taught at the Somali National University in Mogadishu, and when we moved to England, he became a second-level maths teacher in Ealing. Have you been there, Peter?"

I shook my head. I might be half-British but London was just a destination to me, a nice place for a weekend away. Paris is where I learned to write, read, ride a bike along the cobblestones, fall in love with unattainable girls, drink too much tongue-blasting Beaujolais once a year, party too long, and where I have tried to love.

121

London has always been for visiting, like Cork, like Abidjan, like Monrovia. And yet Paris was still foreign to me. Still an exotic place where I could revel in my difference. I was always someone special in Paris. I think that's why I stayed there so long.

I said nothing of this to Burhan. This was his conversation, his show, his indulgence. I couldn't figure out if he was trying to befriend me, scare me, annoy me or if he was just bored, this urbane Londoner stuck in a Somali backwater with big-toed *jihadis* and silent country boys for company.

"I guess you think you know the rest. I have read the articles — these so-called exclusives that purport to know about foreign fighters coming here to join the war. They always portray us as confused, stupid youngsters who don't realise how lucky we are to live in the West."

He stopped, he was breathing harder now. This smooth boy-man commander had his own trigger points. Everyone has them. Tender bruises under the skin that are almost invisible but change the way you move, imperceptibly.

"You've read the stories. Maybe you've even written them. About the preachers in the mosques. The radical imans who proselytise and persuade young men to come here. Some of it is true, I suppose. There is a lot of that in the States, in Minneapolis, in Canada. But it was not like that for me. I am not a follower. I make up my own mind. That is why I have become a leader here."

He waved his hand at the room, seeming not to notice the irony of the gesture.

"I studied at the London School of Economics. I have a degree in International Relations."

He laughed. It was almost a giggle.

"I came because I wanted to defend my country. And I am fed up with how your Western countries are treating Muslims around the world."

His voice was lower now, fiercer but these were practiced phrases. Rehearsed through repetition. Maybe there is no unique way to express these sentiments.

"You cannot imagine what it is like as a Muslim to watch the news every night. To see how we are ground down, unable to practise our religion freely, condemned by your oppressive systems. September 11th was one of the happiest days of my life because we were finally fighting back. When the towers came down, I had tears in my eyes, Peter. Tears of joy because I knew things had changed for ever. You, and your people, and your systems, and your arrogant governments were finally afraid."

"They are not my systems," I said slowly.

I did not want to engage with him, but something about the glibness of his diatribe, coupled with his obvious youth, annoyed me.

If I was going to die, I would not go quietly. I would fight back. I would force this man, and the others, to at least look over the edge, to acknowledge that their reality was just that, their reality. What others considered one of my greatest failings, my lack of ideology, would be my weapon here in this no man's land between life and death.

"What good are you doing here?" I sneered. "You're just a pawn. Out of place, out of your depth. Just like me. You're being played by Al-Shabaab's local leaders. This is their country, not yours. Global jihad? What good is it going to do? For you? For this country? Al-Shabaab is hated here. Your kind is hated here even more than Al-Shabaab. You, and every other foreign fighter who has come here looking for some kind of hippie self-realisation through war games. You won't change anything. You'll be killed here sooner or later, and nothing will change. You had a chance. Your parents gave you a chance. And you've thrown it away."

It was a relief to finally let my frustration out.

The Englishman was glaring at me.

"You know nothing. You, all you journalists, are just part of the machine. You parrot the lies of the Jews and the infidels."

"You can't seriously believe that," I replied. The words were tumbling out now, faster than I could stop them. "I thought you said you studied at the LSE? The preachers did a good job on you, that's for sure."

The Englishman got up abruptly, his face flushed. I stood too. I towered over him and knew that I could easily overpower this man. I could take him, I thought, trying to keep the elation off my face.

"I could knock you out right now and walk out this door."

The Englishman laughed. The shot of anger that had propelled him off the mattress was gone. His eyes were lazy and insolent again. He could see through my bluffing. Could see that what I thought were options were really just illusions.

"So do it. You won't take two steps beyond that door."

"What do I care?" I said. "I'm a dead man walking. Kill me."

A flash just below my line of sight, and out of nowhere, there was a knife in his hand. The blade was thin and the shaft was ornate. Where had this student in international relations got this elaborate knife? Did they give it to him when he got here? As I took two steps back, my mind whispered uselessly, *there's a story in that knife*.

"We won't kill you. Even if you overpower me, even if you get past me, the men outside the door will shoot you. Not to kill, but to bring you down. And then I will come and use this on you. I will cut out your right eye first. And then I will cut off your fingers. We can still put you in front of the cameras. You will still be alive, but only just, and the worst will be to come."

He was inching towards me now.

"The trouble is, you always underestimate us. Just because we kill, just because we are different from you, we are not stupid. It's your choice now."

His tone floored me. I knew he was right. My knees buckled and I sank onto the mat. As I crouched there, heaving with shame and despair, he walked slowly to the door, shouted something in Somali, and again the footsteps came, and the room was full. He crouched down and hissed into my ear.

"You see, you do not understand me at all, Peter Maguire. You think you do. You have already profiled me to meet your expectations. Bored, monied Somali student, looking for a cause, chooses jihad. But what if I like being here for other reasons too? What if I enjoy what I do? Not all jihadis are just *jihadis*. You, of all people, should know how complex humans can be. Or have you learnt nothing?"

He grabbed my hair roughly, forcing my face to within inches of his own.

"You will see what I am capable of very soon. And I will enjoy breaking down your prejudices and preconceptions. Do you see now? You really don't know anything. And that is the problem with all of you."

He flung my head away but I had seen it. The repressed rage, the hatred, and a coldness that turned my stomach. He would cut off my head. He would enjoy it and not necessarily because of the ideology. Or at least not just because of that.

When he was gone, I got up slowly and lay on my mattress, my face to the wall again. I was terrified, but my adrenaline was pumping. The Englishman had shifted the balance somewhere deep inside me, in that dark place where our prejudices, and stereotypes, and unvoiced fears, and hatreds slither over each other. I didn't want to die, not at his hands. I didn't want to die before, but I had felt the weight of circumstance against me. I felt like a nameless victim of politics and forces beyond my control that really had nothing to do with who I was, and everything to do with what I was. What

I am. Now I could put a face to my enemy, and a story, and a character and I would not be *his* victim.

I also had a face I thought could be a friend. I needed to talk to Abdi again. We both needed to get out of here. He had a life to live and I had things to do, mistakes to correct, a life to relive.

As the hours crept by, as the sun sank outside my window, I became a living sea, swaying, undulating, sweeping in and out. I was ecstatic, I would escape, I would make it. And then the wave would break, at its peak, the water turning to soapsud foam that floated away, and could not be made solid again.

I was doomed, I was going to die, horribly. There was nothing I could do. I curled on the mattress, enduring every second as a curse and yet grateful for each infinitesimal gift. More time, but no time to do anything, to stop the clock. I could hardly breathe. I could hardly think. It was getting late.

My sliver of sky had lost its cut-glass brilliance and was fading to a softer blue as the sun set, like a mother heading home and dragging her diamond-bright children with her, removing the colour and the noisy light. I waited for Burhan and his men to come, my breathing shallow, my back to the room, my face almost touching the wall.

I must have slept a little in the end. I heard footsteps and sat up, waiting for the door to open, but there was silence. Then came a rustling and footsteps again, but going away this time. I strained my ears to hear the world beyond my gasping breaths and my hammering heart. I thought I could hear voices. A faint crackling, maybe a fire outside. And otherwise, just the sounds of dusk: the banshee cry of some nocturnal bird, a faint whispering of wind, a wordless shout answered by another.

There was something beside the door. I crept towards it on my hands and knees. Someone had slipped a note underneath the door. I grabbed the single sheet of lined paper and crawled across the floor to where there was still a little light from the window.

The transport has been delayed. I will come for you later. We will leave tonight. Be ready.

It could only be Abdi. The page had been torn from the same book as the pages he gave me to write my letter. He had written in black biro in a small, tight script. Tiny letters that looked like they hardly had the strength to carry this dangerous message.

I huddled in the corner furthest from the door with questions thundering through my head. Why was he helping me? How would we do it? And because these questions could not be answered, I went further. Would we survive? And what then? Abdi was little more than a child. And I wasn't fit or brave, or in any way useful. I was a writer and a watcher, not a doer. I crawled back to my mattress. Be ready. But was Abdi ready?

CHAPTER
NINE

ABDI

I am not a hero and I am not a martyr. I am barely a man. I don't know why I am doing this. Maybe it is because there is nothing else to do, nothing that matters. Since I found out about my mother, I have been ready to die. There is nothing left for me now in Somalia. I will either die here or leave, and if I leave, it may be like dying anyway. I could try to find my mother's brother in Dadaab. I remember him a little, a tall man with my mother's curved lips, my lips, but none of her humour. He used to visit our house when my father was alive. He stopped coming around the time that Nadif became one of them. I cannot say we are close. I am not sure I have ever said more than a handful of words to him, but he is my mother's brother, I am of his clan, and he will have to help me.

I thought about this as I sat outside yesterday, waiting for the foreigner to arrive. It's a plan, maybe even a good plan. But I am tired of being helped. I am tired of owing my life and my future to other people. Yusuf would like me to stay here but he will help me get to the border if that is what I want. But then I am just running away, a child again, running from danger, from decisions, from myself.

I am sick of fleeing and hiding, and what is the point of running when you don't know where you are going? It would be different if I had a reason to live. If my mother was coming with me. But without her, my life feels like a burden.

Not like the prisoner. I think he is hungry for life. He is a man with a past, and with a past, you can dream of a future. I have no past left. The future means nothing to me, and that's how I know this is over.

I do not like the Al-Shabaab foreigner. He scares me. Not just because of who he is, but because his presence has reawakened all my questions about Nadif. I want to remember Nadif as my brother, in the time before them. But he has brought Nadif the martyr back to life. Would Nadif have become like him? Would his eyes have been that cold? This Somali who is not Somali angers me with his very presence. He reminds me of them, the bearded men who pulled the strings of our lives to make them smaller, who took Nadif and turned him into a hater, killers like those who took my father from me.

These men have destroyed my life and this killer-leader with his strange Somali and his strong boots embodies the evil that has cursed my life. He has given me a new purpose. He makes me live, fuelling the hatred that is the only thing that can move me. Until now I did not know I craved revenge. But I do. It came to me when the foreigner clapped his hand on my shoulder, and said, "So this is Abdi. I have heard about your brother. A martyr for jihad. May Allah rest his soul in peace."

The anger was red-hot, exploding in my head like a bomb. I said nothing.

Maybe all we Somalis are just as they say we are. Maybe we can't live with peace, maybe all we can do is kill and be killed, clan feuds going back generations, poisoning our present. I don't care. I want to hurt him. For me, he is them. He has a purpose that I have lost. Or rather that they took from me. For all these reasons, I want to hurt him. And I know how. I will take from him. I will take his prisoner.

We will go tonight. I can get the keys to the prisoner's shack. Nobody watches me here. I know why they expect me to be loyal. The shadow of Nadif, my brother, my keeper. We will head back to Mogadishu. There is no Al-Shabaab between here and Mogadishu, or at least not many, and my clan is scattered around this area. Al-Shabaab are further south. That is where they were going to take the prisoner, so we cannot go there. I thought about heading to the border with Kenya but it is too far and for what? The prisoner will find safety in Mogadishu and I have my own reasons for going back. I want to say goodbye. It is too late, but I must do it. Al-Shabaab are in our neighbourhood but I will be careful and I do not fear them now.

I have stolen a little food from the kitchen and four bottles of water and they are here in the backpack that Yusuf gave me when I told him today that I had decided to go to the border. He agreed that Dhobley was the best place to go.

"You can cross easily there," he said as we sat under the acacia tree, watching the foreigners who had arrived in a four-by-four. They had painted the car but the white paint was peeling and I could see the red of the Save the Children logo underneath. It looks like the child has its hands up, in fear. This is how the war here perverts everything.

The foreigner had gone inside to talk to the Sheikh and the other four men were lounging in the shade. Two of them were asleep, leaning against the wall, their guns between their legs. They did not talk to us when they arrived, but they walked around like they owned the compound, sunglasses glinting angrily. We are nothing to them.

"It will cost you about $50 to get through the border," Yusuf continued. "Trucks go through all the time. But the best thing would be to look for Abdirashid, a member of our clan. He will help you if he is still there. You must ask for him when you arrive in Dhobley. Everyone knows him. This is his business. He will give you a good price in honour of your father and your mother, Allah have mercy on their souls."

I nodded.

"Can you pay me today, Yusuf? I need to prepare for this journey, and I want to hide the money carefully."

"Very wise," Yusuf nodded. "I will get your money now. There are many bandits on the road to Dhobley. They prey upon people trying to get out. They will shoot for a few senti."

"What about Al-Shabaab?" I asked.

Yusuf chewed his khat for a moment, his cheeks bulging as though he had some kind of malignant tumour, then he spat noisily into the dust in front of us. His spit stained the ground like blood. I felt lightheaded and looked away.

Yusuf lowered his voice.

"Al-Shabaab are always a danger. They are moving a lot these days. But there are also other militia. And then you have the bandits. Just stay off the roads, travel by night, hide when you hear guns and don't talk to anyone. Be quiet, be invisible and you will get there."

"How did you make connections with these Al Shabaab?" I asked.

Yusuf smiled, his brown, khat-stained teeth like striated river stones in his wide mouth.

"You know, Abdi, I am a businessman. I must communicate with those who have money. Al-Shabaab has money. They are the ones collecting the taxes from farmers, villagers, even from pirates south of here, near Kismayo. They may not have control of the whole country but they have enough. I need to be able to talk to them. I heard about a white man being held by some thieves. I contacted them. They are nothing, they had been lucky. But stupid too. They killed the man's driver and his clan had vowed revenge, so it was difficult for them in Mogadishu. I offered to take the captive off their hands. They agreed. I paid and now I will make twice as much by selling him to this foreigner. It is always possible to reach Al-Shabaab. Nadif was not the only one. In our clan, there are many who have seen the way this world works. They have joined the strong men."

He spat again and tiny drops landed on my shirt. He was leaning close to me, his hand on my forearm. I had to stop myself from shaking him off. I suddenly hated him.

"But when things change, we will change too. Al-Shabaab have power now but they are too extreme. This is a grey world, Abdi, there is no room for belief if you want to survive. You must know how to be grey. I am grey, and I am alive, and I am becoming richer. I do not believe in anything. I do not expect anything except the loyalty of my clan, the betrayal of others, and the fact that people will always pay for what they want. So when Al-Shabaab go, because everything eventually changes, then I will become friends with whoever fills that space."

Yusuf lectured me for a little longer. He likes to play elder although he is only a few years older than me. He thinks he is a player. I envy his certainty, but I also pity him. We are all being played here.

It is time to go now. The clouds have come and covered the moon. The shadows will help us. Yusuf, the Sheikh, and the foreigner are eating in the big house. Two of the foreigner's men are fiddling under the bonnet of their Land Cruiser. Earlier, while the foreigner was inside with the prisoner, and his men took some time to eat in the kitchen, I tore one of the wires out of the car's engine. My hands were shaking, but I did it. I was grey.

134

Before Al-Shabaab came to our neighbourhood, my father had, for a while, owned a blue Nissan with red doors. It seemed to only run when it wanted to, and my father spent many hours working on it. He was a mathematician but he loved the practicality, the fluidity of engineering.

"See how this works, Abdi. This wire goes here and then this piston moves and then the fuel flows. Isn't it amazing?"

I knew he was really talking to himself. He was more amazed than I was.

They discovered the broken wire when one of the men tried to move the car into the late-afternoon shade by the wall. The foreigner shouted at his driver, the smallest of the silent men who are our guests and masters. The man looked terrified. The foreigner accused him of driving too fast, of hitting a pothole on the track that led from the paved road to the compound. He spoke slowly, as if the driver was an idiot. The man dropped his eyes to the ground. The foreigner never raised his hand but the man shrank from his voice. It made me hate the foreigner more. I hoped nothing would happen to the driver but I have no more room for compassion.

A guard sat on a chair at the gate. His head was tilted, his legs splayed in front of him, his gun resting by the wall beside him. In sleep, he looked harmless. He was one of Yusuf's men and so a hired gun rather than a fanatic, but I didn't plan on using the gate anyway.

I crept out of the shed where I slept. The clouds had swallowed the shadows created by the showy moon. I

135

melted into the wall and skirted around until I was behind the prisoner's shack, just below the tiny window that showed him the sky. I slipped round the far wall, the one furthest from the main house but closest to the gate. No one was looking at the shack. Inside was a dead man and a dead man doesn't move. I got to the corner, held my breath, checked for noise and then made for the door. Within seconds I was inside, in the dark, with the prisoner.

"Let's go," I whispered.

I could not see him on the mattress. I panicked. Had they taken him inside the main house when I wasn't looking?

"Abdi?"

The voice came out of the far corner. And then I saw him, his white face and hands detaching themselves from the gloom. He looked like a man without a body.

"Follow me. Do not speak."

I edged open the door again. The two men were still fiddling with the car's engine at the other end of the compound. The guard at the gate had crossed his legs but his head was still tilted sideways, still searching for a shoulder to rest on. We crept out. I could feel the white man behind me. His breath sounded like screams but then so did mine. I was wearing my flip flops but he was barefoot. I hadn't thought to bring him shoes. A stupid mistake.

I locked the door again, my hands shaking. Hoping my fingers wouldn't betray me like Nadif's had. We made it behind the shack without being seen. I led him along the wall, heading closer to the part of the

136

compound where the men were fixing the car. The white man put his hand on my shoulder. I shook it off. I kept creeping along the wall until we were behind one of the small houses opposite the main house.

The outer wall was slightly lower here. A few bricks had fallen off the top and there was a gap in the shards of glass cemented into the top. If we were careful we would not get cut too badly. Nobody could see us here.

Earlier, I had brought one of the old buckets I used when cleaning the floors in the main house and placed it here. I turned it upside down and motioned for the white man to climb up on it. He did, grabbed the wall and pulled himself up. He was slow, and panting. I could sense the trembling in his arms. I crouched, placed my shoulder under his flailing feet and pushed. He pulled himself higher, scrambled over the wall and dropped.

I froze. The noise was louder than I had expected. I peeked around the side of the house. The men at the car were arguing over something, voices raised, hands waving. The guard was still asleep. I hopped on the bucket and lifted myself. I am as tall as the white man but my arms are stronger. I hefted myself higher and swung my legs up onto the edge of the wall. I felt my skin tear and a bright pain like a burn, but I bit my lip and dropped down onto the other side.

"I cut my leg," I whispered to the dark.

"Lean on me. Let's go."

The voice was closer than I expected. I felt a hand on my arm, guiding me, into the dark. The sky was black, the moon still hidden in the clouds, but to my right, I spotted a single star. We started stumbling forward, staying away from the track that led to the main road. I wasn't sure if this was the right direction, all that mattered was speed. We weaved into each other, like magnets pushed together by some force in the air. My leg was wet. I pulled off my headscarf.

"Wait. A moment."

I wrapped the scarf around my leg. I did not want them to follow the blood.

"Okay, let's go."

The white man said nothing, but his hand was on my arm again. It made me uncomfortable. We set off again, two men without faces, without shadows, walking under a single-starred sky.

CHAPTER
TEN

PETER

This is a new kind of dark, a new kind of prison. Here, I am caught between captivity and the unknown. The sky and the hard ground are one expanse of nothingness. The clouds cover the moon and I am grateful for this lunar modesty. We need to put as much distance as we can between us and the compound before the silver light pours down again. I know we are not moving very fast and maybe not fast enough. I am scared, exhilarated and terrified, my ears straining for the shouts I am sure will come. And the shots that will follow.

I wish I could turn my mind off. I need to be a thoughtless automaton now. Abdi is limping, stumbling on the rutted ground as we plunge deeper into this blackness. We have not talked since he told me he cut his leg. We have half walked, half jogged, our hands stretched before us like soldiers blinded by mustard gas. My feet are hurting but the scratches and bruises do not bother me now. Occasionally, the moon peeps through briefly, bashfully, allowing us a fleeting glimpse of the void around us. Shrubs, thorn trees and dusty, cratered ground. We could be in any of a dozen countries I have visited.

I am following Abdi, my fingers pinching his thin shirt. I can hear his breathing, I can feel it through the thin fabric. Suddenly he stops and points. I can see a darker shadow in front of us. It is a hut, frail and broken but still standing. Abdi motions me to stop and moves ahead, cautiously. There is no light from the hut but that doesn't tell us anything. There is no electricity for miles around. Abdi's shadowy form disappears as if by magic and I am alone, standing on the edge of the world, maybe on the edge of my existence.

My heart is pounding, I am sweating and shivering at the same time. I can hardly believe I am outside again. My body rebels against this disorientation, it wants to shut down. A few weeks ago, I was so free I didn't even feel it. Now freedom feels awkward, like a new shirt, scratchy and clingy in all the wrong places. I don't want to think about where we are, or what we will do. I am not ready yet. So I look up into the inky sky where the clouds have parted to show me a speckling of stars. They are fragile, flickering as if they might go out, and I hold my breath. And then the moon, a queen preceded by her courtiers, slips out from the clouds, spilling her limpid mercury-light across the ground, creating shadows and contrasts, like a painter bringing a picture to life. I watch as if bewitched but I am actually under another moon, on that beach in Monrovia, six years ago, walking with Esther.

We had eaten thick *palava* sauce and fufu at a little roadside café not far from the beach where waves ended their long journey from another world by crashing exhausted on this new shore. It was the day before the first round of the presidential elections, my reason for coming to Liberia. I had filed my curtain-raiser that afternoon and needed to be up early the next morning to go to the polling stations.

But I also needed to see Esther. If I were to explain the attraction, it would sound clichéd. She was beautiful but it wasn't just that. She was damaged and fragile, and different and yes, there was an element of that, although I had slept with women from Mali, and Ivory Coast, and Ghana before. Before Michelle, and since Michelle. I always believed that what happened on the road, stayed on the road. What I didn't realise is that you had to be fully complicit in this deception, and if you could not forget or erase what happened on the road, your deception swept along its own separate, secret alley before spilling into the other better-known roads that together make up the illusion of a single path through life.

After our late meal, I walked Esther back to the rehabilitation centre. We went along the beach, slipping off our shoes and tiptoeing through the unstable, grasping fringe where sea meets land. Her left hand was in mine. There were clouds that night too and some rebel stars that naughtily twinkled their refusal to be dimmed. We were silent. The comfortable silence was one of the things I liked about Esther. When she spoke, it was deliberate as though she had been given a finite number of words at birth and was determined not to waste any of them.

I squeezed her hand and she turned to smile at me. Her teeth were large and bright, but the front two in the centre were slightly crooked. Her brown eyes danced under arching brows. She had dimples in her cheeks and a fine rash of tiny spots across her forehead. She had braided her hair that morning and the oiled plaits shone when the moon finally wrestled the clouds away.

"Tomorrow, you will work all day."

It was more a statement than a question but I nodded my head.

"You will leave after the second round?"

I nodded again, unwilling to tarnish this moment with my foreigner's voice. I felt at one with the sloshing water, the salty breeze, and the far-off sound of cars taking sodden, late-night revellers home. I wanted the illusion to continue. If I spoke, the picture would break into a thousand tiny pieces.

But she was still staring at me, using her eyes to save her words.

"I have to leave then, Esther. But I'm sure I will come back. My editors are bound to want a follow-up story, maybe when the new president is sworn in. Especially if it's Johnson-Sirleaf, and it probably will be. She has . . ."

"But will you come back for me, Peter Maguire?" Esther interrupted.

She stopped walking, pulled her hand from mine and stared at me. She was smiling but there was something sad lurking around the corners of her broad mouth. A tightness that was like the early shadow of a disappointment she knew would be hers.

142

"I don't know, Esther. It's not that simple. Michelle is waiting for me. We have a different life in Paris."

"I don't want to be with you in Paris," Esther said sharply. "I want to be with you *here*. I like you, Peter. You are different from the men I have met, the Liberians and my own people."

She allowed herself a small, ironic smile.

"And yet in some ways, you are all the same. You are complicated. You do not understand yourselves. You don't know what you want, but I believe I can help you. You have been kind to me, you have accepted my condition. And I love you for that. We could be happy together. And have you asked yourself why you are sleeping with me if you love Michelle? I could understand that from a Liberian — we have a culture of mistresses. War has poisoned our very morality."

She fell silent for a while, shutting me out of whatever memory she was struggling to repress or resurrect. I knew she was thinking of things she could barely describe, and that I would surely never understand even if she could speak of them.

"But you are from another culture, you value faithfulness. So what is this?"

I sighed.

"That's not how it is. You're making it much too simple. This is not about different cultures. It's about me. I love Michelle. In my own way. But I have feelings for you too, Esther. You are beautiful and I want you, but does that mean I can't also love Michelle and desire her? I've never seen it that way."

Esther began walking again.

"Does Michelle know this?"

"No," I said, reaching for her hand.

She let me hold it, closing her cool fingers around mine like a blessing.

"She wouldn't agree," I admitted. "So yes, I am being dishonest to her. But it is who I am. I know what I should do and yet I can't."

"One day, Peter, you will have to choose. Unless you have decided already. That would make me sad but I can survive."

Again that ironic smile.

Esther was not pleading. She was offering me a life with her but my younger self didn't know how to say yes. I didn't know if I could say yes. So I chose silence, knowing I would soon be gone, and in my other world, miles away.

Something touched my arm and I was yanked from my past. It was Abdi. He said nothing, just took my hand and led me across to the hut. We passed under the low door, through the ashes of a dead fire in the centre of the room, and across to the deepest shadows at the far wall. The hut was just a frame of sticks covered with woven mats, some of which had rotted away. I looked up through the broken roof at the stars, a poor man's observatory. I took a deep breath, trying to stop the panic rising in my chest. Another room. I felt as though the walls were moving towards me.

"We will stay here for a while," Abdi whispered, unwrapping the scarf around his leg and grimacing as some dried blood tore off with the cloth.

"The moon is too bright now to run."

144

"Where are we going?" I asked, licking my teeth with my parched tongue, hoping to wring some moisture from somewhere.

Abdi reached into his bag and handed me a bottle of water.

"Don't drink too much. I don't know how far we will have to walk before we get some more. We are going to Mogadishu."

Abdi spoke softly, but certainly.

"How far is it?"

"About ninety kilometres. We will follow the main road. It is over there," Abdi said, lifting his arm and pointing across me.

"Will they follow us?"

"I do not know. Yes, probably. For some time, at least. But I have family around here. My clan comes from this region. I am hoping we may be lucky."

It sounded like a frail hook for even the slightest of hopes, but I realised I was completely dependent on this teenager now. I was the foreigner. If we survived this, it would have nothing to do with me. I was still a prisoner, of my ignorance, of my weakness, of my inappropriateness here.

"Thank you, Abdi," I said. "You are taking a huge risk. Why are you helping me?"

Abdi turned his face to mine and in the pale light, he looked even younger than before.

"I don't know. I have no one. So it does not matter what I do. But I am tired of always having things happen to me. My father died. My brother died. My mother died. These things happened to me. I have never done anything except come to my cousin, and work for him here. And still things keep happening to me. I wanted to do something myself."

He spoke slowly, almost as if he were speaking to a child. He looked away again. He was wise enough not to expect or want a response. I didn't know what to say. And so we sat in silence under the woven mats, listening to the bigger silence outside, waiting for the clouds to come.

"When will they find out I am gone?"

"Soon."

Abdi reached into his backpack and pulled out some crumpled pages.

"This is the letter you gave me. You will give it to your mother yourself. If you still want to."

I took the pages, looked at Abdi and tore them into pieces. I scrabbled at the soft earth and I buried each wrinkled witness to my despair. If Abdi was my saviour, I needed to believe in him. I needed to show him my faith. I buried them deep for him, and maybe for me. A scribe's offering to the gods of hope.

"You remind me of the mother of my son," I said, when I had finished and could bear the rustling silence no longer.

"Esther is a survivor like you, Abdi. They cut off her arm in Sierra Leone and she fled to Liberia. She survived the civil war there, saw horrible things just like you. But she is still in Monrovia, caring for our son. She made her own decisions. You are making yours. That is not something I have ever done well."

Abdi seemed to ignore me.

146

"I am sorry I forgot to bring you shoes," he finally said.

I laughed, and it felt good.

"You saved my life," I said, swallowing the "for now" that flashed in my brain like the neon entrance to a sleazy club.

I touched his arm. "Don't worry. I'll put some cloth around them."

I ripped the end of my frayed, dirty robe. I tore off four strips and wrapped up my feet as best I could.

"We will find some shoes."

"Honestly, Abdi, don't worry. If I have no shoes, maybe I can leave no footprints."

Abdi did not smile. He was looking up through the mats to the sky.

"The clouds are back. We must go. We must go as far as we can before dawn."

He stood up and offered me his hand.

"I hope we will make it, Peter Maguire."

It was the first time he had said my name.

"But if we don't, I will have done something at last. I will have tried."

The black of the night was leaking out of the sky when Abdi stopped me again. By this stage, I was almost sleepwalking. I was no longer conscious of my sore feet, or the dark, or the land around me. I was all pounding heart and rasping breath, my whole being reduced to these two cardinal functions. My fingers were still gripping Abdi's shirt, but when he stopped I almost walked past him, twisting his shirt around his waist. His hand pulled me back. We had stopped under a thorn tree. I could see a huddle of huts in the distance.

"There is a village ahead. I have clan there. I must go first and see if they will offer us shelter," he whispered.

"Why would they do that?" I asked.

"Because I am clan," Abdi said, a hint of a smile in his voice.

"There are some things that are hard for foreigners to understand, and maybe this is the hardest. My clan will support me even if it is risky. It is their duty, even though I do not know this family very well. They are on my mother's side, her cousins. But also, they hate Al-Shabaab."

"Why?"

"Because they tax our people. Because they make us obey their laws — no television, no music, beards, veils. Because they have brought the world here, the Ethiopians, the Ugandans, and the others, and because they have turned this country into a playground for violent men from other countries who have no business here."

He stopped as his voice cracked. He took a moment to calm down as he bent to retie the scarf around his injured leg.

"I will go in alone. I must see if Mukhtar is there. He is the leader of the clan in this village. I must speak to him alone first. I will not be long. Stay here."

He limped off. I sat under the thorn tree, leaning against its slender trunk, grateful for the hard ground beneath me. I watched the world turn from black to grey, and prayed to all the Gods I had for so long ignored to bring Abdi back to me. My eyelids were sliding shut but I fought to stay awake. I could not let death creep up on me. The birds were beginning to chirp and the dry earth was starting to sweat when, before I knew it, sleep claimed me.

CHAPTER
ELEVEN

NINA

I woke hot and sticky, wondering where I was. I had slept like a child in the foetal position, but my body can't really do foetal anymore, at least not willingly. As my bones creaked into place, and my brain engaged, I realised I needed to find Edward. I had not seen him since the day before. I could hear purposeful male voices, heavy vehicles revving and above and below it all, was the dull thud of artillery somewhere in the city. The sounds did not scare me anymore.

I was caught in my first gun battle in Abidjan in 1979 — it was a nothing event, not even a footnote in history. Some criminals, thugs as we called them, stormed a restaurant on the lagoon on a sweaty, shisha-filled night as Tim and I ate spicy chicken and rice, swaying to Lebanese pop and laughing about nothing. Three men in jeans, with scarves round their faces and baseball caps pulled low over their foreheads, burst into the main dining room, firing their sub-machine guns in the air. I had never heard gunfire so close.

I dived under the table with Tim, shaking uncontrollably at the thought of those random bullets whizzing around the room with who knew whose name on them. I felt so vulnerable. It is humiliating and humbling to know that there really is nothing you can do. It must be the same feeling people get when the plane starts to go down, or the ship starts to tilt towards the waves, or in that fleeting second when you realise you have lost control of the car. No one was killed that night. We were ordered to our feet and one of the gunmen came around to take our jewellery, wallets and purses. We gave them gratefully, fingers fumbling. I did not dare to look into the attacker's face as he stood beside us. But I remember his smell — strong and sharp. The smell of anger, limitless power and opportunity.

Guns and, more specifically, bullets still terrify me. But years in this business have refined my terror — I know now how to distinguish bullets that will kill you from bullets that are far away, destined for someone else's soft body. Unless they sneak through the air, silently and maliciously, plotting a course that will change your life, and all the while, you stand there, chatting inanely, oblivious.

I finally tracked Edward down to the canteen. He was sitting alone, his laptop in front of him, a mug of cold coffee by his side. I sat down on a plastic chair opposite him.

"Did you get some rest?" he said, without taking his eyes from the screen.

His fingers were flying over the keys and I noticed how delicate they were, thin and long, the fingers of a flautist. His fingers did not fit.

"I slept, or something like it," I said, swallowing a yawn. "Where have you been?"

"I had things to do," he said, and I resisted the urge to laugh.

I hoped he wasn't going to treat me like this for long. I sat, and patiently waited for him to elaborate. Eventually, his fingers paused their cyber concerto, he shut the laptop brusquely and finally met my eyes.

"I have some news," he said. "But frankly, I'm wondering if I should even tell you. I don't want to get your hopes up too early."

"Edward, with all due respect, don't you dare patronise me," I said. "I appreciate you are the expert here, and my son's life quite probably rests in your hands, or pretty close to them anyway. I'm not a novice at this kind of thing, or this kind of place. I know there are things that you cannot tell me, and I think I am smart enough and experienced enough to know what they are, but if you have news about the whereabouts or health of my son, I expect you to pass that on. Now."

Edward smiled.

"Don warned me you would be difficult. Okay, sorry if I offended you. It's just I am not one hundred per cent sure of the information I have."

"How sure are you?" I asked sharply.

"About seventy per cent. We've heard that a prisoner escaped from Al-Shabaab near Wanlaweyn last night."

He held up his hand as I opened my mouth — he's done this before for sure, I thought in the part of my brain that kept working normally despite the emotional whirlwind whipping through the rest.

"I can't tell you how we know, and like I said, the information is not confirmed. I need to make some calls and maybe head back into the city to try to get a better handle on things. I may be gone for a while, but I'll call here to let you know if anything new comes up."

I tried to be rational, to treat this news as any other information I might get on a story. Interesting but the sourcing was flaky. Even if it was true, it didn't mean Peter was safe. Edward clearly did not know where he was. So he was still in danger.

Edward grabbed a laptop case from beneath the bench, slipped the computer into it, and rose.

"Stay here. There really is nothing you can do now except wait. Here."

He emphasised the last word and then he was gone, pulling his mobile phone from the breast pocket of his incongruously crisp blue shirt as he pushed open the door on the broiling sun.

I sat at the table for a moment, but I couldn't bear it. I would walk, just as I had walked after I found out that Peter was Shaun's child. Then, I struggled up mossy hills and plunged gratefully into the cool valleys of the Cévennes in France, breathing in the heady scents of cypress and eucalyptus, hoping their purity would somehow be transmitted to me.

Now, I headed out of the restaurant and went to find Colonel Mugweri, pulling my sunglasses over my eyes, feeling the heat like a hammer through my canvas floppy hat. Mugweri was standing by a block of brick dormitories, chatting to some of his soldiers. They laughed uproariously, and he grinned like a man who is used to making people happy. He saw me, bent his head to whisper to his crowd. Their eyes swerved nervously towards me.

"Did you rest, Mrs Walters? Would you like me to assist you in any way?" he asked as he approached me across the hot sand.

"Would one of your men be able to show me around the base?"

He arched an eyebrow so that it peeked cheekily above his Ray-Bans.

"Why? It is very hot now, and if I understood correctly, you are not here to work but to wait for your son?"

It was a question, but also a reprimand. I have often found men in uniform, whatever their nationality, to be experts in turning any sentence into a barely veiled admonishment.

"Colonel, what do you do when some of your men are killed out there?" I said, waving towards the edge of the sprawling compound of half-finished buildings, bulging, split sandbags, and coiled razor wire.

"Say there is a gun battle and you hear of casualties. Do you rest? Do you drink tea? Do you sit around waiting for someone to come back?"

Mugweri smiled and turned to squint into a sky so perfect it seemed to have lost its way to paradise.

"I am older than you, I am a different colour, I am not a soldier. But like you, I cannot just sit here while everyone else searches for Peter. Get someone to show me around. Let me see a little of what brought him here. I have come so far, and who knows, maybe I will

154

be the only witness to his last story. I hope to God not, but if this place was worth Peter's life, then I'd better see what I can see."

"As you wish," Mugweri said, sighing. He dug out his phone and barked out a few words in what sounded like Swahili.

A few moments later, a short man with a bulldog face and a canine grin that revealed very yellow teeth came marching towards us. Sweat dripped into his eyes from under the rim of his helmet, and his rapid blinking made him look like a peculiarly nervous killer dog. He saluted vigorously, the action extravagant like his appearance.

"Private Nabakoba, this is Mrs Walters. She is our guest. She would like to visit the base. Take her on a tour. She can go anywhere," Mugweri said, adding a few words, again in Swahili.

Nabakoba saluted again, and Mugweri marched off. I extended my hand to my new minder.

"My name is Nina," I said as his fingers grazed mine, and then pulled back quickly.

"What would you like to see?" he asked in a high-pitched tone. This bulky soldier, whose forehead was hiding under his too-big helmet, was just a boy. He was maybe nineteen.

"Nothing in particular. Just take me around the base. I want to see what you do here. My son came here to write about this place. I want to imagine what he might have written."

I left the "in case" unspoken. It hung heavy in the air.

"First, we must make you safe," he said.

He led me to an office, again in a shipping container, where he pulled a faded flak jacket from a pile balanced precariously on metal shelves.

"I am sorry. It is not strictly necessary to wear these on base, but since you are a civilian, and . . ." He faltered.

"Old?" I suggested, laughing a little.

"No, no," he blustered. "But in the circumstances . . ."

"Don't worry. I understand," I said, struggling into an unwieldy, unyielding jacket.

The heft of it, and the stale smell of sweat, propelled me back to Baghdad in 1991, my last real assignment. Then I was doing a job, something necessary, or so I told myself when the bullets and mortars got too close, and my fear saw me huddling behind a wall, all thoughts of being a witness to history buried by a primal desire to survive.

We started walking across the sandy yard. I felt like an ungainly tortoise but Nabakoba strode along briskly, his squat frame bearing the extra weight of the Kevlar easily. Some people are born to wear four-inch heels, I thought, and some to wear flak jackets. It was only 9am, but already the heat was a physical presence. All consuming.

"We will start with the clinic. It is always busy. There will be much to see there," said Nabakoba, gesturing to a building near the perimeter of the base.

"You are from Uganda?" I asked as we walked, pointing to the red, yellow and black stripes on the arm of his shirtsleeve.

"Yes. You have been to my country?" he said, his smile broadening until I shook my head.

"No, I mostly worked in West Africa when I was younger," I said. "Do you come from Kampala?"

"No, I am from a small village in the western district of Rukungiri," he said, dragging the words out slowly, as though he doubted my interest.

"I live with my older brother on his farm."

"How long have you been here?" I asked.

"Six months. So I have three months left on this tour. God willing, I will be home in November and this year, we will celebrate Christmas in style. But not too much style."

He chuckled, a sly, knowing laugh.

"I want to buy my own field. And build a house. I hope to be able to do that after this tour. And then if I need more, maybe I can come back again."

"You would come back again?" I asked, though I was not particularly surprised.

I could imagine his brother's little iron-roofed house on a green hillside. I suppose if nothing else, war offers potential for improvement, if you can just avoid being killed.

"Yes. This is good money for me. I did well at school but there was no money for college. So I was just like everybody else at home. But now I am special. After the bombings in Kampala last year, in fact, we are heroes. When I last went on leave, people treated me with respect. I had no problems getting a seat in the taxis."

He laughed, with the innocent delight of a teenager discovering something new and fresh about life. I remember that.

"They know what we do now. And they know why we do it. And for us, it is good money. We have a future."

I became aware of a soft hum even before we rounded the corner of a bleached wall that marked the edge of the outpatients clinic. Dozens of women and children were squatting in the dust, their sunset-red, brilliant blue and shocking pink veils pulled over their heads. Children sat by their mothers, some still and vacant like tiny statues, others rambunctious, all kicking legs and flailing arms.

A little girl, whose round dimpled face peeked from her shiny green headscarf smiled shyly at me, and I waved back. She must have been about five. Her mother covered her face as I walked past, but the little girl pushed the veil away and kept smiling.

I felt my own smile was insincere. It was not honest. It suggested empathy, which there was, and help, which I could not offer. As so often before, I was just a spectator. I could do nothing for her and I worried, as always, that she took my smile to mean something else. I have never known how to react to children on my travels, especially in poorer countries. I represent foreign interest and for so many, my presence suggests that people outside care. What should I do? Smile and let the hope live? Or explain, honestly and brutally, that the world probably does not care about your war, or your famine, or your slum, or the burns you got because you went to scoop petrol from an overturned truck, but that I am here to try to get them to care. I may succeed but I probably won't. I'm just doing my job. And my job is to bear witness to your suffering, and tell the world, and then you are on your own again.

I walked past the little girl and through the seated crowd. Some children shouted after me, then collapsed into giggles as I turned to them, eyebrows raised. Others were too weak to indulge in such games. Mothers sat, straight-backed and straight-legged with babies on their laps. Some of these weaker children followed me with unnaturally big eyes. Others had their eyes closed, and their mothers fanned them listlessly, swishing away the flies in an endless, futile, almost clichéd gesture of love.

"I will take you to meet Dr Robert Mugyenyi. He runs this clinic," Nabakoba said, steering me through the people.

The shuffling and noise died down as I approached, only for a louder chatter to break out behind me as I moved through.

We entered the clinic, edging past the people standing in a tight queue at the door. There was no place for personal space here. Each eager patient was squeezed up to the person in front, as though they feared any gap would be exploited. They were probably right.

In the dark interior, I felt the shade like a lover's touch.

Nabakoba marched up to an older man who was bent over a little boy on a stretcher laid on a solid wooden table. The child's mother brushed his forehead lightly as the doctor pulled back a pink bandage from his skinny stomach.

Dr Robert Mugyenyi peered over his glasses at me. I knew that look. In the old days, I would have brazened it out. Yes, the doctor might be busy but I had a deadline and needed my five quotes, and some background in the next half hour or I would miss it. I don't think I'm callous but I probably seemed so.

Now I wanted to say, "No, don't worry. I can wait," but he was tilting his head to usher me over. I pulled off my flak jacket and dropped it on the ground near the stretcher. It felt obscene to be wearing body armour here among the thin, fragile, hummingbird-like women lined outside. The young mother glanced at me blankly, but her hand never stopped its rhythmic stroking of her son's head.

"You can hold this for me," Dr Mugyenyi said in a low voice.

Meekly, I took the edge of the bandage he had pulled back. The boy had a two-inch gash on his left side, just under his rib cage. The wound was oozing blood, slowly as though death was willing to wait a while for this boy with the slender, too-long nose, and lips like those of a girl.

"He was hit by shrapnel while he was playing outside yesterday afternoon," the doctor said as he gently touched the edges of the wound.

"His family removed the piece of metal, but couldn't get him here until today because of the fighting."

He said something to the young mother in a language I did not recognise, and she replied with a few words, her voice soft and insistent.

"He needs stitches and antibiotics. But he will live." I guessed he was talking to me again.

The doctor smiled at the boy.

"Eh, Asad."

He turned to the mother, this time speaking slowly in English, but using his hands to illustrate his words.

"We will have to sew him up. Do you understand?"

She nodded.

"But he will be fine. You got here in time. You did well. He has a good and brave mother." A nurse behind him translated in a soft whisper and the young mother smiled and covered her face with her black veil, her giggles tinkling like fresh water over stones. She bent and kissed her son's forehead, who attempted a faint smile.

Dr Mugyenyi pulled off his gloves and beckoned to the nurse. She came up to the table carrying a tray with a needle and surgical string. I moved out of the way, following Dr Mugyenyi as he went to a scratched desk in the corner to write in a long hardback notebook whose pages were turned up and spattered with brown and black stains. He was a tall man with a spare frame that suggested he never sat still long enough to allow fat to settle. He wore the same green fatigues as the other soldiers, but his slenderness was accentuated by the absence of a flak jacket, or a gun. His hair was grey, tight to his head, and his hands were huge. Instead of the regulation black boots, he wore trainers, old and worn with the laces fraying at the ends.

"I do not have much time to talk to you. As you can see, we are very busy," he said, waving to the crowded doorway. I could feel patient eyes on my back. Nobody would challenge me, but everyone was wondering how long I would keep the doctor from tending to them. I spoke rapidly, embarrassed by my uselessness.

"I don't need to talk to you. I just wanted to see what happens here. Perhaps I could sit somewhere and watch you work? Perhaps I can even help. I have nothing to do today. I am waiting for news of my son, but I can't bear to be idle."

"Are you a doctor or a nurse? Have you any experience of first aid?" he said. The words were clipped, but his eyes were sympathetic.

"No, I am a journalist, or I was," I said. "But I can carry things, fetch things, check names, write down whatever you need," I said, pointing to the book. "My handwriting is quite tidy."

Dr Mugyenyi smiled and squinted at his own spider-like scrawl.

"Okay, you can stay. Sit here on this chair." He pulled it forward from the desk.

"I will find something for you to do in a little while."

He gestured to the next patient, an old man with a neatly trimmed, orange beard, a white skullcap stitched in silver thread and a hip-twisting limp. As the old man settled slowly into a chair, Dr Mugyenyi turned to me.

"We are all hoping for good news about your son."

I nodded.

For the next three hours, I swabbed wounds and cuts with antiseptic, I weighed babies so light I felt they might drift out of my hands like feathers. I cut bandages and fetched pills from a medicine cabinet that had more empty spaces than boxes. There were two Somali nurses working alongside Dr Mugyenyi but there seemed to be no end to the people waiting outside. The softly murmuring crowd sitting in the sand stayed the same. After a while, I stopped peering out of the door. I was beginning to understand.

"We see about three to four hundred patients a day. Everything from shrapnel wounds to diarrhoea, to malnutrition, sexual diseases, cuts and arthritis. There are hospitals in the city but they are very under-equipped, and sometimes people are afraid to cross the frontlines to get to them. At least here, they know we have medicines, or at least some. They know we will do our best to treat them. Of course, sometimes it is too late. Or we do not have what they need. Even in war, people still die of cancer."

Dr Mugyenyi spoke rapidly as he scribbled another incomprehensible entry into his notebook. I wondered if anyone ever checked these records. How many people had been reduced to a note of "deceased" in this stained ledger?

The doctor heard it first. A slight disturbance outside. He started towards the door, putting his glasses back on. I followed. By the time I got outside, the noise had taken solid form.

A man was running towards the tent, cradling a body in his arms, blood dripping into the sand. Behind him

163

came a small knot of women and men, keening and shouting. The running man said nothing. He sped through the crowd. He was thin and wore a blue flannel shirt and a red-and-white macawis sarong. He was wearing just one flip flop.

Dr Mugyenyi took the body from his arms. It was a little girl, maybe five. She had an obscenely large bullet hole in the right side of her chest. She was unconscious and her face was covered in blood and dust. But her thin chest was rising and falling irregularly.

Dr Mugyenyi placed her on the stretcher, barking orders at the nurse. The running man collapsed onto the floor in a corner, his head in his hands, his shoulders heaving. He began to moan, a low animal sound that was more terrifying than the wailing outside the door.

I could not help here. I went and sat on the floor beside the weeping man. Eventually, I cried with him as we watched Dr Mugyenyi try to save the girl's life. People crowded the doorway, whispering or watching with blank expressions. Death was no stranger here.

"We must operate," Dr Mugyenyi ordered.

Two Ugandan soldiers, who had followed the man into the clinic, grabbed the ends of the stretcher and carried it out a small door at the back of the room, towards the operating theatre in the main hospital, a short distance away. Dr Mugyenyi raced after them, waving a hand behind his back to indicate that the man should come with him. He rose unsteadily, then followed the doctor silently. He never asked a single question.

The nurse who had remained behind, a pretty Somali in a dark scarf and black robe, beckoned in the next patient. I pulled myself up and went to her.

"Will the little girl be okay?" I asked as I helped her place a child in the weighing scales.

"I don't know," she said in a low tone.

"She was hit by a sniper's bullet. It does not look good. The bullet is probably lodged in her lung. And she is, of course, malnourished. Even if she survives the operation, infection will be a big problem."

She lifted the child out of the harness, and placed him again on his mother's lap. She reached for her thermometer.

"You should go now. You have helped a lot, but you must rest. This heat is tiring, and this place is tiring."

I picked up my flak jacket and walked out into the sun.

I was exhausted and yet I felt as though I had done more good in the last three hours than I had ever done. I could feel the stirring of a ludicrous idea, a brilliant idea. As I walked aimlessly around the base, I allowed myself to imagine something different, a new life. Then I remembered Peter and nearly stumbled with the guilt of having to do so. I needed to find Edward. I headed towards the canteen.

Edward was not there. But Dr Mugyenyi was, his shoulders slumped, his head bent over a steaming cup of coffee. I sat opposite him, and then, without really realising what I was doing, I placed my hand on his large one, and I didn't need to ask. I knew the girl hadn't made it. We sat in silence for a long time. There

165

was nothing to say. I pulled my hand back as a group of soldiers came in for their lunch of watery, too-tough meat stew and too-hard rice.

And then, as plastic trays clattered and tin spoons scraped on cracked china plates, I told a man I had only known for three hours, the story of my son. A truth I had only told a handful of people, and belatedly, too belatedly, my son.

CHAPTER
TWELVE

NINA

"How did you find out?"

Dr Mugyenyi had finished his stew while I was telling him my story. Until now, it had really been *my* story. And Tim's story, I suppose, though really he was a secondary character. I told the quiet doctor with the sympathetic, silent stare about my trip to Liberia in 1980, about my brief affair with Shaun, about his death. And about how, two months later, as I tried to put the pieces of my life back together in Abidjan, I found out I was pregnant.

"I didn't find out that Peter was Shaun's son for a while. I knew it was a possibility. Actually, I knew or at least, I *felt* he was Shaun's son from the moment he was born, but I just refused to confront that possibility. It was only when Peter got malaria when he was about two that I found out for sure. They did a blood test at the hospital in Abidjan. Peter is AB. Tim and I are both type A. It was not possible. That's when I knew, or rather that's when I had to face what I always knew. But I didn't tell Tim for many years. In fact, I only told him after I had told Peter, and that was after Peter's own son was born."

"I didn't know he had a son. He is married?" Dr Mugyenyi asked. "In our internal memos, he was described as a single man in his late twenties."

"It's a little complicated," I said, smiling despite myself. "As you can tell from my own story, I have never been good at simple, and it seems my son has inherited this trait, as well as some of my other failings. But his eyes, those are Shaun's."

Dr Mugyenyi sipped his now cold coffee slowly, his eyes fixed on the table. Suddenly, I felt stupid and self-indulgent. How odd for this Ugandan doctor to be listening to a stranger's convoluted life story in this clanking canteen on a military base in Mogadishu. But then, aren't all our stories the same? What changes is just the context, and perhaps the culture and the language in which we tell of our foibles and fuck-ups. There are no new stories in the world, they say. We are doomed to relive the dramas, and mini-tragedies, and banal drudgeries of everyone else. We just think it is special because it is ours.

"How did Peter react when you told him?" Dr Mugyenyi asked, after a quick glance at his watch.

He had not spoken about the little girl who had died, and I got the sense he didn't want to. Maybe that is also why I spoke so freely. I needed a listener and I felt he needed a story to take him out of this place, even just for the duration of his lunch break. The ideal distraction.

"He was furious. He felt as though I had deliberately lied to him and worse, deliberately forced him to live a lie. I thought he would be sympathetic. He had fathered

168

an illegitimate child — although I hate that term, but I suppose there isn't any other way of saying it. I thought he would understand what happened to me. I suppose I wanted sympathy. We make such harsh demands on our children."

"And did *you* ever understand what really happened?"

The question surprised me. It upset my narrative and that rarely happens to me these days. I have a finite number of stories, and I have told them all. I don't expect any revisions, or corrections, or indeed questions. And this particular story was always too painful in the telling to invite rational discussion.

"I don't know if there is that much to understand. Perhaps that is where we go wrong. We always want a reason for everything. But most of what happens to us is without reason. Or at least without the kind of empowering, fulfilling reason that we like to believe governs our lives. I don't believe in life as a whole. It happens in pieces, and some of the pieces make no sense. They could happen, or not happen. It's not fate because that is too grandiose. We are not governed by fate but by the ineluctable, inevitable power of the random."

Dr Mugyenyi smiled.

"You are a cynic. That's good. So am I. I have to be. I see the power of chance everyday. That little girl who died on the operating table today. You can't tell me that was part of something bigger. It was not. She was in the wrong place at the wrong time. Her father did not have a car to get her here quickly. And here we did not have what she needed to save her. These are all random events and circumstances and they came together to end her life. There is no greater meaning, much as we wish there to be."

We sat in silence, listening to the clatter of dishes from the kitchen, the hum of the air conditioner creating a fake, mini-climate.

"My marriage collapsed because of my secret," I said. "When Peter was born, I could not love him in the way a mother should. He was living proof of my betrayal, of my fickleness, and of my loss. I don't know if what I had with Shaun was just a war-time romance, a chemical byproduct of high levels of adrenaline and fear. But every time I looked at Peter in those early years, I was reminded that I would never know. And the sorrow I felt because of that unquantifiable fact was unbearable. It poisoned my relationship with Tim. I always knew I would have to tell him, and tell Peter, eventually. Everything I did happened in the shadow of that certainty. So my present was crushed between the mistake of my past and the certain betrayals of the future."

"Aren't you being too hard on yourself?" Dr Mugyenyi said. "You say these things are random. So how can you take responsibility for the random?"

"The events themselves are random," I said, measuring every word. It was important to get this right. I had spent so many years trying to understand.

"How we react to them, shouldn't be. I think that is where my failure lies: I did not have a strong enough moral compass, or ethical grounding, to be able to deal with what happened to me. That is where I have let myself and my family down."

Dr Mugyenyi's phone rang. He answered it, listened for a moment, grunted and hung up.

"There is someone at the main gate to see you. They would not tell me his name but he is Somali, a civilian. Nabakoba is coming for you. Are you expecting anyone?"

"No," I said. "I didn't think I knew anyone here. Maybe it is someone from the British embassy?"

"They would not have to wait at the gate. I must go."

Dr Mugyenyi rose quickly, stuffing his phone into the pocket of his trousers. He extended his hand formally.

"It was very nice to meet you. I wish you the best of luck with finding your son."

I shook his hand, suddenly feeling embarrassed. Hoping he hadn't felt my revelations were inappropriate. Perhaps he was simply shrugging off another story of woe, just one of the many that peppered his days with other people's tragedies, the way shrapnel will reach far and wide, wounding as many as possible.

A second later, Nabakoba was at my side.

"Please come with me, Mrs Walters."

"Who is it?" I asked.

"He says he has information about your son. But we cannot let him in yet. You must speak to him."

"But I don't know who Peter knew here," I said, feeling inadequate, a bad mother again who did not take enough interest in her son.

"Maybe you know more than you think," Nabakoba said over his shoulder, his pace quickening as we passed the medical centre and approached the razor wire strung between two columns sprouting from the walls surrounding the base.

"There he is," Nabakoba pointed.

On the other side of the wire stood a tall man with deep-set eyes, carrying a little girl. Standing behind him, hiding in his sparse shadow, there was a small, fine-featured woman supporting an older woman wearing a white veil. The older woman's eyes were tiny, wrapped like raisins in folds of flesh.

"Can I go and speak to them?" I asked Nabakoba. He nodded and ushered me past two soldiers in a narrow alley of sandbags that weaved towards the gate in the wall.

I stood in front of the little family and held out my hand to the young man. He turned slowly, handed the little girl to the woman behind him and extended his arm to mine, offering his wrist with his hand hanging limp. He did not smile, his face was neither friendly nor hostile.

"My father was killed when your son was kidnapped," he said in a low voice that trembled at the edges. "I am Ahmed. My father was Guled Adan. He worked with Peter. And he was his friend. He was shot when they took your son."

I had not expected this, and suddenly I was ashamed of my negligence. Of course, I had heard of Guled. Edward had filled me in on the details of the kidnapping, as far as anyone knew them. I had heard of the fixer who was killed, and had felt sad and somehow responsible, and then I did not think about it anymore.

172

I was as guilty of dismissing collateral damage in my life as any military general. And yet, I did not know this man. I had never met Guled. I thought back to the last conversation I had had with Peter, a few nights before he left.

"It's only for a couple of weeks, Mum," Peter said, sprawling long-legged on my couch.

"I'll be with Guled. He is going to sort out security. It'll be fine. Mind you, Michelle's not too happy. We were supposed to go to the Loire Valley this weekend."

He smiled, almost naughtily, and I laughed, rejoicing in this professional complicity that required a hurt third party to really work.

So, yes, I had heard of Guled, but I had not bothered to put a face, or a family, to the man who had perished, driving my son around Mogadishu.

"I am so sorry for your loss," I said now. "My prayers are with you and your family."

"We have little use for prayers here," the young man said quietly, jerking his head back towards the potholed street that stretched from this fortress into the city.

"I have information about your son. But you have to give me something too."

The little girl writhed in the young woman's arms. Her mother pulled the toddler's pink hat down further, crushing tiny beads of sweat on the child's forehead.

I turned to Nabakoba. "I need to talk properly to this man. Can he and his family come inside?"

"I must ask for permission, and they will have to be searched. Let me call Colonel Mugweri."

We stood staring at each other as we waited — an old woman, a bird-like man and his family.

"Is that your daughter? Your wife?"

Ahmed nodded, the slightest tilt.

"And your mother?"

Again, a faint nod. I studied the older woman. She was probably younger than me, but grief had aged her face, drawing the wrinkles deeper. Or maybe it wasn't grief. Maybe it was just time, unadulterated by expensive creams promising to stop the clock while only managing to slow it slightly.

Nabakoba came back and nodded the little family past the soldiers manning the gate. The little girl's eyes were wide with fear, but she did not make a sound. When her mother put her down to be searched, she hid her face in the folds of the woman's gauzy blue skirt. She never said a word but her tiny hands seemed to be shaking. A puddle formed in the sand around her bare feet. I wanted to scoop her up in my arms, and hold her to me, but how terrifying that would be for her. I would not use this child to salve my own guilty conscience.

Nabakoba ushered us to a block of pre-fab offices, half hidden behind green sandbags, and into a small room with three cream plastic chairs and a stained white plastic table.

Nabakoba left to fetch Colonel Mugweri and I excused myself to call Don. The family barely acknowledged our departure. Ahmed was standing by a window looking into the yard where Ugandan and Burundian soldiers were oiling their guns, kicking around a flat football, or working on some stranded armoured cars. The older lady sat on a chair, staring at her hands in her lap. The younger woman had her daughter on her knees. She had removed the pink hat and was stroking her dark, curly hair and whispering in her tiny ears. The child was not smiling, but she was no longer shaking.

I could hear Don asking me questions down the line.

"They are here. At the base. I don't know what information they have. I am waiting for the colonel to come. But how am I supposed to tell if this is really Guled's son? Don't you have any records, Don?"

"You know how it is, Nina."

Don's voice was faint and scratchy but I could feel his impatience.

"This was an arrangement made by Peter himself. Of course, he claimed expenses for Guled. We have records of that but we didn't have any details beyond the man's name. And his location. You know the way it works, Nina."

"Okay, okay. Sorry. But are you going to do something for the family? You have to, Don."

My voice was harsher than I meant it to be. I was not angry with Don, not really. I was angry with myself. I had ignored these people since arriving in Mogadishu. I had been so immersed in the story, Peter's story, that I had forgotten that this was not just his story, or my story. There were other people involved.

I had broken every rule I had ever made as a journalist. I prided myself on always trying to safeguard the dignity, the humanity of the people in my stories. I didn't want to treat them as quote machines, fluffy details, or necessities that demanded little more than the journalism equivalent of bagging and tagging. But here, I had forgotten Guled, or at least not given his story its due. I had treated his death as a detail.

"Of course, we will do something for them," Don said, his justifiable hurt at my anger cutting through the static.

"But we will have to investigate a little more. Edward can help us with that. Where is he?"

"I don't know," I said. "He went out this morning and I haven't seen him since. I'm going to look for him after this. I have to go and talk to Ahmed now, Don. I'll let you know what he says."

"Be careful, Nina. This could be a scam. I'm sure people know you are there. This guy, Ahmed, might have nothing to do with Guled, or with Peter."

"I know," I said impatiently. "But Don, he is here with his whole family. That suggests something else, doesn't it?" I said, hoping I didn't sound as desperate as I felt.

Don was silent. I clutched the phone to my ear, losing myself in the hypnotic crackles and hisses of the invisible world between us. My fingers were sweaty and the phone kept slipping. I was outside, hugging a wall, trying to disappear into its meagre shadow.

"Talk to him and call me back," Don said and hung up.

I headed back to the almost-bare room where all my hope was now stashed. As I opened the door, I heard confident footsteps.

"Nina!" Edward was striding towards me. He was sweaty and dusty, and he looked more at home now than when I had first met him at the airport in London. He had swapped the shirt for a dark green T-shirt with sweat stains under the arms, and faded chinos that might have been dark brown once but were now a feeble beige. He wasn't wearing a flak jacket and yet somehow he looked, not invincible, but hard to harm.

"What's going on?"

I shut the door again and filled him in quickly.

"This could be a trick . . ."

"I know, I know," I interrupted impatiently, tired of having the obvious pointed out to me at every turn.

"But we should hear him out. Where have *you* been? Okay scrap that, you won't tell me. What have you learnt?"

"I've confirmed that Peter escaped. It happened last night. The good news is Wanlaweyn is not too far from here, and if he is heading to Mogadishu, he should not be travelling through Al-Shabaab territory. The bad news is we don't know exactly where to look, and this is Somalia so we are never quite sure where Al-Shabaab are, or indeed who they are. And then there are the militias, the clans and bandits. And we don't know who he is with. Maybe this man will be able to tell us more, but in any case, I'm going with AMISOM towards Wanlaweyn as soon as we're done here."

Inside, Ahmed was still staring out the window. The little girl seemed to be sleeping against her mother's chest. The old woman had not moved. For a fleeting second, I wondered if she was dead, and then her eyes flickered towards me. It was the briefest of glances but I felt she was reproaching me. I had borne the boy who had taken her husband. What would she do now?

Ahmed turned and glared at Edward.

"Who is this foreigner? I want to talk to you, not to any government."

"He is here to help me, Ahmed. He has been looking for Peter too. He does not work for any government," I said, realising as I said it that I was not quite sure if this was true. Edward said nothing. He stayed a few steps behind me.

The door squeaked open and Colonel Mugweri and Nabakoba came in, somehow filling the room with grunts and shuffling. The little girl woke up. I guessed she must be about two.

"I am Colonel Mugweri. Welcome to the AMISOM base."

He held out his hand to Ahmed. They were about the same height but Mugweri was bulked up by Kevlar, with an extra inch added by his heavy boots.

"I am Ahmed, this is my wife, Ubah, my daughter, Lila, and my mother, Aisha. I can take you to Peter Maguire but I will not travel with soldiers. I can take the mother and her friend, we will travel with my clan, and in return, you will offer places on this base to my family."

The words came out in a rush, as though Ahmed was afraid he would forget a piece of his plan if he hesitated.

I glanced at his mother. She was looking at her son, and I thought I saw a faint smile around her lips. His wife looked scared, her eyes flicking from side to side as if she was watching a table tennis match. I guessed she did not speak much English.

Edward, Colonel Mugweri and I all spoke at once, our words fizzing in the silence that followed Ahmed's speech.

"That sounds risky," said Edward.

"I'm afraid I can't agree," said Colonel Mugweri.

"Let's go."

Colonel Mugweri glared at me.

"With all due respect Mrs Walters, this is not your decision to make. I cannot make such guarantees on one man's word, whose identity we have not even confirmed."

"I agree with the colonel," said Edward. "It could be a trap. It is not safe out there. Let me go with some soldiers. We'll get him back."

"My son is *out there*," I said. "I am willing to take the risk. And I trust this man," I added, nodding at Ahmed. He did not react.

Colonel Mugweri shook his head.

"I will not permit this. If the authorities were to hear about it, I would be fired. And his condition for cooperation is impossible. We cannot offer safe haven to civilians. We'd have the entire city in here. Or what's left of it. It's out of the question."

I turned to him, willing myself to stay calm.

"I will be their guarantor. I will take responsibility for them. I give you my word I will sort it out with your bosses, with the Somali authorities, with the British, with whoever you damn well please. When I have my son back, I will have nothing else to do. But now, I do not have time to argue with you. Peter is out there. He has escaped. This man can take us to him. We can bring him back. I don't think, with all due respect, that you can stop me. I am not a soldier. I am free to do as I like."

"You are our guest. You must obey our rules."

Colonel Mugweri almost growled the words, no longer the gentle giant.

I ignored him. I would not be held back now.

"I will come with you, Ahmed. I will take care of your family afterwards. They will not leave this place without me. I give you my word. How do you know where my son is?"

Ahmed opened his mouth but he looked scared now, as if he had drained his reserves of courage and confidence with his audaciousness in coming here.

He looked at Colonel Mugweri who was still scowling. Edward gave him the slightest of nods.

"He is with a man called Abdi. Abdi is one of my relatives. We belong to the same clan. Abdi was with the kidnappers, not Al-Shabaab. The others who were to sell him to Al-Shabaab. Your son is now with Abdi in a village, about 50 kilometres from here. But you cannot go without me; they will not accept you, and they might even fight you. I have also heard that Al-Shabaab are looking for him so if you want to go with me, we need to go now."

"Al-Shabaab do not control the territory in that area," Colonel Mugweri interrupted.

"Al-Shabaab are never where you expect them. They move like ghosts," Ahmed said quietly. "And do you really think they are the only ones who will harm him? If so, then you have learnt very little about our country."

"I'm going with this man," I said. "Edward, you can come with me or not. Colonel, we have to do this. I will not sit here when my son is so close."

Mugweri glared at Ahmed.

"Why are you doing this? Why do you want to help this woman? Her son is the reason your father was killed."

The words were like knives. I looked at Ahmed. He replied to Colonel Mugweri but his eyes were fixed on mine. And I could feel Aisha's eyes on my face too. I knew that I deserved this scrutiny.

"My father liked Peter. He hated Al-Shabaab. I know it was not Al-Shabaab who killed him. I know who they were, but that is my problem. I will take care of that. And that is why you need to take care of my family. I have work to do after this. But my father will not rest in peace if I do not help Peter. He was our guest, he stayed in our home. He was a friend. My father would have defended him. I am my father's son."

"Thank you," I whispered, fighting to rein in the tears of gratitude and shame that were filling my eyes.

"Can you give us an escort to the edge of the city?" Edward asked Captain Mugweri. "Can we do that, Ahmed?"

The thin man nodded, slowly.

"I will meet you outside the new port. May I go now? I will get my own transport," Ahmed said.

Captain Mugweri nodded. "Daylight is fading. We have about three hours until sunset. I want you all back on base by then. That is not a request."

Edward nodded.

Ahmed walked to his mother, held her frail hands between his for a few seconds, then kissed her bowed head. He did the same with his wife, and with Lila. But as he was walking to the door, Lila leapt from her mother's lap and ran to him, wrapping her tiny arms around his legs. She was sobbing. Ahmed lifted her, held her to his chest, rubbed her back and whispered in her ear. She lifted her head, nodded sadly and pulled his ear. He smiled and his face was transformed. He put her down again and she walked slowly to her mother, climbing onto her lap and burying her face in the folds of her robe. Ahmed was still smiling at her as he left the room.

CHAPTER
THIRTEEN

ABDI

When I went back to the thorn tree with Mukhtar, the prisoner was asleep, his head tilted to one side.

"You have brought us a tough man then, eh, Abdi," Mukhtar chuckled as we drew close.

Mukhtar kicked the foreigner's dusty, bruised feet.

"Wake up. This is no time to sleep."

The prisoner stirred but it took some time for his eyes to open. Maybe he did not want to come back to this world, to the sunrise that would soon banish the shadows and shades of the night. I too would have liked to lie down under that tree and sleep. I wouldn't want to wake, and maybe if you didn't want to, you wouldn't. Could you sleep forever if you believed you had no reason to get up?

The prisoner stood shakily. He rubbed one of his thin hands over his long face.

"You are starting to look like Al-Shabaab," Mukhtar grinned, pointing to the hair spreading across the white man's chin and cheeks.

"Maybe you could join them. They have people from your world too. But if you did that, you would probably be killed by the militias. It is difficult to cheat death in this land. It is not yet clear to me if your time is up, or if you are meant to go free. We will know in a few hours, I suppose."

The prisoner seemed not to follow Mukhtar's words although my cousin's English is excellent. He studied in Canada when he was a teenager, came back when Siad Barre was still in power, and later taught English at Mogadishu University for a few years until a mortar crashed into his home, killing his wife and six-year-old son, and scorching the flesh on the right side of his body. In our family, we call him The Professor, although I think he never actually had that title. He is not the oldest clan member in this village, but his learning means that most people defer to him. He has been abroad, he has lived in Mogadishu, he has taught, he can quote from the classic Somali poems as well as other African authors, whose names I learned in school before education became a luxury we couldn't afford.

"My name is Peter Maguire."

The prisoner stepped forward and extended his hand to Mukhtar, who smiled like a man enjoying a private joke, before stretching out his scarred right hand.

"I am Mukhtar Salah. Or you can call me The Professor. You must come with us now. We must talk to the other clan members and decide what to do. Abdi, the son of my cousin Faduma, may she rest in peace, has presented us with quite a dilemma. This should be interesting."

Mukhtar chuckled again and, taking the prisoner's hand, began to lead him back to the village. The sun

184

was slipping above the horizon now. We were men with shadows again. I followed.

The last time I had seen Mukhtar was when I was perhaps seven. He came to our home after Abdulkassim Salat Hassan was elected president and returned in triumph to Mogadishu. I remember Mukhtar as a tall, dashing man, with a head of dark hair that seemed to have a life of its own, as though it was shot through with his own personal electricity. He would have been about thirty then, an old man to me, but somehow he seemed younger than my parents. He smiled a lot, joked with Nadif and me, brought sweets for us, and then magicked them from behind our ears. He was not a close relative, but he stayed for a few days, and his presence made the house ring with laughter, his shameless chuckle rising above our giggles, my father's deep laughter and below them all, silent but supportive, my mother's indulgent smiles.

Mukhtar led the prisoner to his hut. It was small and away from the perimeter fence of thorn branches.

"Stay here. You can sleep, and perhaps you will dream of your future. While you do that, we will discuss it. Do not leave, please. You may want to rush to Mogadishu but the roads are not safe."

"Is this area controlled by Al-Shabaab?" the prisoner asked, his eyes flicking nervously to me.

I stayed silent. This was Mukhtar's home and this was now his problem. I had made it his problem but I was grateful that we stumbled upon his village. Perhaps the gods of destiny have decided to take my side. At least for a short while. This is just one moment. I have no illusions that it means anything. In this land, moments come and go but you can never trust them to last. Peace is fickle, war is random, death is the only constant. We are not dead yet, but that just means that we could die at any moment.

Nadif used to say he was not frightened of death. And then, later, when his eyes grew hard and his face dark, he would say that he welcomed it. I think I am finally beginning to understand what he meant then. Though it took his loss, and the loss of my mother, to bring me to this point.

"No, Al-Shabaab do not control this area," Mukhtar mimicked the foreigner's accent with a smile.

"But, it is not clear who does. It depends on what you mean by control? Al-Shabaab come here, certainly. What is to stop them? This country has become their playground. But we also have militias, our own and others. You have been to Disneyland, perhaps?"

The prisoner shook his head, managing a bewildered smile.

"Shame. It looks very . . . bright and shiny. This is East Africa's Disneyland. There are rides, kingdoms to explore, treasures to find. How do you say it in the US? Ah yes, *where dreams come true*. That is Somalia in a nutshell. Although we can also do nightmares."

"I'm not American. I am British. Or Irish. You can take your pick."

For the first time in days, I heard anger in the prisoner's voice. It cheered me. Anger is a force for life. I would like to feel more anger. But I have no one to blame for the past six months, and everything that went before. I have no one and everyone and that is the same. Who should I blame? The dead? The living? Myself? The foreigners? The other foreigners? Anger cannot thrive in this confusion.

"My apologies. We are a simple people. You are a foreigner so we make assumptions. Perhaps you can understand why."

Mukhtar's words were conciliatory, almost apologetic, but I could hear the laughter underneath.

The prisoner rubbed his face again. He started to say something, stopped.

"I owe everything to Abdi. I will wait for his decision about what to do next. Thank you."

He bent to enter the hut.

Mukhtar waited until he was gone.

"Well, Abdi. I think you have become what they like to call in the West a hero. Let's see if the others agree."

I did not think they would. We headed to a large hut in the centre of the village where Mukhtar would meet the other elders, where the prisoner's fate would be decided, and by extension, mine. I knew I was in no immediate danger. Nobody in this village would kill me, but they could kick him out and that might amount to the same thing. I cannot abandon him now. I have changed his fate, and I must stay the path.

Inside, the hut was thick with smoke. In the gloom, six men were faceless mounds of shifting shadows. The fire had withered to a whisper of flame and a sliver of acrid smoke.

Mukhtar found a space and I crouched beside him. There was silence. A silence that speaks of the absence of something powerful.

Mukhtar spoke, all trace of laughter now gone. He had made light of the situation with the prisoner, but in here, in this dark hut where the deepest of our thoughts and traditions were gathered, there was no place for jokes.

"We have a decision to make. Abdi, our cousin and our kinsman, has brought this man to us. We can debate his decision another time. I will simply say that this is the son of Faduma and Omar, both now dead, may Allah welcome them into his presence. This is a good boy and his decision will not have been made lightly."

There were some grunts, some shuffling of feet and clearing of throats. The shadows were full of unseen eyes, all focused on me.

"We must decide what to do with the prisoner. Al-Shabaab will be looking for him. They may come here. If they do, we will deal with that. The prisoner needs to go to Mogadishu to be safe. Will we help him? Can we help him?"

For a moment, nobody spoke. Then a voice came from our right.

"There is more to this than you say, Mukhtar. Abdi is your cousin and our kinsman. But Guled Adan was also the cousin of some of us here, a member of the sub-clan."

I stiffened. I had heard what had happened to this Guled, of course. When I was sent by Yusuf to be with

188

the first group of kidnappers in Mogadishu, before the prisoner was transferred to Wanlaweyn, they told me a driver had been shot. I did not realise he belonged to one of our sub-clans. This was bad news.

"Guled, may he rest in the arms of Allah, was killed because he was with this foreigner. There is a debt to pay here. The foreigner must pay it."

There was some murmuring of agreement. I could not see the speaker. Mukhtar leant towards me and whispered.

"That is Ali. You do not know him. Now you see, Abdi, this is more complicated than you perhaps thought."

Clearing his throat, Mukhtar spoke.

"This is true, Ali. And yet the foreigner did not shoot Guled. It was a Somali who did that. What kind of person shoots an old man for being in a car with a foreigner? This was a crime and I trust that all of you from Guled's branch of the clan will deal with that man in the correct way."

"It will be done," said Ali, leaning for a moment out of the shadows so that I saw thick brows, eyes like pools, and a wide mouth. "Ahmed, Guled's son, is taking care of that. But now, Ahmed needs to know of this new development."

Mukhtar nodded.

"I will contact him," said Ali. "I will be happy with whatever he decides. It is his decision to make."

There was a rustling and Ali rose, slipping out of the hut on long legs, and already pulling his mobile phone from his shirt pocket.

"Would anyone else like to speak?" Mukhtar asked. "Are there any other issues to consider in this?"

"I agree it should be Ahmed's decision," said a thin voice from our left. I recognised the weak tones of Abdulghani, another of my mother's distant cousins.

"But I also say we should support Abdi. He has taken this step, he has sought refuge here. It is our duty to protect our clansman and by extension, his . . . his companion. We must do what is right."

Abdulghani was a trader who had had a small business selling phone cards in Kismayo in the south of the country. When Al-Shabaab took over the town, they forced him to pay protection money, beat him when he was late, and stole his produce. He came north earlier this year, leaving his wealth, his new home, his hopes. He was a bitter man. He had never dreamed he would have to work on the land again, eking a living from this poor, unreliable soil. He was also a lazy man. My mother called him a wastrel, and rolled her eyes to heaven whenever his name was mentioned.

His speech was followed by some muted sounds of assent. Al-Shabaab were no friends of my clan. Some of the men here had lost family members to this latest war, some had lost money, some had been forced to move. All felt humiliated. Mukhtar never knew who fired the mortar that destroyed his family, and scarred him on the outside as well as the inside, but in these situations you blame those you already hate.

I wondered if these men knew about Nadif. They must do, but my father's kindness, generosity and dignity would have carried more weight with these

190

elders than the mistakes of a teenage boy. And then, they would understand Nadif's reasons for wanting to take up a gun.

"Thank you, Abdulghani. I see your remarks are not without support here," said Mukhtar, the lilt of a chuckle returning to his voice, like a shy teenager entering a room of elders, quietly, hugging the walls, hoping to pass unnoticed.

"Let us wait to hear from Ahmed. Until then we will do nothing."

We sat in silence for a while, but this was a more serene silence. Some of the men began to whisper among themselves but the voices were tame now, the urgency was gone. I tried to relax. There wasn't any more I could do.

Ali came back, pushing aside the blanket in the doorway and bringing with him a rush of fresh air and a burst of light. I had forgotten it was day already.

"Ahmed is coming. He says we must not harm the prisoner. This foreigner was his father's friend. Guled respected him and Ahmed says he does not blame the foreigner for his father's death. He said this man deserves to live."

There was some disgruntled murmuring from around the walls but I knew now Peter Maguire was safe. I suddenly felt exhausted. I whispered to Mukhtar who quickly clapped his hands and declared the meeting over.

"Let us wait for Ahmed. He can take the prisoner back to Mogadishu. He is coming with men?"

Ali nodded.

191

"There should be no problems on the road from here to Mogadishu. The militias are fewer and we know people on the roadblocks. Ahmed will choose good men from among his own people."

"He will not bring the foreign troops?" Mukhtar asked.

Ali shook his head, and murmurs of approval rose alongside the grunts and sighs as six bodies rose awkwardly from the dirt floor and filed out of the hut into the hard light of a fresh day.

I went to lie down in Abdulghani's hut. There was a thin mattress on the floor and I fell onto it. But Abdulghani wanted to talk. He had lost everything in Kismayo and had he been a braver man, he might have found a way to nip at the heels of the "dogs" of Al-Shabaab, as he called them.

"I had a good business and hope for the future. And then, these teenagers come, waving their guns, racing their technicals up and down the streets, scattering the dogs, and the chickens, and the people. They think they own this world and the next, these children. In my day, we would have grabbed them by the neck, beaten them well and taught them to respect their elders. They have no respect, these foreigners. And make no mistake, many of them are foreigners. Bringing their Wahhabi rules and hunger for power and greed to our land."

Abdulghani paused and my eyelids slipped lower. I hoped he had finished but he wasn't there yet.

"I tell you, Abdi, they have ruined this country. I am old enough to remember the past and to appreciate it. Siad Barre was bad, but under him, we could at least pull together something of a life. Then we had the chaos that followed his death when brother fought brother. But nothing has been as bad as now. These Al-Shabaab brought the Ethiopians to our country. They made the US see us again after we had managed to turn them away in the 1990s by showing them that we could not be beaten in our own land. But now, now we are being defeated and humiliated, by our own misguided youth. I have lost everything, Abdi. You see me here, back in the village, back in this land of nothingness, me, a man who had a house, a shop, a livelihood."

He shook his head sadly, but also triumphantly, because here, everybody has a story but his, in his eyes at least, was one of the most tragic. A kind of victory in a country where broken lives were all that was left. One-upmanship of sorrow.

"And these suicide bombings? Who are these boys who blow themselves up? Why do you need to kill yourself here? Life will sort you out soon enough. All this talk of seventy-two virgins waiting for them, and rivers of honey? Okay, maybe getting honey here is difficult today, but virgins? Are not our women, here and now, beautiful enough to make a man live? Why put off until paradise what you can have now?"

Abdulghani chortled in the way single men do when they talk about women. I know this laughter. It is the laughter of a man who knows nothing about women, a man who tries to cover his ignorance with noise. Before, before everything, I might have joined him. Not now. I couldn't listen anymore.

"Please, Uncle. I am very tired. I do not wish to be rude but I need to sleep."

Apologising, Abdulghani left the hut. I sank into the mattress, closed my eyes and thought of Nadif. And the time we had argued about the virgins.

Nadif had been long gone from our home but I bumped into him one day a few streets away. It was after midday and since the fighting had died down, as it did everyday because of the heat, my mother had sent me out to see if I could find some flour to make bread for our evening meal.

I didn't see Nadif at first. I heard the roar of the technical and without looking, I moved closer to the crumbling walls of the small shops and shacks along the street. I always felt nervous walking too near those walls. Mogadishu seemed like a city that could fall on you at anytime, burying you quietly, undramatically so that nothing would be left except a pile of rubble that looked exactly like all the other piles of rubble. I kept my eyes down. We have a saying: *Do not walk into a snake pit with your eyes open.* But what if you live in a snake pit? Best to keep your eyes lowered.

"Abdi! Abdi!"

I looked up. Nadif was standing like a hero behind the machine gun welded into the flatbed of the pickup. He yelled at the driver and the beast slowed. He jumped down. A checked scarf covered his face and his eyes were hidden behind dusty sunglasses. I felt a pang of envy. Here was my elder brother. He was somebody, with a gun hanging casually over his shoulder. He was a

194

master of these roads. I was less than the chickens that scattered out of the way as the technicals roared past, a puny seeker of milk and flour.

"My brother, how are you?"

Nadif hugged me fiercely, as though he needed to make up for the past six months when we had hardly seen each other. He smelt of men, tobacco and something else that was strong and dusty, and had traces of the sea and spices. He smelt like adventure would smell if you could buy it in a ruby-coloured bottle from the medicine men in Bakara market.

"Let's get a drink."

Nadif led me to a kiosk where he bought two Cokes. Behind the casual way he handed over the money, I could sense his pride. He could now offer me a Coke. The last time I drank a Coke was at my father's funeral. Then, I drank it quickly, shamefully. I enjoyed it, but I did not want anyone to see that I could be so superficial as to enjoy such a thing at the funeral of my father. I remember being surprised that Coke could still taste the same, in this new world where I would grow up without a father.

Nadif led me to the mango tree beside the football field, where we had sat so many times before. Some little boys were perched on the wall when we arrived, pushing and jostling, and laughing when one of them slipped off. They scampered away, eyes big with terror and delight, when Nadif approached.

"How is Mother?" Nadif asked, as if he was talking about a distant relative.

"She is okay. She looks thin. She worries about you and sometimes it is hard for us to find food now that there seems to be fighting every day."

Nadif nodded solemnly.

"Soon, we will have taken the rest of Mogadishu. The government's troops are nothing, and AMISOM . . . They are their own worst enemy. Most of their soldiers can't even shoot straight, country boys from backward places! Soon we will force them to leave. You saw what we did last week? The attack on the base? They cannot even secure their bases. That was Mohyadin, remember him?"

I thought of the plump boy with very hairy eyebrows and a thin fuzz on his head. He used to sit near me in class. He was a joker and got me into trouble more than once with his quips about our teacher. He would whisper a joke, and I would burst out laughing. Mohyadin would paste a look of total innocence on his face, his bushy eyebrows climbing up his wide forehead like caterpillars.

"What do you mean, that was Mohyadin?"

"I mean," Nadif said, "that he was the one who drove the bomb into the base. He messed up though because they spotted him. Still, he managed to detonate the bomb, and three or four of the enemy were killed."

Nadif laughed loudly, maybe even a little too loudly.

"I told them he was too nervous for the job. They thought he was ready to be a martyr. He was ready but he wasn't good enough."

"What about you?" I asked nervously. "Are you ready to be a martyr? And what does that mean, Nadif?"

Nadif turned his face towards me, but kept those big-man sunglasses on so that all I could see was my own reflection.

"I am ready," he said in a soft voice. "Ready and able."

"But why would you want to kill yourself, Nadif?" I said.

Today, here, now, that question seems naïve. Today, I can imagine a host of reasons to kill yourself. If I had that conversation with Nadif now, maybe he would not have become so angry.

"I am fighting jihad, child," Nadif said scornfully. "It is my duty. I am ready to go to Allah, and enjoy the rewards of the faithful."

"Like the seventy-two virgins?" I asked.

Nadif laughed.

"Yes, like the seventy-two virgins. Let's hope there is quality as well as quantity," he said with a snigger that showed me my brother was still there, inside this eyeless face of a warrior.

"It seems a stupid idea to me," I said. Maybe that snigger had allowed me to relax a little.

"Why kill yourself for something you cannot be sure of? However bad things are here, at least we know what they are. I think being a martyr is stupid."

Nadif's arm came out of nowhere and suddenly I was sprawled on the ground, the Coke bottle spinning in the sand beside me, the delicious liquid leaking away just inches from my mouth, which was full of dirt and grit.

"Don't you ever say such a thing again," he growled in a low voice.

I lifted my head and squinted into the sun. Nadif stood like an executioner above me, backlit and featureless. He swung back his boot and kicked me in the ribs. I gasped and coughed, spit sticking bits of grass to my lips.

"I mean it, Abdi."

His voice was kinder now but it almost sounded like he was pleading for something I couldn't give him.

"You desecrate the names of the martyrs. People we know, who have decided to do what is right, to support the jihad. You lie here, like a worm, keeping your head down, doing nothing to avenge our father, and all the fathers, and you dare to question the martyrs. I am hungry for the chance to join them. I am eager to die, Abdi."

He lifted his gun onto his shoulder and turned to go.

"It is unlikely we will meet again. I am going out of town for a while. I don't think there is much for us to say to each other anymore. Goodbye, little brother."

Nadif was right. I did not see him again until they brought the pieces to our house. I guess he was not technically a martyr. He blew himself up by accident. Maybe he wasn't as ready as he thought. Nadif was always good at talking himself up. I will never know what went through his head in the second between his mistake and his death. There must have been a moment. I wonder, did he think of the seventy-two virgins, or did he worry he would be shortchanged because he was dying in an accident?

As I lay in Abdulghani's hut, I thought of one of our more famous, or perhaps notorious, proverbs: *I and Somalia against the world. I and my clan against Somalia. I and my family against the clan. I and my brother against the family. I against my brother.*

Nadif was dead. He had made his choice. He had not lived long enough to reach the end of the proverb. I had lived less but already I was there. And now I knew what I was going to do once I was free of the prisoner. I had nothing left to live for, and there was one job where that would be an advantage. I smiled as I finally felt sleep claim me. There was, after all, a place for me yet in this land.

CHAPTER
FOURTEEN

PETER

The sound of distant shooting woke me from a sleep I half hoped might be something else. For a moment, it was dark around me and I could feel another world fading into the corners. I tried to hold onto the dream, but trying to catch the fragments of Esther, of Godwin, was like trying to close my fingers around smoke. Before they had even faded, those images were fake. I haven't ever seen Godwin in the flesh. My son turned five on July 15th. I had wired Esther some money before I got here, and asked her to buy him a present. It did not calm my guilt. The gesture, for that is all it was, taunted me with its futility.

Another burst of gunfire. I could hear shouts outside and bare feet slapping into the hard earth. With consciousness, fear returned, but I was so worn out, I couldn't bring my body to react. I rose sluggishly to my knees, shaking my head. For a moment, I felt the strongest urge to lie down again, pull the thin blanket over my head and curl up. Maybe everything would go away.

As a child, I used to listen to pop songs on a wheezing transistor radio under my duvet. It was a teenage rebellion, I expect, but a hidden one. I was supposed to be asleep, instead I was whispering the lyrics under my breath, dreaming of adventure and love, and indulging in the kind of sentimentalism that only teenagers can really understand. The songs made me believe I could be a rebel, live whatever life I wanted and to hell with the consequences. Breaking hearts was good, as long as it wasn't mine that was being broken. I know better now.

Mukhtar ran in, carrying an AK-47. His hands were steady though his voice shook, and I suspected The Professor was excited rather than scared.

"Get out. They are coming for you."

I straightened, my breath already coming in gasps as if the sight of the jocular man, stripped of his lopsided smile, had dealt me a physical blow somewhere below my diaphragm.

"Al-Shabaab. They are outside the village, coming from the main road. You need to head to Mogadishu, now. Someone is coming for you. Ahmed, Guled's son. Abdi will go with you and Abdulghani will drive. We have a car at the back of the compound. Go. Allah be with you."

He disappeared again, slipping through the door without looking back. The gunfire was coming closer now. I edged out of the hut, my head reeling as I tried to digest this new information. But there was no time to think. Mukhtar was with seven or eight other men, all armed, standing by the weak walls of the village compound, near the main gate. In the distance, I could see two technicals roaring towards us. They were

perhaps 300 yards away. This time, we would not make
it.

Mukhtar and his men seemed to be holding their
fire. The heavy green gate in the wall that marked the
edge of the village was closed, and they were huddled
behind a piece of corrugated iron they had dragged
behind the stones. I wanted to tell them that the rusty
iron would have no hope of stopping most bullets. I
remembered that from our hostile training. Crouching
and cursing my height, I ran behind my hut, heading
away from the gate. Running again, but this time I had
shoes — Abdi had brought me a pair of dirty white
trainers just before I slept.

"Here, Peter!"

It was Abdi again, my guardian angel. He was sitting
in the passenger seat of a faded red Sedan. The door of
the back seat was open and I jumped in, grazing my
shin on the running board. I collided with a man-boy
clutching a sub-machine gun. He shifted slightly. He
had the beginnings of a beard and a manic smile that
made me wince. His fingers looked too small for the
trigger they were wrapped around. I resisted the urge to
slide the barrel away from me. The driver said nothing
but I could see his eyes in the rear-view mirror. They
were neither hostile nor friendly. He glanced at my
reflection curiously, then turned the key, muttering
something in Somali to Abdi.

There was a small gate in the back wall of the
compound. A young boy of about eight swung it open
and we roared onto a bumpy plain that seemed to
stretch endlessly to the horizon.

202

"We will have to stay off the road for a while," Abdi yelled.

I put my hand up to grab the handle above the door but there wasn't one, and my head smashed into the window. The man-boy beside me was bouncing around like a metal shot in a pinball machine, his finger still caressing the trigger.

I pinned myself back in the seat, trying to get as far away as possible from the barrel of the gun.

"How did they know how to find us?" I yelled above the wailing motor and the distant sound of guns.

Abdi was silent for a moment.

"Maybe they asked Yusuf about my ties in this area."

"Who is Yusuf?"

"He is my cousin. I was working for him at the other compound."

"Did he know your plans?" I asked, my mouth dry and gritty already from the dust we were churning up around us as we tore through a flat plain of scrubs, thorn trees and termite mounds reaching for the sky like sandcastles abandoned by giant children.

"No, no. But he knows my family. He would have known about Mukhtar. They are cousins too but they have fallen out."

"Still, why would Yusuf lead them to his cousin?"

Abdi was silent. I kicked myself for the question. Despite everything that had happened over the past weeks, I was still trying to impose a foreign order on this land. I was still alienated by my fixed ways of thinking. I could see my young saviour's face in the wing mirror, but I saw him in flashes, disjointed. I saw

Abdi's eyes, then his nose, his jaw. But the overall impression was of a boy who understood too much and he knew the knowledge was dangerous.

We fell silent. The other men said nothing. Our driver's fingers were white around the steering wheel as he struggled to control the car. I caught his eyes studying me again in the mirror. He said something in Somali. Abdi replied.

"What did he say?" I asked.

"Abdulghani was wondering how much Al-Shabaab were going to ask for you. The ransom."

"They would have killed me anyway," I said flatly.

"Of that I am sure," Abdi said, nodding.

"Will Mukhtar and the other men be all right?" I asked, acutely conscious of the childishness of my question.

"I don't know," Abdi said shortly.

"I am sorry," I said, and that was it. I felt as if something had broken inside me, some last fragment in the wall of certainty that surrounded my life. Everything was gone.

"I am sorry," I whispered over and over.

I could see Abdulghani's eyes widening in the rear-view mirror as he watched me muttering, rocking back and forth, my breaths coming like strangled sobs. The man-boy next to me seemed not to notice. He was staring out the window at the nothingness flying past.

I wanted to explain but I knew it didn't matter. I was not scared. I was distraught because I was the perfect victim. I had let myself become the perfect victim and in my shallowness I had dragged others down with me.

204

Here in this strange land, I was doing what I had always done. Fucking up other lives through my ignorance and my carelessness. Fucking up my own life by refusing to acknowledge the definites. We hold these truths to be self-evident. I had to accept the evidence of my self. I had a son, I had a woman who loved me, and another, I had two fathers. I needed to stop fleeing these truths. It might not be the life I wanted, or the one I had planned. It might not even be a life I could deal with, but I had to try. These were the cards I had been dealt. I hoped I would be given a chance to try.

The car jolted, there was a teeth-tingling screech of metal, and then we were on tarmac.

"This is the road to Mogadishu," Abdi said. His words had the timbre of a prophecy.

I ran my hands over my face. My eyes in the rear-view mirror were bloodshot and small. The sudden silence filled the car. The road stretched before us like a ribbon, flat and winding.

"Will we meet any roadblocks?" I asked, trying for a normal voice, trying to swallow the trace of tears.

"I don't know," Abdi said.

He was leaning over the dashboard, peering into the hazy distance. Abdulghani cursed as we swerved to avoid a pothole, then we all fell into a tense silence. We had gone maybe thirty minutes when Abdi muttered something in Somali. Abdulghani leant forward, peering through his small round glasses. The man-boy sat up straight, pushing against me as he leant into the gap between the two front seats. A car was coming. No, it was a technical. As it sped closer, I could see a man standing behind the mounted gun, scarf fluttering in the breeze. On this empty road, the speeding car had the force of a vision, getting sharper by the moment as it ate up the distance between us. Abdulghani floored the accelerator and our car leapt forward. For a wild moment, I thought we were playing some bizarre game of chicken. Red racing towards white on this empty road under a cobalt blue-and-violet sky, and a sinking sun. If we crashed, it would be a rainbow.

"It's them, it's Ahmed," Abdi said.

Abdulghani sighed and released the accelarator as though the breath he forced out came from his very feet. We slowed to a stop, not even bothering to pull in. We had passed no traffic since leaving the compound. The technical screeched to a halt some ten yards ahead of us. The man behind the gun stayed where he was, legs splayed, hands on the gun. His scarf had fallen onto his shoulders, exhausted, twitching. Behind him I now saw three other men, crouched in the truck's flatbed. They jumped out, two taking up positions at the back of the truck, facing back the way they had come, facing back to Mogadishu, the city that could give me back my life.

The other man moved forward. He was tall, white, stocky, with a crewcut. He wore aviator sunglasses and carried his sub-machine gun easily, like a hockey stick. No one had moved from our car. And then the door of the pickup opened. It took me a second to recognise my mother. I could see her but it didn't make sense. My mind didn't seem to be able to compute the messages being sent to it from my eyes. She had her hands over her head and as Abdulghani finally cut our wheezing engine, I heard her calling, "Peter, Peter. It's okay. We've come to get you. You are safe now."

I looked for Abdi in the side mirror. He nodded. I got out of the car slowly. I did not run to my mother, I stood with my hand on the top of the car door, shielding my body and looked. My mother started walking towards me, her hands outstretched in an empty hug.

After everything, it seemed too easy. I squinted past her. Another man had climbed out of the pickup cabin. I recognised Ahmed. He lifted his hand from the barrel of the AK-47 he was cradling and waved. A brief flash of fingers, but he did not smile. Guled's shattered head flashed before my eyes like those vivid bursts of nightmare that sometimes light up the back of my eyes in those moments before I sleep. When I finally had the courage to leave that car door and walk across the road, I was heading to Ahmed and not my mother. My mother belonged to another life, one that I knew I would have to reconstruct. Ahmed belonged to the now, to the here. I needed to apologise to him. As useless as I knew it would be. If everything that had happened to me since I was kidnapped was some kind of dream, or half-life, then Guled's death was the last time I had felt part of reality.

"I'm okay, Mum. Really."

She tried to hug me, I grabbed her hands as she raised them to encircle me and brought them in front of my chest, squeezing them harder than I meant to. She was covered in a fine dust and there were sweat patches under her arms, but her eyes were bright, and she looked younger. I had seen what she was looking at in fragments in the car's mirrors — bloodshot eyes, dirt, a beard, matted hair. I didn't recognise my own face.

"I must see Ahmed."

She nodded and somehow untangled her fingers from mine. I had not stopped squeezing.

"Ahmed, I am so sorry about your father. Please forgive me."

I didn't dare extend my hand. Words might be weightless, maybe even pointless, but a formal handshake seemed like it would be offensive. Ahmed looked at me for a long moment.

"My father liked you, Peter. I have come to get you to honour his name and your friendship."

"How is your mother?" I asked.

"She is at the AMISOM base with my wife and Lila. They are fine."

My mother had joined us with the white man.

"Peter, this is Edward. He has been helping us find you. We really need to go now. It will be dark soon."

"Give me a minute. Just a minute. I need to talk to Abdi. He's the one who helped me escape, I owe him my life."

I turned my back on the trio standing by the pickup truck, my mother sandwiched between the two men, one black, one white, both armed. Abdi was still in the sedan. Abdulghani had lit a cigarette and opened his door, his feet resting on the road. The man-boy had got out and leant his gun on the roof of the car. I recognised the self-consciously nonchalant pose of the teenager.

The first shot rang out before I got to the car. I heard something ping off the pickup behind me, and in that second of silence, I spun around, falling to the ground, looking for my mother. As I pirouetted into the dust, I caught a glimpse of a cloud of dust, maybe two, heading towards us across the scrub-covered plains to our right. I knew it was them. There was an inevitability to the roar, the dust, the gunshots.

The man with the scarf, still standing by the machine gun, started firing wildly, screaming something angry and ritualistic. Spent casings ricocheted off the floor of the pickup and onto the road, their tinny pings like xylophone notes ringing out over the booming of the gun. The air quivered and I covered my head with my hands. I pressed into the ground but it would not give.

I started to crawl on my elbows towards the pickup. My mother was running now, the white man had one arm around her and was firing his gun towards the dust clouds coming ever nearer. They made it to the back of the pickup. I was almost there when I felt the air crack and heard a sick gurgling. I looked up, the man with the scarf had slumped over his weapon. The back of his head was gone, the black-and-white scarf was turning red. I staggered to my feet and sprinted to the back of the pickup truck.

They were upon us now. The two technicals screeched to a halt twenty yards from the red Sedan. The white man and the two Somalis were beside us, all huddled at the back of the pickup, but for a second no one did anything, no one said anything.

A silence descended that was thick with absence. I chanced a look over the tailboard. Abdulghani's body was sprawled on the tarmac, his feet sticking out in front of the tyre. The man-boy was standing as he had been before the firing started. His gun was still resting on the roof of the Corolla in a spreading pool of his own bright red blood. I couldn't see Abdi. The passenger door was open.

"Don't shoot yet."

It was Edward.

"We only have one chance to get out of here."

He motioned to the two Somalis huddled beside us, his palms open, his head shaking. They looked terrified. They were just teenagers.

"Al-Shabaab," whispered one.

I nodded. I couldn't even pity them. I had nothing left except a selfish terror and an overwhelming fatigue that made me want to lie down in the shade of the pickup, close my eyes, and let events take their course.

"They are coming," the white man whispered.

"What are we going to do, Edward?" said my mother, her voice trembling.

I looked at the white man too. I didn't know who exactly he was or what he was doing here, but I hoped he'd have an answer. He shook his head and his shoulders slumped.

"Where's Ahmed?" I asked.

He had been standing with my mother when the bullets started flying. Another shake of the head from the white man. I chanced another look around the side of the pickup.

They were coming. It was Burhan and the four others, all armed, all walking toward the pickup. They had almost reached the Sedan now. We had seconds to live and I couldn't think of anything to do. I crouched lower, pulling my mother with me. I cradled her head in my chest and whispered, "I am sorry, so sorry. It's all my fault."

Edward looked at the two Somalis beside him and nodded. I could feel the three men tense. Edward hoisted his gun, squared his feet.

"You have to get to the other car with her. We'll try to hold them off. Get to the car and drive away from here."

"Peter Maguire!"

It was Burhan. He sounded cheerful.

"Why don't you surrender? Come out and we'll see what we can work out. Otherwise, this is going to end very badly for all of you."

My mother clutched my robe. "Don't."

It was the tone she used to favour when she caught me cursing as a teen, or when I came back drunk from those early, almost-innocent parties when the world seemed to be waiting for us to make it spin faster, or better, or longer.

There was a heavy thump above us. I looked up and saw Ahmed leap over the side of the truck and push the dead man's body from the gun. It all happened so quickly.

Edward shouted, "Get down! Now!"

I fell on top of my mother, feeling her softness give way. Ahmed was screaming and shooting, angry bullets and sharp bellows. Edward and the two Somalis were shooting too. There was screaming and smoke, and the smell of my mother's hair under my face. Then it all stopped, in an instant, as though I had imagined the whole interlude. I put my hands on the tailboard and pulled myself up.

The sun was sinking towards the horizon, pouring its limpid, golden light over the road, which stretched empty behind us. Ahmed stood at the gun, one dark intense eye open, staring wildly through the blood that covered his face. His other eye was gone. He was gone. I could feel my mother's hand in mine, and behind her I heard Edward panting.

The bodies of the Al-Shabaab fighters lay like discarded dolls in the middle of the road, all strangely bent limbs and loose scarfs. Abdi stood above Burhan, who was trying to crawl back to his truck. Abdi's back was to us and in the fading light, he was all shadow. He let the injured man crawl past the first body, then a second, following him slowly, haltingly. Burhan's legs left long streaks of blood on the tarmac. Abdi stepped around them.

He had time now. He was in control. For the first time since I had met this teenager, no one was calling the shots. Burhan faltered, his head fell onto his outstretched arm, his legs lay still. I thought he had gone but after a few seconds, he started his pained, pointless crawl again. Slowly, Abdi bent towards him.

212

He kneeled at his side, like a mother checking on a slumbering child.

That's when I saw the knife in Abdi's hand. It caught the slanted rays of the sun and stung my eyes. Abdi bent lower. He seemed to be whispering in Burhan's ear. Burhan had stopped moving now. He drew his outstretched right arm back towards his body. I couldn't see if he was answering Abdi. The teenager grabbed a handful of the prone man's hair, pulled back his head and the knife flashed once. Abdi dropped Burhan's head. He stayed kneeling there, rocking gently in the dusk, his head bowed. He looked like he was praying but the sunset wind brought snatches of his words to me: names. He was reciting a list of names.

CHAPTER
FIFTEEN

ABDI

It is night. Everything we did today has disappeared in this darkness. If there is no light, then no one can see us. No one can see what we did. We are driving through the streets of Mogadishu, heading for the AMISOM base. There are no cars. We could be the only people alive in this ghost city, if it were not for the noises. There is gunfire coming from the north, where Al-Shabaab hold the pasta factory, but it is faint and infrequent, a Mogadishu lullaby.

Two AMISOM Casspirs met us as we entered at the western edge of the city and since then, I have felt safer. But I know this feeling is only temporary. I have killed an Al-Shabaab commander, a foreign *mujahideen* and they will find me. If my death felt like my shadow before today, a black shape fluttering at the edge of my field of vision, now I am certain that I am unlikely to see out this year, maybe even this month. I know this as a fact that does not really concern me.

I am sitting inside the first armoured car, squashed between two very large Ugandan soldiers. They have not spoken to me since I leapt from the bed of the pickup, slipping on Ahmed's blood, and climbed into

214

their moving safe house. In here, it is green, a soft green like the inside of a wave. I can peek out the small windows at postcard-sized fragments of Mogadishu as we fly by, but there is not much to see now in the dark. So I relive the day that this darkness has so discreetly, and so kindly, hidden away.

We sped from the place of killing just minutes after I slit Burhan's throat. I felt no pity as I sat in the back of the truck, looking at the bodies on the road. Without life, we are nothing more than piles of rags, good for nothing. I looked up and the vultures were already circling. They too know that what we do is always the same. They know they must just bide their time. In the end, someone always dies.

Maybe it is true that eventually compassion dries up. I have almost nothing left now for anyone. I did feel a flicker of pity for Ahmed, whose body lay crumpled in the corner of the truck. I could not see his face but there was something sad about his outstretched hand, reaching towards the tailgate. That hand was the hand of everyone I had ever known and lost. All their hands were reaching out, trying to touch something, trying to hold on. But I did not really know Ahmed either. Yes, he saved us, and he sacrificed himself to do it, but maybe he had his reasons. I can imagine reaching a point where letting go would be easier. I am almost there. And maybe it is less letting go than realising that there is less and less to hold on to. I will shed no tears for Ahmed. I have no tears left for such deaths, be they mundane, heroic or futile. In the end, they are all futile.

As we sped away from the bodies, away from the vultures, chasing the fading light to Mogadishu, I knew I was not empty of *all* feeling. Rage was building inside me. My anger had been unleashed, and was jumping and barking like one of those foamy-mouthed dogs we used to see in my neighbourhood. I feel it even now, and I do not know if I can tame it again. I don't think I want to. It may be the only thing keeping me alive.

It felt good to kill the foreigner. It felt right and it felt just. But perhaps, more important than all this, is what I didn't feel. I wasn't disgusted, or remorseful, or afraid. I could do that again. And again. I feel closer to Nadif now, although what motivates me is so different from what motivated him.

But is it really? Did he join them because he believed what they said, or because he hated the white and Ethiopian foreigners and wanted our country to be free? Whatever that means.

Maybe he joined them to avenge our father's death. Or perhaps it was a bit of all of that. And maybe even something else, less pure. He was just a teenager after all. Just like me, and I know what it felt like when I picked up his AK-47. I know now what it feels like to kill a man, to watch his blood pour onto the dust, to reduce a man to a pile of bones and flesh, to leave him for the vultures. I felt like a god. I felt invincible. I felt pleasure, yes, great pleasure. It was like the first time I scored a goal on that dusty football pitch near the mango tree. Nadif and his friends ran over to me, clapped me on the back, nearly knocking me over, hurting me, and yet I felt so proud to finally be one of

216

the big boys. Killing may turn a boy into a man, but it may be the boy inside who drives the desire. I don't know yet.

As I catch glimpses of my humbled home city through the small windows of this steel car-giant, I find it hard to believe that this place of nightmares can be saved by anyone, much less these stone-faced soldiers beside me, who speak to each other in Swahili, a language I still find hard to understand. The lights of the pickup behind us, like mini-moons, shine on piles of rubbish that have been on the streets for as long as I can remember.

As we turn a corner, raising dust because to drive slowly is to court disaster, the lights spotlight an alleyway and I see a headless robe disappearing through a doorway. I see the feet clearly in the camera flash of lights, and the dirty white of the robe, but nothing else. This unreal night has made my city real to me. Before, it was a place of love, of home, of friends, of faces I knew in the street, even as we ran from the approaching gunfire, faces that winked a warning as the technicals of Al-Shabaab roared up. This night-time city of faceless ghosts running soundlessly between the buildings is now more true. Maybe I had to lose everything to see the Mogadishu that other people see, the Mogadishu that Nadif used to show me on the Internet when we were still allowed that tiny window on the world.

We pass through AMISOM roadblocks quickly, despite the unusual presence of the battered pickup in the middle of our convoy. We are important. Or at least the white people huddled in the Casspir at the back are important. Maybe that is why I am in the first vehicle. If there is a roadside bomb, this Casspir, or the pickup, will surely get hit. Peter Maguire and his mother and that other white man will have time to swerve. It is as it should be, or at least as it has always been.

"Do you speak English?"

One of the Ugandan soldiers turns to me. I see big eyes, bloodshot with exhaustion.

"A little, yes."

"Why did you leave Al-Shabaab? Why did you save the *mzungu*?"

This Swahili word I know. Why did I save the white man?

"I was not Al-Shabaab. I am nothing. I am just a Somali. I don't know why I saved the white man. What does that mean? We were all there."

I am tired and I do not want to answer his questions. To find the answers, I need to lift many stones in my mind and I am afraid of the scorpions that might be hiding there.

Why did I help that man escape? It is true that I didn't like what Al-Shabaab were planning. I did not like Burhan and his killer's eyes. I did not want to be part of reducing a man to less than a goat to be slaughtered when he has no way to defend himself. And yes, I liked listening to the prisoner talk. Maybe I even liked him, if such a feeling is possible between two people from different worlds. Maybe what I liked most was that he was a man who was free to make choices, and still made mistakes. He was humble, he accepted his faults without feeling the need to promise to get

218

better. I liked the world he showed me. I liked its greyness. I did not want this grey to be reduced to our black and white. There were many reasons that man should not have died here, and maybe I liked all of them. Or maybe it was because of Nadif. Or my mother. Or my father. You see, I too can live in the grey. I would like to always live in the grey, in a world where there are no absolutes, nothing to fight for, nothing to kill for, nothing to preach for. One of my father's favourite Somali proverbs was: *A madman does not lack wisdom*. I like a world that can keep both those ideas together, a world where nothing is as it seems, and there is room for everyone to be mad and wise at the same time.

Sitting in the Casspir, banging my head on the ceiling as we bumped through Mogadishu, I realised the truth was probably something simpler, something purer. I think I did it for me. To save myself. In that compound, under that acacia tree, I was losing myself. When I heard my mother had died, I was ready to die too. If I had done nothing, I would have stayed with Yusuf out of apathy, out of not having anything else to do. And bit by bit, I would have drifted closer to Al-Shabaab, and I know I would not have had the willpower to stop that descent once it started. I could see that happening, as unstoppable as the waves that are washing up now on the beach that I know lies just beyond the broken streets. I sit in the green, inside my steel wave, still being carried along, but at least this is a sea of my choosing.

We arrive at the AMISOM base beside the airport. I have never been inside the base before. Four years ago, I stood outside these gates with Nadif and watched the soldiers at the entrance. They had just arrived and we were awed by their guns, and their helmets, and their flak jackets, and their organisation. Until then, guns had meant chaos, a sudden shot ringing out at the market, signaling the start of a battle. Shots followed always by breathless running, flip flops slapping the dirt, single shoes abandoned in the middle of suddenly silent streets.

I asked Nadif, "Why are they dressed in so many clothes and heavy things? It is too hot for all that."

Nadif, who, like me, was wearing a T-shirt and frayed shorts, laughed. He was nearly sixteen and I worshipped him. Our father had been killed the year before and Nadif had become even more to me. I thought he knew everything, although the cynicism and anger that was to take over later was already building.

We stood among a group of teenagers and children, watching the foreign soldiers who seemed so big and well-fed compared to us. Some of them were placing sandbags around the edges of the camp.

"They are dressed like that, little brother, because this place is dangerous."

Nadif laughed long and loud, and thumped me on the shoulder, and said it was time to go home. I wish I had listened more to that laugh. I thought that laugh was part of the world. I didn't know it would run out.

The base looked different now. It was as though it had grown down into the dust and soil, had put down roots. It no longer looked temporary. We drove to a yard around the back of the first group of buildings.

"You can get out now," the soldier said.

Behind me the two Somalis, who had come with the white man, crept out. Their guns had been taken, their eyes darted like small sparrows pecking the dry ground. I knew that look — as soon as they could they would disappear into the night that forgave all.

My legs hurt and I was afraid for a moment that I might fall. I leant against the side of the Casspir. I was shaking too. Or rather, my blood was shaking, deep inside my veins, skittish blood-dogs running around my body. I wanted to sleep and my head fell forward. I had never felt so tired but I knew I could not sleep now because a decision had to be made. I had no interest in looking around.

A hand touched my arm. It was the prisoner. Dust covered his face and his thin beard. I realised I must look the same after speeding to Mogadishu in the pickup. I wiped my face. My hand came back white. We were both white in the dark night.

"Abdi, are you all right?"

I nodded. His hand was still on my arm. It made me uncomfortable and I edged away. He let his arm fall but his eyes clung to my face. As if he hoped to ignore the thousands of miles between us, the worlds that separated us. But I could see them. For a few days they had disappeared, but there was no ignoring them now. Our time together was over. There was nothing to say. So I did not say anything.

"They are going to need to question us. But don't be afraid. I am here. I will tell them what you did. They will believe me."

He spoke with the confidence of a man who expected certain things from life. It almost made me smile. His certainty had returned. That was one of the deepest trenches between us.

I understood what he was trying to say. They would not believe me, a Somali teenager with the blood of the man he had killed drying on his shirt.

"I do not want to answer any questions. I want to leave. If you want to do something for me, you will get them to release me. I need to go."

I surprised myself by mimicking his firm tone. I surprised myself with the words. But as I said them, they became stone, they became the only possible reality.

"You are just a boy, Abdi. If they let you go, you will not be safe. The others may be looking for you. Better to stay here, in safety. I can look out for you here."

"How? You are going to stay here?"

He looked away.

"No, you are going to go home as fast as you can, to your white girlfriend, to your world. You have a life to return to. I have to make a life. I cannot do that here on this base. If you want to thank me, get them to release me. That's all I want."

I spoke slowly so that he would understand. I felt angry but I did not want to show it. It was not his fault, and yet it was. His fault and everyone else who came here to play whatever game they were playing in our country. I wanted to be rid of them all.

He left me then, walking slowly towards his mother who was talking urgently to a Ugandan with many stripes on his shoulder. I think the prisoner wanted to say something else, but I am glad he did not. What is there to say? Our paths crossed, we walked a little of the road together, but now it is time to return to our separate tracks. Exhausted, I slumped to the ground and put my head on my knees.

Someone tapped me again. It was the white woman. She was bending over me and when I did not move, she lowered herself onto the ground beside me, grunting a little. She must have been at least fifty, but she looked much younger than the fifty-year-old women in my neighbourhood. Life is fast and hard here, and it does not tread lightly across a woman's face.

"My name is Nina Walters. I am the mother of the man you saved. I wanted to thank you. You are a brave man and I . . ."

Her voice trailed off. I said nothing. I did not know what she wanted from me. Did she want to shake my hand? Did she want me to tell her why? Why did everyone assume there was a reason? What kind of lives did these people live that allowed them to think there was always a reason?

I stared at her. If I had done nothing, this woman would have been reading the prisoner's letter now. I had spared this woman those tears. I allowed myself a moment of pride. The prisoner would have a chance now to make his apology in person. I had given them time. *I* had done that.

When the white woman put her hand on mine, on top of my knee, this time I did not pull away. I looked at her hand. It was so white, with blue raised veins and light brown spots. I had never seen a white hand so close. Even when I cared for the prisoner, I kept my distance. I did not touch him then and afterwards, during our flight, it was dark and we were just shadows. I stared at this hand, but saw another. This hand was my mother's hand on mine. Warm and soft.

"The Ugandans have agreed to release you. Peter told them you were not involved with Al-Shabaab. They had thought you could give them some descriptions, you know, of the fighters, but Peter has promised to do that himself. You should leave now, before they change their minds. Do you know where you will go?"

I nodded slowly.

"Peter told me your mother died recently. I am so sorry," she said, and her hand squeezed mine. For a moment, I wanted to put my head down there too, so that she could stroke it like my mother used to when I was frightened. But this is not my mother. I pulled my hand away. I was not angry, but it was time to pull apart these worlds that had collided.

"I will leave now."

I got to my feet and walked away quickly.

And I am still walking. I feel like walking tonight. I am not scared, I feel invisible, and my tiredness seems to be slipping away with the night. I am one of the living dead. In my other life, Nadif had a comic book with stories about zombies. He got it from a friend in the days before it became impossible to have such things.

I remember the pictures. Skinny people in rags, walking with their arms stretched out in front of them. They called them the living dead. We are all the living dead here.

The sky is grey now, and I escape the city for the seashore, the only place where you can turn your back on this place and stare at something beautiful, something pure, an ocean that stretches to other lands where people live on streets that are clean and silent. In these other cities, I imagine the day breaks softly, sunlight bringing hope, and that priceless sense that nothing will change. In the distance, I can make out the misty shapes of ships on the horizon, and onshore, the tall cranes at the port. They are stretching their arms to heaven, but I don't think there is anyone there.

My father was a Muslim and a man who loved life more than the promise of the afterlife. He drank, he smoked, he smiled, he loved, as if love and laughter were his religion. I suppose I am a Muslim too although we have never been strict about religion in my household. We prayed every day when my father was alive but the habit died with him. Some people find comfort in their faith at such times. We did not. My mother obeyed the obvious rules, doing the things you need to do to get by, but you could tell her heart was never in it, and as the list of what you had to do became longer and longer, her lips tightened and her eyes hardened. I think whatever little was left of her faith disappeared in the dull, dusty thud that tore Nadif apart.

I can't imagine my mother dying with any hope of an afterlife. But I wasn't there. They say people change when their time comes. I like to believe that she didn't. I expect nothing from the afterlife. My family is lost to me here, what further punishment can the afterlife contain? And if there is no punishment, how can there be reward? I cannot believe that all this suffering is leading to some great glory. I have no reason to believe this and so many reasons to believe the opposite.

I walk along the seafront and down onto the beach. I take off my flip flops because they are sticking in the wet sand. My toes are stained with drops of blood. I walk into the shallow water to clean them. The tiny waves tickle my toes. Even here in this dangerous city, even after everything that has happened, I enjoy this feeling, and the sand between my toes, and the tang of salt on my lips. I realise I am thirsty and hungry. I walk past colourful boats swaying in the sea. I make my way slowly towards the old lighthouse. My father always used to tell Nadif and I to stay away from here.

"It's falling down and dangerous. Full of khat chewers, and layabouts, and criminals. No place for good boys."

We loved this place. We used to come down here sometimes instead of going to school. We would climb the crumbling staircase inside the tower, Nadif always running ahead, daring me to go faster, to be more reckless. We would sit at the top, looking out to sea, hoping somebody would catch a shark. I loved

226

watching the fishermen carrying the sharks and swordfish across their shoulders as they headed up the beach to the fish market in Hamarwein. With the sun at their back, casting them in shadow like moving statues, they looked like magical beings, half fish, half man.

But today, I do not want to go into the lighthouse. It is still too dark, and I fear the memories that may rise out of the shadows. The sun will be here soon, and then I will go and see my mother, and Nadif, and my father. But for now, I want to sit here and watch the sea.

Beyond the lighthouse, there are square stones like giant steps. I will go and sit there, and let the spray wash over me. Nadif used to dare me to jump from one giant step to another. And he would laugh, with his head thrown back, when I stumbled and swayed on landing. Then, we would sit together, he would smoke, and I would wish the steps would stretch all the way to the horizon, so that we could jump away from here, step by slippery step.

I sit until the sun rises. It is beautiful. The soft purples and pinks come first, and then the sharp golden light as the sun eases over the horizon. For a moment, the sea is golden, the spray that spatters my face is cool. I shiver a little but I savour the moment because I know that later I will sweat. The fishermen drift onto the beach. They prepare their nets, and load them onto their low blue-and-white boats and head out into the golden waves. I imagine it feels good, to head out into a huge ocean, to feel free, to believe for a moment that you could just keep going.

CHAPTER
SIXTEEN

NINA

I am getting used to the heat. Or maybe I am just rediscovering the joy of sweating profusely, and publicly. I remember that from Abidjan. When Tim and I first arrived from Paris, I was horrified to discover visible sweat patches under my arms and on my back. The stains would break through before 9am, and linger stubbornly for most of the day. I carried spare T-shirts, reapplied deodorant throughout the day, and once even bought one of those little hand-held fans on a trip to South Africa, but the patches were not to be tamed by such man-made frivolities. Finally, I learnt to live with my imperfections. It is the same here but the process has been quicker, maybe because my vanity did not survive my fifth decade.

It has been three months since I came to this military base. I still live here but I hope that one day soon, I will be able to join Aisha, Ubah and Lila in Medina where they live on a noisy street of tumbledown shops decorated with child-like drawings of loaves, fish and unidentifiable car parts. Their two-room home is near the hospital where Ubah works as a volunteer nurse. She is paid irregularly, whenever the Red Cross is able

228

to donate some money for wages. I have been to visit her with Dr Mugyenyi, who does some consulting there on his increasingly rare free days. The fighting has died down since Al-Shabaab withdrew most of its forces from the city in August, but the streets are now filled with the small, patchwork tents of the hungry. They have come from the barren fields to the south and to the north, a human tide of silent rebuke washing over the slowly reawakening city. Their fragile shelters fill the empty spaces between shot-up buildings, rising like the domes of coloured Easter eggs across the sand, and turning the entire city into a refugee camp. Internally Displaced People is what they call them here. It is a clinical term for a recurring tragedy.

The first time we visited the hospital, honking and swerving through jammed, narrow streets in a three-vehicle convoy that seemed both obscene and useless, I was shocked. It is a place of blood, broken windowpanes, crooked and creaking iron beds, dirty tiles and mattress-filled corridors. In Mogadishu, the hospitals are honest: they don't try to hide the truth behind clean curtains and disinfectant. I have seen this before, of course, but this place, built from echoing shipping containers, made me think of very large, steel coffins. A place where dying is a luxury.

For the first twenty minutes of that first visit, I was depressed beyond words. The consideration and pride of the young doctor with the stained apron, barely-there moustache and fuzzed chin made everything worse. But when Dr Mugyenyi put on his own white coat and got to work in the wards, with me trailing behind like a wide-eyed shadow, I felt the first stirrings of hope. The way patients grasped his hands after he examined them, the gratitude, the flurry of activity that followed his every pronouncement. By the time I left, I was elated, and I had a new purpose.

That was about a month after Peter left. At first, I stayed in Mogadishu more out of apathy than because of any notion that I could help. I did not make a decision and that was it. I wandered around the dusty base, visiting daily with Ahmed's family, teaching Lila to draw with biros and paper magicked up for me by Private Nabakoba. At first, the little girl was bemused by my imperfect drawings of teddy bears and rabbits, but she became comfortable enough to laugh at me, and in that time of confusion, those high-pitched chortles became my lifeline. There were tears as well, for her father. But she could not really understand his death. More heartbreaking than the tears was the look on her face whenever anyone knocked on the door of the container that had become her home. That look has faded now.

Nobody asked me to leave the base. So I stayed.

I sat for hours with Aisha and Ubah, who had been allowed to remain on the base, again, I suspect, more out of apathy and inefficiency than because of a conscious decision by the authorities to shelter them or help me honour my promise to Ahmed. On those hot, sweaty days before the rains came in October, I felt like a time traveller. I sat on a woven mat with the other women outside the container, and we stared ahead of us, our eyes resting lazily on the soldiers cleaning cars, laughing and smoking in corners, or filling sandbags, seemingly endlessly, making soft bulwarks against steel. God knows, sand is one thing this place has in abundance. Sand, and the bullets to bury in it.

And then I visited the hospital and discovered a purpose in its clanking, sombre, green-walled rooms. I helped Ubah get a job there, and now I help out too. I have learnt to decide quickly which patients need immediate care, and who can wait. It's not as easy as it sounds when really, every single one should be seen immediately. I can stitch basic wounds and set up IVs. I am keenly and gravely aware that I would not be allowed to do this anywhere else. I feel privileged and lucky that I can, despite my age, be of some use. I have been reborn here but the price of that may be a total and irreversible renunciation of my previous life. I am not yet sure. I have not yet had to make that decision. It is as though time is standing still. I am happy here and I suspect that happiness is fragile. If I went back, my contentedness would evaporate and all I would have would be those fragmented memories that sometimes make you smile when you least expect it.

I guess I will have to go back to Paris one day, at least for a time. There is a flat to get rid of, dead plants to throw out, a fridge to turn off. The other day, I tried to remember where I kept the cereal in that kitchen. I can't. It's as though my life there is a photograph fading in the sun, so that the details are losing their edge. Soon the print will turn to sepia, becoming an inherited, treasure-box trinket showing people and places that no longer exist. In a way, when I go back, I will be doing my post-death clean-up. What Peter would have had to do if this had not happened. I like the idea of sparing him that. There is still too much on my life's credit side. I feel guilty because of what I did to him or, more precisely, because of the burden I bequeathed him.

Part, and maybe a large part, of what I am doing here is seeking redemption. It is a common idea, but what are we if not stereotypes? I am not here because the Somalis, or Aisha and her family, need me, I know they don't really. And not because I feel responsible for the deaths of their men, although you could argue that I share some measure of guilt. I am here because I need this place. If it seems selfish to demand personal salvation from a place like Somalia, I agree. It is. I have long abandoned any pretence at perfection. I am who I am, and I need what I need, and I am trying to make up for my failings as a wife and as a mother, too late, I know.

I play with Lila because I did not play enough with Peter, not in those first years. Of course, I did not blame him for who he was. But my baby, with his flailing fists, piercing cries, and wide, green eyes, was also my conscience. His long lashes berated me. I was terrified that Tim would one day ask why Peter did not look like him. But then of course, Tim thought he *did* look like him, or like his family, a cousin today, a dead but fondly remembered uncle on another day.

We see what we want to see. I always saw Shaun in Peter's eyes. The same long lashes and lazy lids. But as he grew older, he developed his other father's

232

mannerisms: a hint of lilting Cork in his accent, something you would never notice unless you were looking for it; the way his middle finger scratched his thumb when he was anxious.

My fears faded as the years passed and my secret became more of a memory and less of an unexploded mine buried in the expanding no man's land between Tim and me. I knew I would have to tell Peter one day, but I learned to live in the now, and I also learnt to love him for who he was, not for what he represented. That took time and those first years of trepidation and uncertainty took their toll, on me, on Peter, on my marriage.

I lived in denial and eventually, because I had got away with it for so long, I wondered if really I needed to tell Peter. I know my decision was selfish. Age brings self-knowledge and if I still do not know why I fell so madly, swiftly, and ridiculously for Shaun, I know why I did the things I did after that. I did not want to get hurt, or cause hurt, and the two are interchangeable.

It was only when Godwin was born that something in me clicked. The birth of my grandchild — Shaun's grandchild — made me realise that this secret was not mine to keep. Perhaps it was the tenuous, unresolved nature of Peter's relationship with his son. When he told me about Godwin, haltingly in my little sitting room in Paris, I imagined this child, so different from me, so fundamentally different from his father, and I knew that I could not hide the truth any longer. I could not risk betraying another child. A child I had not met then, and still have not met, and shall probably never meet because that is the path I have chosen from the roads I was shown.

When Peter paused, after telling me that he would care financially for Godwin but could not commit to anything more right now, I told him about Shaun. The blunt, raw facts that made up his very being.

What else was there to say? Peter looked hurt, disbelieving, and betrayed. I expected nothing less. He did not speak then, though later, much later, he would ask me to explain the inexplicable. Before he walked out, without his coat, without his phone, I asked him to forgive me. But his step did not falter, he did not turn around.

He returned after midnight. I heard the door open, his steps rang hollow in the hall. I heard him enter the sitting room, those empty steps again, and then the soft click of the front door, closing. In the morning, his phone was gone. We did not speak for months.

I have not heard from Peter since he left on August 16th. The British were keen to get him out. His gaunt face did make the newspapers, and his quotes were as banal and cookie-cutter as we had both hoped and feared, but they were mercifully hidden away on the inside pages. Peter had to give one or two phone interviews but with a sex scandal hogging the British headlines and a hurricane threatening a beachside retirement village in Florida, he was, at best, a filler. To be honest, he didn't give good story. A single man, to all intents and purposes, held for only a few weeks, a journalist rather than an unfortunate civilian. He lived, and so his past remained buried. Except to Michelle, and that too was my fault.

He was debriefed by AMISOM and some British suits, who turned up with Edward the day after that macabre standoff on the road. Peter and I talked about the killing later the same day as we lay on our separate camp beds in the shipping container. He spoke quickly, as if expelling the words would expel the memories. He did not tell me much about his captivity, but then again what could he tell me? I wouldn't be able to imagine his fear, his boredom, his panic. He did tell me about the foreign fighter from Al-Shabaab, and if there was fear in his voice, there was also wonder.

"He sounded just like anyone else, Mum. I mean, like everyone else I have ever met. I expected these people, these fighters to be somehow exotic, to sound different from the ordinary. Like blockbuster villains. I wanted him to be as bizarre as the life he was leading. But of course, it was only bizarre to me."

He paused.

"I wrote you a letter, but I tore it up when we escaped."

I had to strain to hear his voice. It echoed with the metallic ring of the container. It was a new voice, a voice for here, not the voice of my son, the man I thought I knew.

"I wanted to apologise for all the time I spent being angry at you, for all the time I locked you out. I never apologised before, not properly, and I thought I was going to die. The fear, Mum, it was like a physical pain in my stomach."

"Darling, you have nothing to apologise to me for. And you never will," I said, feeling my eyes fill and my cheeks flush. My punishment is eternal and I must forever seek forgiveness. It will never be mine to grant.

I couldn't bear the distance anymore. I went to him, and lay on his bed. I held my boy's head against my chest while he sobbed. I didn't need words. Neither of us did. As I held him, I remembered all those other times, and I was a mother again. At last, the complications were superfluous, and the distance that had grown between us evaporated. We cried together, a flood of tears to cleanse the world so that we could start again in our dark, humming, metal womb.

A few days later, Peter was flown to Nairobi, where he was going to be debriefed again at the British High Commissioner's residence, before heading back to Europe. At the time, I had no idea what he was thinking. I suppose I should have guessed.

If I could not summon the energy to go back to my life, why did I assume that Peter would just pick up where he had left off? I suppose because that is what we are supposed to do. Keep going. I had opted out, but I didn't think Peter would be able to do the same. I was wrong. I underestimated what had happened to him. Or I overestimated his strength, just as I have always done.

CHAPTER
SEVENTEEN

PETER

When I left Somalia, I did not know where to go or
what to do. We use that phrase, "I don't know", so
often, and it has grown to mean so little. It can mean
confused, a little lost, unsure. I was beyond that. I don't
know if it was a delayed reaction to my captivity, or to
the trauma of my escape with Abdi, but things had
changed. I had changed.

I was passed around. I answered questions, and more
questions, my voice boring even myself. I didn't have
much to tell the nameless men, all hewn from the same
rock: hard-faced, hard-eyed, the angular men. I didn't
know where I had been held, I didn't know anyone's
name, except for Burhan and Abdi. And I wouldn't tell
them about Abdi.

They probed, their disappointment sharp behind
their glasses, and in the twitchy fingers ready to
scribble down anything I gave them. I like to think I
gave them nothing useful. It's not that I am
ungrateful. I know the British helped rescue me. At
times Edward Chadwick, pops up in my thoughts,
but he is always a shadowy figure. He came with me
to Nairobi, but I never saw him again after the first

day. I imagine he returned to wherever he came from.

We did not speak on the short flight from Mogadishu to the Kenyan capital. I leant against the window, watching without feeling as we flew over the pristine beaches, over a land crisscrossed with green lines of scrub on a sandy background. From the air, it looked like the very earth of Somalia was fracturing, pressed upwards by some giant determined to shove it off his shoulders.

"Where will you go afterwards?" Chadwick asked as our diplomatic car drew up at the British High Commissioner's house in the richly quiet, green suburb of Muthaiga. I was numbed by the journey, by the endless traffic jam that had kept us on Nairobi's Mombasa Road for over an hour and a half. I had used up all my energy not thinking. I felt that if I engaged my brain, it might explode.

"I don't know," I muttered, and as I said it I realised this was true. The implacability and irreversibility of those words hit me with the force of a jackhammer. I turned from the window, noticed the car had stopped, and repeated, "I don't know."

This answer lit a slow-burning fuse that went off hours later as I lay in my room, alone for the first time in the blur of days that had followed my weeks of near total solitude. I wept like a baby, curling in on myself, still in my dusty clothes on top of the soft, cool duvet. I traced its pattern of gaudy irises. I recited names through my tears: Michelle, Esther, Godwin, Mum, Tim, Abdi, Guled and Ahmed. Each name made me

238

feel nauseous with guilt. Even then, I knew I was crying out of self-pity, not just because I had failed all these people in the little things, and sometimes the big, but because I now could not deal with this burden.

When I woke again, the television was flickering and the bedside light was on. As I lay there, wondering if I was expected to get up again, I knew that I had left one name out of my litany of self-confession. Shaun. I said it out loud just to hear myself. I tried to imagine the face that went with the name. I had nothing. For the first time, I felt curious. It was a faint stirring but I dared myself to believe that filling that blank where my father's face should be would help me. I could redefine myself. I could change. I could at least try.

After Nairobi, and the endless, pointless briefings, I headed back to Paris. I landed at Charles de Gaulle airport as dawn broke. Exhausted by the steel, the corridors, the customs officials and the sheer regularity, I sat in the soulless pavilion and ordered a coffee. I had not spoken to Michelle since my escape. After my mother confessed she had told her about Godwin and Esther, I thought it would be crass to call. I would either have to ignore the fact that she knew, or explain something that even I couldn't understand, over a bad phone line from Mogadishu.

Michelle did not call me either. There was too much to say and nothing to say at all. I knew she wouldn't want me now. Michelle hated secrets — her first serious boyfriend was a serial cheat, who loved her, but not only her. Years of deception and painful, tear-filled reunions had left her with a horror of even the most trivial of omissions. I once asked her how she knew I remained faithful when I was away. On reflection, the question was callous, and my cheeks burn now remembering my casual cruelty. It was a smug, condescending humour. It should have been beneath me. It was certainly beneath her. She was blending soup and when she did not answer immediately, I assumed she hadn't heard me. I was glad as I was already regretting my rash defiance of common sense.

My mother had recently told me about Shaun, and I had just that week received a letter from Esther, with a photo of my one-year-old son. I was leaving for Baghdad early the next morning and Michelle was making dinner. I don't know why I wanted to provoke her. I remember, at the time I had the distinct feeling that my life was spinning out of control. All my certainties had turned out to be mirages.

The blender stopped and the silence felt heavy. I could feel Michelle's eyes on me so I lifted my head from the rucksack I was packing with delicate superstition — everything arranged according to a precise order in special pockets. The journalist's equivalent of a footballer putting on his boots and socks in a particular way. She didn't look angry, but there was something fierce about the set of her mouth and her slightly too-open eyes.

"What kind of question is that?" she said quietly. She paused. "But if you must know, I don't worry because if you do screw around, I will always find out. And if I do, I know what to do. I will never live with lies again, and you know that."

She turned back to the blender, and its angry buzz filled the kitchen.

I finished my coffee. With nothing else to do, I left the airport. Outside the concourse, the chill of an early September morning made me shiver. I had missed the taxi rush and gratefully sank into the first car in the queue. As I leant back into the seat, trying to draw warmth from the cold leather, I realised I didn't know where I was going. I didn't want to go straight to our flat. Michelle would be there. After a few moments hesitation, I gave the impatient driver my mother's address. We left the rank with a squeal of tires, as if he was trying to make up for the seconds I had foolishly squandered pondering such a basic question.

My mother's apartment was cold, and as soon as I walked in, I felt sure she would not live here again. After that night at the base, when she climbed onto my camp bed and held me, we hadn't spoken much. As I waited to board my plane out of Mogadishu, standing on the tarmac with Ugandan soldiers huddled nearby exchanging insults and cigarettes, she hugged me for a long time. The wind was roaring, the sea was in a fury, and her hair was whipping around her face. She looked more like herself than she had in years.

"Be safe," she whispered. "I'll call you when I know what I am doing."

I hugged her back but I had nothing to say. I knew I was going to be safe. I had already talked to Don about a leave of absence. He said yes to everything. I am not the only one lugging a satchel of guilt through this life.

My mother stayed on the tarmac until the plane took off. I leant into the window as we taxied away from the terminal, towards the sea. I doubted she could see me, but I pressed my head so hard against the plastic that it hurt. I could not stop myself waving as we picked up speed. Of course, she did not see me then, but then sometimes goodbyes are more for ourselves than the ones we are leaving.

Her apartment seemed to have said its own goodbye to the woman who had lived there for so many years, trying to create a fantasy family out of a shrouded tragedy. What secrets could these walls tell me about the woman I never really knew? The woman who lived inside the mother? What despair did these walls see, what sighs did this sofa hear, what tears were shed on these pillows? I will never know and though part of me feels like the story of me-and-her-and-him-and-him needs an ending, what happened in Somalia has left me with a distrust of logic and endings, and maybe even beginnings.

I spent two days sleeping in the flat. On the third day, I phoned my father. I had spoken to him in Nairobi, of course. Then, he had sobbed down the phone, thanked God, asked about my health, and repeated how worried he was until it became a mantra, to fill the awkward silences.

I couldn't talk about what had happened. I had put him through enough. I had pinned him like a butterfly to a board. My very existence had probed the recesses of his marriage. My captivity had smashed the tranquility he had every right to expect in his final

242

years. He did not escape the reporters, although thankfully their interest was brief. Tim is a shy, reticent man. He is a man I have always admired, the kind of decent man I thought I could one day become. But then my faith in some kind of delayed genetic goodness was dashed. Perhaps I already knew I could never match him. My philandering, my fickleness, my inability to return love. These faults were magnified in the light of his sacrifice, even if, initially, it was unwitting. He had loved me, and raised me, and cherished me as a son. I could never match him. I had abandoned my own son, and his mother.

I found it hard to speak openly to my father after I discovered my mother's secret. I knew she had told him, but we never really discussed it. It was too late. We had lived without that shared knowledge for so long that to embrace it, or even acknowledge it, seemed pointless, almost cruel. So instead, we contented ourselves with platitudes, banalities that cast shame on me, and that betrayed our shared past. But he was too old and tired to fight, and I did not know how to reach out. Of such little tragedies is life made. None of us is immune, I suppose, but we work hard to quash individual pinpricks of pain, because if we felt each one, we would be like prisoners dying from a thousand strokes of a torturer's thin-bladed knife. And after all, life must go on, or so we believe.

This time, my father was calm and the conversation was less stilted. I told him where I was, and where I was going. He listened. I wanted to tell him, pathetically, that it was not about him but about me, not about our

243

relationship but about a gap that I needed to fill, it was additional, not instead of. But that wouldn't have been entirely true, and I have always favoured silence over the outright lie. It's one of my virtuous vices, I suppose.

He wished me luck and said goodbye, but the phone didn't click and I held on, not wanting this to be the end, although unable to articulate what I felt I should say. This man who had taught me to talk, and walk, to catch a ball, who had read me Hardy Boy stories until my eyes closed on dreams of derring-do. He deserved a moment. He, a man of courage always, filled it.

"I have always loved you as my son, Peter. At the beginning, of course, I knew no different," he said, his voice melting into his home lilt as it always did when he was upset or excited.

"But then I loved you as my son, because you *were* my son. The details didn't matter to me. I'm sorry they do to you. But I understand. I think I might do the same if I was in your shoes. What I *have* learnt over these many years, is that not knowing is worse than knowing, and that imagination is a powerful foe as well as a friend. Sure, I'm guessing you know that better than most now. *Go n'eiri an bothar leat, a mhac,*" he said. Then the line clicked.

May the road rise with you, son. It was one of the few phrases I knew, handed down over the years by a father who had left his land and his language but needed to hold onto a few straws to steady himself in the world's wild winds.

After hanging up the phone, I packed a rucksack and left. My mother would sort out the apartment. She

244

would know how much of her life here she needed to keep. I felt sure it would not be much. I felt sure she would not come back. I made her bed though, in case.

I walked to the bank, weaving my way awkwardly through the people thronging the narrow, cobbled streets. Paris always has tourists. When I lived here, I felt a native's disdain for the camera-clickers, the sky-gawkers, the gaspers. But my favourite time to be in Paris was actually at the height of the tourist season — August, when the city's residents head for the beaches, mountains and lakes further south, or to the cool, clear north, seeking adventure while acknowledging that nothing better is to be had outside their sacred borders.

I withdrew all my savings. It wasn't much but it would do for now. I only had one mission. I was incapable of planning beyond my immediate destination. But before I left this life behind, I had one more thing to do.

I stood on the steps of the bank for a moment, looking for something to explain the rushing crowds, the charging cars, the shiny shops all selling the same thing. From the steps, I gazed across the road to Les Halles, and the Saint-Eustache cathedral, that giant, unwieldy, smog-stained building. It seemed diminished by the clutter around it, the shoppers strolling from Rue Montorgeuil, the teenagers heading towards the escalators that led underground to a sunken mall where they could cruise cheap, slightly seedy shops in a half-world that always smelt of urine. I turned away, heading towards the other side of the city, towards the canals, down roads I knew so well, but that looked garish and strange now. My mind had changed, and the world had not changed with it. The ordinary would have to be relearnt. I was not ready for that yet. It was the perfect time to leave.

I texted Michelle to say I was coming. It had been two months since I had seen her, and I had missed her. Despite it all, despite what she might be feeling, I had missed her. I ran down the steps from the street to the path that ran alongside the water. I wanted to be as alone as possible in this crowded city.

Small yellow leaves crinkled under my feet. They had gilded the edges of the softly lapping water. The sun was soft on my bare head, there was a slight breeze. I thought of the harsh heat of Somalia. It must be another sun.

I tried to compose my apology to Michelle in my head. I had brought a photo of Godwin with me. I still was not sure if I would show it to her. I didn't know what I hoped it would achieve.

Would there be tears? Would Michelle cry over what we had lost, or rather what I had destroyed? Or would she be angry, beat me with her fists? I realised I did not know her well enough to even hazard a guess. The thought slowed my steps.

I knocked softly on the door, my door. The key was in my pocket but I had forfeited the right to use it.

Michelle must have been waiting because the door opened immediately. She looked beautiful and tired and sad and resigned, like a Renaissance Madonna. She stared at me, and I could see the emotions glide across her face. I knew I looked different too. The man who

246

had stared at me from the mirror that morning was haggard, unshaven and pale. She motioned to me to follow her down the hall.

We went into the sitting room, and sat opposite each other. I felt the room and its furniture, its pictures, its smells reaching out to me, goading me with their implacable certainty. I knew this place, I should feel at home here, and yet I did not.

Michelle sat quietly opposite me. Her eyes raked my face. I could not meet her gaze. She was looking for sorrow, and that there was. She was looking for love, and that too there was. And above all, she was looking for a reason, and I still did not know what to say. My brain felt slack under the enormity of this burden.

"How are you?" I surprised myself with the triteness of my question. We always fall back on what's gone before. There is no other way.

And for a moment, the Michelle I knew, the woman I left in this apartment before I went to Somalia, was back. An ironic smile twisted her lips and she raised an eyebrow. I smiled back.

"And you?" she asked. Perhaps it was convention, perhaps she did care. I chose to believe the latter. I needed to tell her, and she needed to hear. We were locked together in a macabre dance of truth and we would not be able to move on until the last note had faded.

"I am . . . I am lost, Michelle. I can't find my way back to whatever it was that I had before." I spoke like a child, each word pushed out laboriously, filling the air with prisms of pain and neglect and remorse, and yet it was not enough. I had to try harder. I needed to find the right words to explain something that was, still, inexplicable to me.

"I am so sorry. I didn't mean for all this to happen. It's not an excuse I know, but it's the truth. I didn't set out to be unfaithful. I was so young, and stupid, and careless about what I had. I didn't mean for you to find out from someone else in this . . . this terrible way. It broke my heart to know that you would. I am so ashamed, Michelle. And so sorry."

I lifted my head. My hand rose from my lap, hovering somewhere in the air between us, unsure where to go. I lowered it again. It was not yet time.

"Did they hurt you?"

Her voice was reluctant. I understood her effort. I loved her for it, and hated myself even more.

"No, they beat me a few times, but it was nothing really. There was a Somali man, his name was Abdi. He became my friend. Well, that's probably too strong a word for it. I think he pitied me. I don't think friendship can be built on pity. I guess love can't either."

I needed reassurance, but it was not mine to demand. I was in the confessional, Michelle was the priest. I had to keep going until my sack of sins was empty. I knew there would be no absolution.

"He helped me escape, and we ran to a village where he had friends. I think, in some ways, he was as lost as me. He was as much a prisoner as me. It's hard to explain."

248

I stopped. This was not the story Michelle needed to hear.

"What are you going to do now?" she asked, her head bowed.

"I'm leaving. Today. I'm going to go to Colorado. I need to find Shaun's family. I can't explain it, Michelle. I feel as though I have been beaten, pulped into tiny fragments. I have no sense of myself anymore. This is my only chance to put myself back together. Maybe it's post-traumatic stress, but I don't think so. I think it's something that goes deeper, maybe some kind of nervous breakdown that has been brewing since I found out that my father was not my father. Maybe that's it. Maybe what happened in Somalia just provided the trigger. Maybe I'm reading too much into it all. But I feel like this is the only thing that will keep me going right now. Otherwise, I might just stop. I might just lie down and not wake up."

She came to me then, knelt by my feet and put her head on my knees. Her arms came around my neck and we hugged for the last time, holding everything we had had and would not have in that small space between our bodies. One last time.

"Did you ever love me, Peter?"

I barely heard the words, but of course, I had been hearing them for months. The question resonated in my brain long before I went to Somalia, it came to me as I lay on that mat in that first cell and later as I stared at the moon through my barred window. Did I ever love her? How could I not? But perhaps I was asking the

249

wrong question all the time. Could I ever love? Did I have that capacity? Could I have that capacity?

I took a deep breath. I looked into Michelle's face. This was the moment when I must stop and think, really think, and then move forward with whatever knowledge I had gleaned. Love was not a state of mind. Love was action, life, everything together, spun into the soul, running through the veins so that it was the gold filament of life. Love was desire and sacrifice and the other. I had not yet learnt to love. I was still an unfinished man.

"I thought I did," I said. "I did to the best of my ability. And I still do. But I know it is not enough. It was never enough for you. You deserved more. I'm so sorry. I don't think I loved Esther more than you. Or less. I don't love my son, because I don't know him. All these things are wrong. I cannot live feeling like this. I need to find a way to love, and then, I need to start with Godwin because he is my son. I have hurt you too much, I know. I hope one day you will forgive me. I really hope so. I don't know what else to say Michelle. I fucked up."

"You really did," she said. "I would have loved you for ever, Peter. We were good together, maybe not perfect but I wouldn't have known. I could have gone on for years with you, we could have had a family. Maybe it would have been fine. And what does love mean anyway? If we were happy, we would have thought we were in love. And we would have been happy. Probably most of the time."

250

She was right. And wrong. Because we would not have been happy in the end. I would have fucked up again. I had not been ready to love. I was perhaps not ready now, but I owed it to my son to try. It was late but there was light in the sky yet. I could sleep or I could set out on a new road.

We sat for a little while longer as the afternoon died and the room filled with a limpid late autumn light that speckled the floor and the walls and then slipped away as darkness crept in.

"Will you leave Paris?" I asked.

"Yes," she said. "For a while, at least."

Michelle rose, her dark hair catching the last rays of light as the sun skipped behind the buildings across the street. It was not just the day dying. The apartment had fallen asleep. As we had talked, the essence of these rooms had slowly slipped away and now we were alone with just walls, a roof and some denuded furniture.

I walked to the door, stopped and turned. I wanted to say something that would somehow be great, that would do justice to Michelle, that would sum up something that had been very good, something that did not deserve to die this way.

"I will miss you so much," I said.

She paused, and then with a smile, she whispered, "Good luck."

And she closed the door.

CHAPTER
EIGHTEEN

NINA

Today is November 14th. I am in the AMISOM clinic with Dr Mugyenyi. I will go and visit Aisha and Lila later. Nabakoba told me a patrol would go to Medina after lunch. They will drop me a street away, so as not to draw attention to the house, or the women inside. Anyone watching will only see a small veiled figure scuttle along the path and through the blue iron gate. My trainers will be hidden under my long brown *abaya*. My disguise is crude but adequate. We are told that Al-Shabaab has mostly withdrawn, and AMISOM has claimed victory, but beyond the amorphous idea of Al-Shabaab, there are people, fighters who have always lived in Mogadishu, and who still do, men who have buried their guns, for now, in backyards and sandy courtyards. But they are still there. And then there are the bombs.

A few weeks ago, a truck packed with drums of fuel exploded near the K4 roundabout, outside the education ministry where scores of students had gathered to learn if they had won scholarships to study in Turkey. That was a busy day at Ubah's hospital.

252

Around seventy people were killed, but many more came to us, some even walked. Faces without eyebrows, heads without hair, hands without skin, bodies deformed so that the humanity was hard to see. That is, of course, what they want. We worked all day, and into the night. When I stepped outside to clear my head several hours after the explosion, parents were still wailing at the gate, begging us to let them in. We couldn't. The corridors were already crowded with bodies, writhing, screaming and bleeding bodies. When Dr Mugyenyi and I returned to the base, passing the roundabout where the bomb had twisted trees into grotesque shapes and sent red-hot shrapnel into soft flesh, we sat under the stars, gazing at the sea for an hour. We did not speak.

Today began as all the others do, with a slow realisation that my eyes were open and staring into the dark. I had no idea that everything was about to change again. We never do. We start each day with the assumption of continuity when really we shouldn't. I know this, but while I may be old, I am not yet wise enough, or brave enough to accept the randomness of change. So the charade goes on.

The patient was silent when he hobbled in. He may have been in shock, although he was not shaking. He was leaning on a smaller boy, a child really, who had his right arm around his companion's waist. The first thing I noticed, I admit now with shame, was the older boy's T-shirt. It was black with a big yellow Batman logo across the chest. And then I saw that he was missing a foot. And a hand. His right foot and left hand. Bloody rags covered the stumps, but the one around his hand had unravelled and trailed to his knee, like a tattered flag of surrender. Dr Mugyenyi rushed towards him, catching him as, slowly almost gracefully, he fell forward.

"Cross amputation," Dr Mugyenyi said in a low voice as he laid the teenager onto a stretcher.

He began to unravel the bandages, while the younger boy retreated to a corner and sat on the floor, his eyes wide, his stare blank. Halima, a gentle nurse from the southern town of Afmadow, appeared at my side. She breathed a few prayers under her breath and, as she helped Dr Mugyenyi remove the bandages, she questioned the younger boy. His answers were slow and stilted. Halima translated them so that the revealed story seemed to bear no relation to the series of tired almost-moans that came from the figure huddled on the floor. The older boy had passed out by now. It must have been excruciating, even though Halima and Dr Mugyenyi removed the bandages as gently as they could.

"His name is Minhaj, he is seventeen. They said he was a thief, but his brother says that is not true. Minhaj was picked up from the market in Afgoye a week ago. He was sentenced to have his hand and foot cut off. His brother says it was unfortunate they chose the left hand because that is the one he writes with. Wrote with. The brother says that they cut him first in a football stadium in Afgoye. Then they took him back to the house where he was being held. A few days later a sheikh came and

254

said they had not cut the right place on his foot. So they cut off another two inches."

Halima fell silent. The bandages were off now and the boy's wounds were exposed. I was shaking. I took a step back from the table where Dr Mugyenyi was hooking an IV to the boy's slender arm. I tore my eyes away from the mashed flesh, from the exposed white bones.

Minhaj's face was peaceful now. He could have been sleeping. I looked at Dr Mugyenyi. He was cleaning the wounds, slowly and cautiously, but he was muttering under his breath, and the sunlight sheen on his glasses meant I couldn't see his eyes. I went to the boy on the floor and sat by him. I held his hand, helplessly repeating, "It's okay. He'll be all right now. He'll be all right."

I knew it was a lie. What would this disabled boy do after we had treated him? What was out there for him?

Another nurse came into the tent. Her eyes found me on the floor and she beckoned me out.

"You have a phone call. In the commander's office."

It took me a moment to understand what she was saying. I had a mobile phone, but only Peter had the number. If someone was looking for me through the base commander, it must be about Peter. I jumped up, dropping the quiet boy's hand. He didn't seem to notice. His eyes were closed now and his breathing seemed heavier. Maybe he was sleeping. How would *he* survive after this? These thoughts chased me as I rushed to the door. Dr Mugyenyi looked up and I shook my head to his silent question. Peter's name rang through my brain as we crossed the yard towards the commander's prefabricated office — a container with a noisy air conditioner hanging outside the window, dripping onto soft sandbags below. *Peter, Peter, Peter.* That word, which had for so long meant more than any other word, became the rhythm of my steps, my heartbeat, my breathing.

The commander, recently arrived from Kampala, was standing beside his desk, holding the phone. His face was sombre. He avoided my eyes. There are no new ways of transmitting bad news. No new ways of mourning, of loving, of losing. We must copy those who went before, we must bow to conventions.

When I put down the phone, my heart was still beating to a name, but it was not Peter's. And as I stood there, looking out the window at the tiny dust devils skipping around the bleached yard, I realised I had forgotten this rhythm, this name, but that once my heart had thrilled to these three letters. Tim.

I didn't need to cry. I didn't want to cry. It seemed almost trivial to mark this with tears. I wanted to sit and think, and so I wandered past the silent commander into the sun. He lifted a hand, maybe to pat my arm, but I was gone. Outside, I went straight for the skinny shade under the thorn bushes. I needed to be alone.

It was Tim's sister, Bernadette, who had called. She couldn't locate Peter. I told her I would try.

"What happened?" I asked.

"A massive heart attack, Nina. They said no one could have survived it. You know, he's been ill for months. He had no energy, the poor man. I think his system just shut down," she said, her rolling accent opening a portal to Tim's small kitchen, overlooking the sea.

The phone became a seashell of memory as I drank in the sounds behind her — was that murmuring the wind that blew open the windows, startling us both, last time I visited my ex-husband? Surely that faint whistling was the old black-caked kettle that Tim insisted on using because it had been his mother's? When I put down the phone and looked around, I was surprised to see the grim-faced commander, to be in Somalia.

For the next hour, in the shade of spindly branches, I travelled — to Paris, to Abidjan, to Liberia, to Tim. Then I lifted myself, feeling my mortality in every aching bone, and wished like a child that I could share this part of my life with the man who shared my youth. I went to lie down. I needed oblivion.

Dr Mugyenyi came to my dark room later. I woke to him stroking the hair from my face, and that's when I finally cried. Because that is what Tim used to do a lifetime ago when I was trying to sleep. I would turn to face his body, he would open his arms, I would make myself small as I slipped into his embrace, nuzzling my head against his collarbone, my legs snaking around his, our bodies locked like pieces in a perfect puzzle. That is how our attempts to make a Peter invariably started. But we never could, and maybe that too is part of the web of whys that meant I found out about Tim's death in a troubled city on the edge of Africa.

Dr Mugyenyi played magician that night. His soft surgeon's hands brought Tim's hands back to life, but also dug deeper and brought back memories of my mother's hands. Soft and plump and sweaty from the kitchen, pushing back my hair which was always falling into my eyes as she dropped to her knees to hear my latest story, and comfort me after whatever injustice had poisoned my little life. And later, much later, hands that were papery and impossibly cold, lying inert on the off-white hospital sheet. I held her hand as she passed away in a disrespectfully bright room. I didn't notice the moment. My mother passed away as gracefully and unobtrusively as she had lived. She never wanted to rock the boat, even when she was getting off.

Dr Mugyenyi stayed with me for hours. And at some point, he climbed under the sheet and joined me on the camp bed, holding me in his arms. When I mourned Shaun, I mourned in secret, and in shame. I mourned Tim in the arms of another man. As I lay there, after the doctor had fallen asleep, his head just centimetres from my own, our bodies squashed together, I knew I would not go to Tim's funeral. There was even less reason for me to leave this place now. My past had moved from this world to the next, I was nobody's business but my own.

I needed Dr Mugyenyi, in whatever way I could have him. I needed his magic hands and this dangerous, vibrant city where I could finally forget myself. When dawn broke, I crept outside. The base was still mostly quiet, but then I heard a boom in the distance, like a gong signalling the start of the day's chaos. I heard the engine of one of the ungainly Casspirs roar. A shout or two. And the squeal of a kite, black on grey in the dying night above me.

I am here now. It is cool. One day soon I will go to Lido beach in the city. They say it is safer now. I will go with Dr Mugyenyi and we will take off our shoes and we will paddle in the foam, and I will hold his magic hands. But today, I must visit that other country, the past. I must tell Peter about his father. About the man who loved him as a son. The end of our story must be written for our boy so that he can start to write his own story, without restraints. Tim is no longer of this world. The world has given up on me, and I have given up on the world, and I have found my place. I can be happy here.

CHAPTER
NINETEEN

PETER

I wake suddenly, forced back into the world by the contractions of my dreams. I am sweating and my head and throat hurt, as though I have been screaming or crying. Maybe I have. There is no one here to tell me. I rub my face but if there were tears, as there have been before, they have melted into the beads of sweat. I throw off the covers and lie still, relishing the crisp slap of cold air on my sweat-soaked legs. I will never feel too cold again, even here in the shadow of snow-covered mountains, in a room where the long, shivering night has sucked the heat from the fire, leaving nothing but ashes. I will never again curse the cold.

The nightmares have become part of my life, so much so that I am sometimes not sure what really happened all those months ago on the road to Mogadishu, and in the long weeks before. I wake sodden, not because I am reliving the shoot-out, but because in my dreams, Abdi turns on me and pulls the trigger, and he is smiling. Or my mother turns to me with a knife in her hand, raises it and plunges it towards my chest.

Maybe this is the only way my brain can cope with what happened. Instead of trying to forget what it knows, it attempts to blank it out by making the horror worse, by gilding it in absurdity. Somalia is a land of immeasurable horror in my brain, a place where anything can happen, because it did. The unthinkable became real. You can't fear the worst when the worst has happened. And yet I do. I fear, but I fear myself, not the world. I fear my ability to live on.

That is why I am here in Colorado. I am not ready for normality. I am done with telling other stories. I am done with mining other people's lives to give meaning to my own. I don't want that kind of vicarious existence anymore. I am happy to have survived. I don't want or expect anything from the future. I have withdrawn but my cave is not in a desert, but in another time. I am a time traveller. It's as though I have come to a chasm in my road. I cannot go forward, so I must go back, and find something that will carry me across the abyss.

This is a place of pinched faces, small eyes above scarves, muffled greetings, a place where words are to the point, functional. Who wants their face to freeze while they declaim an idea that can be presented just as well in a word or two? Outside my window, I hear the muted sounds of a frozen city coming to life. The gritting trucks snarl because the frosts have come early this year. If I got up and pulled back the curtain, I would see the sun gleaming on the Rocky Mountains. It is a peacefully static sight. It lifts the viewer's eyes to the horizon, and maybe that is why this type of vista

261

makes us feel so tranquil. It suggests endless possibility. Snow-capped chimeras.

As I return slowly to the day, I remember that my father is dead. Or rather, let me phrase that correctly: Tim is dead. My mother tracked me down yesterday, an electric bolt of low voltage distress that crackled out from Mogadishu, through the spark-plug that is and ever has been Don Struddle, into this nondescript room making the cheap Nokia on my coffee-stained bedside table vibrate. Only Don knew where I was.

"Tim died, Peter. He died two days ago. It was a heart attack."

My mother was never one to surrender to emotion, but the emptiness of her words were sufficient. Tim had been a million miles from my thoughts as I continued the internal debate that had kept me cooped in this carpeted hotel room for two days. Gripping the phone, I felt a hot rush of guilt, sadness and something deeper, a regret so sharp it hit the back of my throat and crumpled my legs.

"How?" I asked before realising she had already told me. Mum said nothing. Or maybe she had not heard me. The line was poor, an unworthy medium for such a call.

"I mean, when?" I asked helplessly. She had already told me this too. But if I had the what, where, when and who, what else was there to say? I sat silent for a long minute. I had no father now. I was no longer any man's son. I must be my own man.

These ideas ripped through my brain, jumbled, half formed, rebellious, unwanted. I didn't even try to sort them. Time enough for that later. I let them rush through, waited for the noise to subside, for the mob to surge past, and then when all was still and white and blank, I asked my mother, "Will you go?"

"I don't think so. No. What purpose will it serve?"

I could hear my mother inhale deeply. "And maybe I am a little afraid of going, Peter. I have found a new life here. I am working in a hospital. I don't want to go back to where I was. I know I am weak. If I leave now, maybe I will not have the strength to come back."

"I will go," I said. "When is the funeral?"

It was a sudden decision, an elemental one. It was always this way, and would always be. My own words surprised me and for a moment, I felt calm. I would go to Cork, and I would say goodbye at a graveside, and then, and then . . . But first, I would go to another grave. If I could, and if she would take me. If I could bring myself to knock on Selena Ridge's door and present myself as the illegitimate son of her long-dead brother. I felt overwhelmed by this latest role.

My mother told me I had about a week to get back to Cork. Tim would be buried in the same seaside graveyard as his parents. I liked the thought of him in that wind-swept place of salt, bobbing dandelions and moss-encrusted stones. I did not have much time. This journey across thousands of miles of land, heart and soul must end now.

Don had helped me find Selena. I could have asked my mother for the little she knew, but I wanted this to be my journey. Even after Mogadishu, I did not feel we could talk about this easily. I did not want to hurt her, and I had finally begun to accept her personal tragedy in all this. She is happy now. I did not want to reawaken her demons.

I worked from the *Post's* office in Washington, where I stayed with Don, until I hit a solid lead. A local paper with an article on a young man who had been killed in 1980 in a freak shooting. It happened in a place called Monrovia, in a country called Liberia, where the US sent its freed slaves so that it would not have to face its shame. Outside a Freemasons' lodge, of all places.

The local reaction of shock and confusion had been captured well in the *Denver Post*. There was a picture of the family. Without Shaun. As though they had prepared for the day when this would happen. A tall, straight father, a smaller mother with a big smile and her son's eyes, a lanky, self-consciously casual twenty-year-old woman, who seemed to be grimacing at the camera. Perhaps her brother took the picture. It was a study in tension, as all family photos are.

The mother's right hand is reaching for her daughter, who seems to be tilting away. Of course, it means nothing. It was just a moment in time. But it was preserved for ever in the digital archive of the newspaper, out of context, reframed for tragedy. I found one other mention of my father in an article on journalists' deaths, this time in a national newspaper. There was a small snapshot of a man wearing sunglasses and a loose green scarf. He was half turning from the camera and stepping from a muddy verge onto a road. The caption said Sierra Leone. 1978.

264

I sat on the street outside his sister's house, feeling like a criminal in this place of tidy lawns, clean cars, towering plane trees and leaves that crackled beneath the feet of rosy-cheeked, shuffling middle-aged joggers. This place did not resonate for me and suddenly I felt scared, and embarrassed, and I turned the key in the engine to drive away. But I knew there was nowhere to go that did not start here. I switched off the engine, got out, walked up the garden path, and knocked the lion's head against the door. I tried to remember if I had looked in the mirror before leaving. Could I remember myself shaving? I ran a hand over my chin. I had not. I should have made an effort.

The door opened. She was still slim, but the sharp lines of the young woman in the photograph had softened. Her long face was creased. She had laughed too much, and cried too much.

"Come in, Peter."

I followed her into the house, down a dark corridor and into a back sitting room that dazzled. The bright midday rays of a wintry sun flooded the room through French doors, but the heat was from the blazing fire. The walls were decorated with black-and-white photographs of boy soldiers, rice paddies, mist-covered mountains, market places with mango stalls. My head spun.

"I find as I get older that I need more heat. I hope it is not too hot for a young man. Please sit down."

The room was prettily worn-down. You could tell children's toys, and pencils, and teddies, had once covered the low coffee table, and filled the corners on either side of the fire. Two Barbie doll stickers on the French doors hinted at a busy life long gone. I sat on a cream sofa. It looked newer than the other pieces of furniture. An empty-nest purchase.

"You said on the phone that your mother, Nina Walters, worked with Shaun? In Liberia?" Selena said, taking a seat opposite me in a dark easy chair with a frayed cover.

She smoothed her skirt nervously, and patted her short white hair. There was tea on the table between us. She gestured, I nodded. I thought she must have done this before, a lot, but probably not for some time.

I croaked a "yes", then coughed. I had not expected my voice to fail me but it had been some weeks since I had spoken to anyone other than waiters and taxi drivers.

"Yes, she was a journalist, and she met Shaun in Liberia, just before he was shot."

Selena shook her head. "It still shocks me to hear people say that."

I made to apologise, but she waved me away.

"No, no, I don't mean it like that. He *was* shot. It just still seems so far-fetched that I cannot believe it happened to Shaun."

"I understand it was something of a freak accident," I said, wishing I could sound more caring. I was finding it hard to concentrate on Selena's words. I didn't know how to ask what I wanted to ask. How I could say what I needed to say?

"I have to confess. I remember your mother. She called a few months after it happened to talk to my parents, but they couldn't take any more calls. There had been so many, and they were tired, grieving. They had had their fill of tributes, which I suppose in some ways helped to dull the pain in those first few weeks. Or maybe it is because the tributes made Shaun seem less real to us, more like the kind of person who could get shot in a dangerous place. Of course, we always understood he took risks. But he played them down whenever he came home. By the time your mother called, my parents had gone silent, they had retreated into their own twosome. I think maybe they could only have the silence they wanted together. You see only they really understood what each one was going through. He was nobody else's son."

Selena stopped to hand me a mug of tea. It had *I heart NYC* printed on the side.

"That was Shaun's mug," she said.

My hand trembled, some tea sloshed onto my jeans. I set the cup down. I was still digesting her words, still finding my own. I looked up and Selena was smiling at me.

"I'm sorry," she said. "I know why you are here. I guessed as soon as you called, and said you were Nina Walters' son. I have always wondered whether you existed. I thought you might. I am so glad you have finally found us, or at least me. My parents are dead now, of course."

"I don't understand," was all I managed to whisper.

CHAPTER
TWENTY

PETER

Selena settled back into her seat.

"You will have to forgive an old lady for hoarding her secrets," she said. "Shaun was my hero, but of course, also my brother. Feted yet fallible, funny and annoying, my hero and my nemesis. Do you have any siblings?"

I shook my head. I too had eased back onto the sofa. There was something hypnotic about her soft voice, with its slow drawl. Maybe there was something here. I felt comfortable. I felt like someone was taking over, and it hit me that I had been longing for this for weeks. I could listen. This voice was not just in my head.

"You said you had seen my picture in the paper when they reported his death. The one of me and my parents? I remember. Shaun took that. I was home from college for Thanksgiving, I was studying to be a teacher. It was 1979, I think. Shaun was home for once. He had been gone for a while, got married, that failed, and now he was back. I think he had just been to Northern Ireland; Derry, I think it was. He was full of it. Confidence, enthusiasm, passion and a kind of madness. He didn't talk about the risks he took, but he did talk about the danger to others. When he got going, he was hard to stop. He talked like his words could change things." She laughed a little.

"But he was preaching to the converted. We all idolised him. Our whole world view was Shaun. What he said was right, where he had been was interesting, what he thought should happen should. We Americans can be quite introverted, but when one of ours is involved, we can care. I see that now with Iraq, and Afghanistan, although there is a fatigue creeping in too."

She stopped, hesitated, and then, as if deciding something, pushed on.

"I shouldn't bother you with this, but my eldest daughter, Maria, is a widow. Her husband, Dean, was killed in Afghanistan last year. I know it's terrible, but I think, thank God there were no children. Maria has taken it very badly. She was in college, but has dropped out. She lives with her sister, Belinda, now. They are in New York. I don't always know what they are doing. Belinda's at art school, I think. They're still so young. Maria says now that she wants to be a journalist, to go to Afghanistan, to tell the truth about what's happening there. She has done some reporting here, but honestly, what does she know about going overseas? I hope she has put it out of her head. Of course, I'm worried, and biased, and probably just an old woman ranting at the moon, but I don't want her to go. I've already lost one person to war, a war that was not for me or mine. A war he wasn't even fighting. And then Dean. Such a waste. I don't want to lose another, and not Maria. She is too fragile now. But of course, I can't speak to her. She doesn't want to hear me. I thought you might be able to reach her, because of your profession, and your . . . experience."

"I could contact her. At least make sure she knows the risks," I said.

I don't know if I meant it, maybe it was just something useful to say after this outpouring of common-day tragedy that seemed too large for the pretty room where I was sitting, the little house I had invaded to make myself feel better, to cure myself, never thinking that there were people here who needed help more than me. Selena seemed to sense my discomfort.

"But how rude of me, these are not your worries," she said.

She leant forward to throw some more heavy logs on the sputtering fire. When she sat back up, her eyes had lost the sheen that had threatened to spill onto her thin cheeks when she was talking about Maria.

"Thank you," she said, as if just hearing my offer now. "I'm sure that would be helpful."

She sounded tired and sad, as though she did not believe I could help but she knew, for sure, that nothing she could do herself would work.

"Where was I? Oh yes, I was talking about the photograph. Shaun was clowning around. He said I was too tall, like a giraffe with the interesting bit out of frame. He knew I was sensitive about my height. He always knew which buttons to push. When the call came telling us he was dead, I picked up the phone. I can't remember who was there, an editor I think. But I do recall I thought it might be one of his friends, that he had organised a prank. But even as I tried to believe this, I couldn't really buy into it, not even for those few seconds. He could rib me but he was never cruel. The next few days were hell. My parents collapsed. Then we had the slow monotony of the return of the body, the wake, the burial. If anything, that whole process pushed Shaun further from us, as though death really was another country. We could not find Shaun in any of this. Then weeks later, your mother called. Again, I took the call. I was staying here in Colorado at the time, I had postponed my final year to help my parents. My father had stopped working, and my mother rarely got up. Of course, they eventually picked themselves up and carried on, and even had some happy moments before they died. But it was a harsh sort of life, that happiness was hard-won, and always paid for later in long silences, my mother peering into her tea as she pretended to watch television, my father topping up his brandy and staring into the fire, until he fell asleep where he was. When he did that, I wasn't able to move him, so I would leave him, with a light on and a blanket Shaun brought him from Kenya over his legs. He was always gone by morning. I hate to think of those awakenings. That return to reality, that slow climb up the stairs, that realisation that sleep had come and gone and the world was still without their boy. Who knows what he dreamed. He never said. He wasn't that kind of man."

"Did my mother tell you about her and Shaun?" I asked. I was gripping the mug between my hands now.

I noticed, and afraid I would somehow crush it, I went to set it down on the table. Selena seemed to follow.

"It is yours now. You can do what you like with it," she said. "No, your mother said nothing. But I could tell she had been close to Shaun. First of all, she called so much later. She had been grieving. And she was still grieving. And what she left unsaid was interesting. She didn't tell me about the kind of man he was, or how good his work had been, or say what a shame it was to lose such a talent. She just said, 'I didn't know your brother for very long, but I will miss him and I wanted to tell you how sorry I am.' She said a little more, but the line was bad and I could tell she was upset. I knew she had been with him when he was actually shot, that was in the papers. I found out the rest from Shaun."

She paused. I was lost in thought, imagining my mother at that time, how pained she must have felt. She would have been pregnant, just. She would have been back with my father in Abidjan. Did she leave the house to call? Did he know about the call? He was such a smart man. I was the fool for not asking him when he was still alive.

Slowly I registered Selena's silence, and then I registered her words.

"Shaun told you? I don't understand."

Selena rose from her chair and crossed to one of the black-and-white photographs hanging on the wall. It showed a skinny child, staring brazenly at the camera, defiance and dignity, and a gun in his thin hand.

She brought the picture back to her chair, sat down and turned it over. From behind the cardboard backing of the frame, she pulled out several folded pieces of white paper.

"I don't know why I keep it inside here. It's stupid really. But I told you, old ladies like secrets, and maybe I hoped that one day someone would find this, and it would be exciting and life-affirming and magical, partly because of its hiding place. My daughters and my husband don't know about this. I didn't see any point in telling them. I didn't know you would ever come, and I knew Shaun would never want me to seek you out. You see, he loved your mother. He would have loved you, but he would have understood what had to happen. Read this. It's addressed to me but I think it's really more for you."

She put the letter into my shaking hands, stood up and left the room, shutting the door softly on me and my father's words.

Dear Selena,

It's 4.30am here in Monrovia, and the rain is hammering on the roof. I'm not sure if that's what woke me, or maybe it was the gunshots across the river. I'd been lying awake for a while, and I suddenly realised I needed to talk to someone. I don't want to wake the woman beside me (more about that later, and, Sel, it's not what you think!). In any case, the conversation I have to have with her is different.

I need you, Sel. Your pragmatism, your sharp tongue, your common sense. I've been lying here, thinking about what the gunshots might mean, and about what I saw today, and wondering what you, all the way over there, would make of it all. Sometimes, I think I might actually be in a different world here, perhaps the plane I came on just kept going straight up after take-off, into another dimension. This room with its bare wood floors, the sensuous, sinister smell of the rain thundering down outside, the rat-tat of unseen lives being lost down on the streets, the fear in the air — it's galaxies away from Mom's call to table, the chicken pie, the radio news, the summer camps. It's ridiculously remote even from my more frenetic life in London, a life I hope you'll come and see one day, when you finish college. Do come, Sel! I miss you.

Today, I saw thirteen men shot to death on a beach. They were tied to posts — I think they were tree trunks meant to hold electricity wires — and then slowly, horribly, inefficiently they were shot. They were members of the old government, but above and beyond that, they were just middle-aged men, terrified fathers, brothers and husbands. They had to square up to death as crowds yelled at them. Worse, they faced death with my camera in their faces. I've sent the pictures out on a flight to London. You might see them soon. I tried to capture whatever dignity they had left. I framed my shots so that I didn't show the urine pouring down one man's trembling legs. I shot from behind, and to the side when one man's face dissolved into tears and snot as the firing squad raised their guns to him. I took rolls of film and I sent them all back. Who knows if anyone will publish them? It's hard to get a sense of what the outside world thinks. It's hard, really, to believe there is an outside world here. What if we are all trapped in a nightmare, a horrible collage of all our worst fears, our deepest knowledge of evil?

I've been feeling lost since I got here. It's been two weeks now. Another week to go, I think, and then back on a plane, first to Abidjan and then onto London, and my new apartment where the furniture is still finding its feet, settling into the floor. Thankfully, the whole business with Janine is now over. The lawyers have done their worst, and the papers have been signed. I can see you nodding your head, biting your lip to stop yourself from saying, "I told you so." I know you never liked her, and perhaps I should have paid more attention to your raised eyebrows, the snide looks you exchanged with Mom, your pointed questions. But I thought I knew what I was doing. Of course, everything you thought but didn't say was true. Ironically, I think Dad, despite his taciturn nature, or what you call his "one sentence a month budget", came closest to influencing me, but too little too late.

Did I ever tell you what he said on our wedding day? I don't think so, and I think I know why now. I was afraid he was right and too scared to repeat what he said in case it would somehow make it come true. I guess I always knew he had hit the nail on the head. When I was pacing behind the marquee in the garden, and Mom was fussing about the roses on the ends of the seats, and you were getting ready, he came up to me, touched my arm and said, "Let's go sit." He led me to the bench among the pine trees, where you and I used to smoke when we were teenagers, and sat me down. He didn't say anything for a while, and we just listened to the magpies. Then he said, as if picking up on a conversation we'd been having before, "But are you sure Janine loves you, for you, inside?"

He was staring at me with what you used to call his X-ray glare, the one that made you think he could see right into your brain. I think I said, yes, or sure, or something stupidly banal. That was it. He grunted. We sat for a while longer, and then he said, "Time to go, son," and off we went. At the time, I didn't dwell on it. To be honest, as soon as I saw Janine and that dress, I didn't think of much beyond getting her into bed! I know you and Mom disapproved but man, you have to admit she looked hot! And it wasn't as if it was a church, just our garden. You've sunbathed topless there, so what's the difference? Okay, okay, I'm just trying to annoy you. Admit it, you're smiling now.

Anyway, as things went sour with Janine, and I have to say the speed at which they did surprised me, I remembered Dad's words more and more. I think now that Janine did think she loved me, but the idea she had of me bore as much resemblance to me as those studio photos you can get done in India. You know the ones — all paradise backgrounds, gaudy bright colours. She had me, we looked pretty together, I had an exciting job that reflected well on her. With her PR business and my in-the-field macho job, we were in demand as a couple. I think she even wanted us to work together — to become the core of some kind of advertising behemoth. Which in and of itself shows you the problem. Can you imagine me doing advertising shoots? Right.

Anyway, sorry, I'm rambling. It's just I have a particular reason to bring this all up, and we haven't seen each other much since the divorce. I know I was home last year but I didn't really get a chance to talk to you without Mom and Dad. And then you were studying, and grumpy! Yes, you were. I know I annoy you. I see your point. You put in the time with the folks and I waltz in, stealing your thunder, telling outlandish tales, laughing off my failed marriage, easing their pain with tales of distant places. I'm not proud of this but I don't know what else to do. How can I manage the relationship better? Maybe one day you'll tell me, oh-so-nearly-teacher.

I promised to tell you about the woman beside me. No need to curl your lip like that. She's not a whore, and how many times do I have to tell you not to believe everything you read about photojournalists? We are not all out to take drugs, have sex and exploit poor people. Well, maybe we can't help but do the latter, but the rest is a choice.

The woman in this bed is a journalist. But she is married. We only met a week ago and . . . Damn, now I've decided to tell you everything, I don't know what to say. She was at the beach today. It's not an excuse, but an explanation. But it's not even that. I know you'll say people who have been through traumatic situations gravitate towards each other, you'll try some of that amateur psychology they force you to swallow before you take control of the minds of the future, but I don't think it's just that. I would say there is a connection between us. I would, except that I can hear your guffaws from here, even here in this fourth or fifth dimension. Okay then, we clicked. And she's cute, very cute. And fragile, and all the things you've told me I like in women. To my detriment. And of course, she's unavailable, or at least she is technically unavailable because she is, nonetheless, behind me in the bed, her hair covering the pillow, her arms crossed across her chest, her knees drawn up.

Sel, I don't know how to explain this but I want to see her like that every morning. It's ridiculous, but I've never been as certain of anything in my life. I think this could be it. But I have no idea what she thinks. That's the conversation we must have. Later today, or tomorrow, or if I have to, I will follow her back to her home in Abidjan and have it there. I won't be able to let her go. I know that. Not without asking her if we have a chance, and surely, we must have. I can't just be a fling, can I? Okay, okay, that was fishing. Did you smile generously? You know what I mean. God, I wish you were here.

Dawn is breaking. It's been over a week since Doe killed Tolbert. I can't describe this place to you. I will show you the photos when we meet again. The town is like something from the south, at least in places. There are clapboard houses, shacks, a broad river crossed by two bridges, banana plants on the roadside, and fear in the air. I think that is the most terrifying thing. The fear. It clings to you. It's worse than the smell of death, although of course there is that too. Bodies by the roadside, dumped for the dogs. I don't photograph those too closely. There is no dignity there, no story to tell because you cannot know who that person is, why they ended up there, and the brutality I can show in other ways. With pictures from the beach, for example. Those men had names, and they still had faces. They had an identity in death. Faceless, nameless death is an affront to the individual that was. I can leave that to people's imaginations. I did photograph one body yesterday, but just the feet. They were on the roadside, the rest of the body had slumped into the ditch. But when I crouched down, I could frame the feet and the soft, pink dog roses growing around them. There was dignity in that. A final resting place, a grave of sorts, a moment of respite from the horror. Does that make sense, Sel? Of course, you can't know. I will send you that photograph when I get back to London. You will tell me what you think.

Now, the birds are making an almighty noise. She will wake up soon, and I want to get her coffee. That should tell you how powerfully I feel about her. There is no room service in this hotel. I will have to go down to the kitchen, through dark corridors because the generators have not come on yet, shining my torch ahead of me, find the cook, wake him up, give him some change, wait while he fills a saucepan with water, boils it, finds the coffee, and then annoy him with my request for sugar. She takes sugar. See how much I have learnt? Janine did not. I don't think I would have felt like doing all that for Janine. At least not at the end.

Later, we are going into the city together, looking for stories, looking for messed-up lives and broken dreams. Once we have dealt with that, perhaps it will be time to deal with our own messed-up lives. I hope so. I can't wait to ask her how she feels. Whether she believes this is more than, well, more than what it has been, more than what it would seem to outsiders. I feel full of hope and bravado and excitement. The day is beginning, the world is new, this love is new, this love is strong. I feel like a teenager. Do you remember feeling like that? That energy, that madness, that over-the-top, no-reason exuberance.

I haven't felt that in a long time. I can't believe it's happening here, despite everything else.

Here in this room, that is the feeling that surrounds me. I must grab this feeling and lock it away somewhere safe, so that when I am out there, where all hope seems to be gone, I can do my job properly. Thankfully, these ridiculously pompous photographer jackets we all wear have plenty of pockets, for hope, and love and later.

I am glad we talked, Sel. I am sorry it was a little one-sided. I will post this on my way back to London. That way, when we speak, you will be ready to tear into me.

Shaun

CHAPTER
TWENTY-ONE

PETER

I have come back to the beginning, or at least as close to the beginning as my limited human intellect can fathom. The plane cruised across the Mediterranean from Paris, then bumped over the vast Sahara desert, blank and dark, until finally, plunging through clouds, it fell towards the sun-sheened iron-roofed homes and we landed in Monrovia.

I hadn't been to Liberia since 2005. Then it was October, election time, the country was in a fever. I was in my own delirium, running away without making a move, open to possibilities because they would themselves destroy the budding certainty of my relationship with Michelle. If I behaved as I always did, I knew I would be free again. I was hungry for this freedom. I was also twenty-five, invicible, immortal and puffed up with the pride of a young man with an important job in an unknown land. Empires have been built from less but given there were no longer any empires to build, I opted for wanton destruction of my own life. I am here now to sift through the rubble, but I am very late. Maybe too late.

I got a taxi from Robertsfield, a squat-bummed yellow car with one jaunty blue door and a driver who held my hand too long and my bags too carelessly. When I was last in Monrovia, the rain lashed down for hours, the roads were slick and treacherous and the very air seemed pregnant with moisture, always about to give birth to another downpour. This time, the road from the airport was dry and the palm trees swayed in a sea-salted breeze that made me nostalgic for something I couldn't name. I couldn't be nostalgic for Monrovia. I had only ever spent a few weeks here. This was not my home. I looked out at the almost obscene explosion of green, stretching towards the low mountains on the horizon, as my driver asked me about "the purpose of your visit". It was a good question. I had written "tourism" on the form at the airport, but that was a lie. Business was not right either. Redemption might be more accurate but I didn't fancy explaining that to the forbidding immigration officials.

Monrovia has not changed much. A little more ragged, a few obvious attempts to stem the tide of time with look-at-me tall buildings and even new solar-powered street lamps, rising distant and aloof above women balancing bundles of life's necessities on their heads. I looked for her as we drove deeper into the city, my eyes finding the right arm of every woman, checking and then moving on. Even if I had found her, I'm not sure what I would have done.

Selena had taken me to see Shaun's grave in the Grandview Cemetery, a place of softly winding paths between towering trees that linked the earth to the sky. Shaun was buried with his parents.

Shaun Ridge July 9, 1951 — April 23, 1980.
From my rotting body, flowers shall grow and I am in them and that is eternity.

"I chose the quote," Selena said, as we stood there, two strangers mourning different men — a brother and a father whose life had been reduced to one handwritten letter on yellowing paper stamped with the words *Ducor Hotel*. I didn't know what to feel. I felt sad for the young man in the photo, whose road ran out too soon. I felt sad for myself, but what right had I to demand anything from this man? I did not know him, he did not know me. It was nobody's fault. And finally, I felt sad for my mother because I now knew that her dreams, however wispy and unformed, had been buried with this man. Standing at that graveside, I understood, for the first time, my mother, her strange moods, her bitterness, and now her exile in Mogadishu. She would never use such flamboyant language, of course. She is made of tougher stuff than me.

After leaving Colorado, I headed for Europe, pausing briefly in Washington to speak to Don. He was in the office he rarely used because he preferred to be in the busy newsroom, standing impatiently behind his desk, his right hand beating a frenetic SOS on his mouse.

"Did you find him?"

I nodded and sank into the chair in front of him.

"My father, Tim, is dead. I'm going to Ireland for the funeral. I leave tonight."

Don ceased his tapping. He stood for a minute as if unsure what to do. His heavy hands hung by his side. His face furrowed, the ever-present wrinkles deepening and darkening like a storm.

"I'm sorry, Peter. Is Nina going?"

"No," I said. "She doesn't want to. She is staying in Mogadishu. I think she is happy."

It would be trite to say my mother had changed. That wasn't it. It wasn't my ordeal, or her ordeal in searching for me, or even that earlier ordeal in Monrovia. She had simply come to the end of one road, taken another, and was moving forward. She was happy.

"I need to be happy too, I think. I am tired of searching and trying to understand things that were written before I was even born. I need to take what I have now, and go to a new place. I think I need to start again, Don."

Once again, my words skipped ahead of my mind, or maybe I mean my heart. The idea had been there, lurking around the edges of those amorphous days in Colorado. I had just not shaped the thought with the appropriate words. I had not let it out, but it had escaped, running to Don, the only father figure left to me.

He nodded and came round the desk, putting an arm around my shoulders, a clumsy gesture all the more endearing for its gaucheness. I felt I should comfort him. He had been through it all with us, we had all made him carry our burdens, he even knew about

Esther and Godwin. He bore our secrets with grace. Even now, he did not pry, he did not question, and he did not judge. He just sat with me, until it was time to go.

As I left the building, he told me I had a job anytime I wanted.

"I don't think I'm going to do this anymore," I said. "I don't think I have any curiosity left. I want the small things, Don. I crave silence and peace, and a long, fucking boring life doing very little."

We laughed then, newsmen again marveling at a life that wasn't dictated by deadlines and headlines. I knew he didn't believe me.

Two days later, I stood alongside Tim's sister, Bernadette, and a damp huddle of heavy-coated silent men and women in a graveyard just two miles from the cottage where my father's big heart had finally given up. An overly sharp sun, sulkily making up for its lack of warmth with an eye-watering frigid glare, cast gimlets of gold onto the waves, while the wind whipped the bald priest's words from his mouth, tossing them over the low stone wall, across the sand and into the sea. I didn't need to hear them. I had spoken little myself since arriving, and even my normally effusive aunt seemed not to know what to say or do with me; the gangly son of her brother, who was not even actually that and never had been, an almost-stranger who had been broken in a land she had barely heard of. The cousins I once played with — her three sons — and their friends were the same, and different. A heaviness around the jaw, hair not quite where it should be, a slight thickening of the limbs. Nothing too dramatic yet, but almost more poignant for that — these barely there changes were the sly harbingers of age, and death, undeniable here on the edge of the sea.

How did we all end up here, when just moments ago we were down on the sand, cart-wheeling, cursing, thumping and whining as the man now in the box followed us along, laughing softly to himself? After I dropped a handful of clay on his oak coffin, I turned to the beach. I wanted to see him there, one last time, instead of holding that image of him lying in the coffin the night before, waxy and empty. I would not have recognised him in that box, but I could see him now, down on the sand, picking flat pebbles so he could teach me how to skim. I would never have a father now. It's a simple thought, an obvious one, but so shocking. I would never have a father, and that would never change. I think it was at that moment, looking down at an empty beach and seeing the ghost of a man I now knew I had loved more than any other person, it was at that moment that I decided to go and find my own son. I left Ireland the next day.

I needn't have hurried, of course. Liberian bureaucracy doesn't care about your issues or about your epiphanies. And neither do the French. It took several weeks to get a visa, and to tidy up my few affairs. I spent my time drifting below consciousness in my mother's flat and then wandering Paris by night — past the Hotel de Ville, along the Seine, through the courtyard of the Louvre, down to Place de la Concorde, up the Champs-Élysées, jostled by excited tourists or snarled at by young men who had ridden the metro to gawk at the splendour and excess of the city. I didn't mind being jostled. I was walking to fill the time. I had no destination in mind. I just wanted the colour of the city, its heartbeat to rise up through the concrete into my own shell so that I could stop thinking for an hour or two. It also helped me sleep, especially after stopping for a few cognacs in the anonymous bars along the Rue Montorgueil on the way home. I got to know the barmen the way one always knows barmen.

Finally the fog lifted, and after the weeks of half-life, I surged into action like a man rising from his own coffin just before the lid is nailed down after some terrible medical error. Now I am here in Monrovia.

I had an address from the payments I used to send. She was living in the western part of the city, north of Broad Street, and close enough to the Mesurado River to smell it on a heavy day. Like today. I asked the taxi to drop me on the main road — I needed to compose my thoughts and my toothless driver's chatter about rising prices, water shortages and the perfidy of the ruling class was not helping. I thought I could probably find the house on my own. I had a vague idea of the direction after pouring over maps before I boarded my flight in Paris. But how could I tell them why I had come when I couldn't quite explain it to myself? And why should I expect them to accept me? I had little enough to offer — a broken spirit, a few thousand dollars, a bag of worn clothes, a few pictures, and an idea of redemption, which seemed ever more absurd as I pushed my way down a crowded side street, past hawkers selling charcoal, corn on the cob and shoes to fit all feet in a city of bare soles. I now kept my eyes down, partly to stop myself from tripping over the plastic bags, empty milk packets and bits of fruit peel, partly to stop myself making eye contact in a city that still shamed me, and my heartless, youthful self.

Eventually, I had to ask for directions. I had veered off course, finding myself walking along the edge of a wasteland where a few boys were kicking a ball of twine around. A big-hipped seller of mangoes pointed me down the road, indicating a corner marked by a Coca-Cola emblazoned kiosk. "The family there. I know the brothers, but her, I don't know well. She stays alone."

I bought some mangoes, thanked her and headed off, the plastic bag of over-ripe fruit dangling from my hand. I felt a small smile tugging at the edge of my frazzled mind. Esther always did keep herself to herself.

I knocked loudly on the iron gate, feeling the eyes of men across the street boring into my sweaty back. This was big news here. Esther might have been a mysterious figure before. She would be notorious as the news of the white man's arrival spread round the neighbourhood. Unsure if I was ready for this, or if she was, I knocked again.

A young man opened the gate. He was thickset and sweaty in a dark blue T-shirt and oil-stained jeans, but despite the stocky build, he had touches of Esther around the eyes, which opened now in surprise.

"I am Peter Maguire. I have come to call on Esther, if she is willing to see me."

The young man — whom I now know as Joseph, a hard-working mechanic who will never forgive himself for not being able to defend his sister and mother in a forest in Sierra Leone when he was just a boy, and who drowns that guilt each night in a bottle of palm wine — looked over his shoulder. Following his gaze, I saw them.

They were sitting in front of a small brick house with a curtain for a door. The red lace fluttered in the evening breeze off the river, and caught the dying rays of the sun, casting a supernatural sheen over the tableau in front. Esther was seated on the dry ground, her legs straight before her, her head bent as a young boy traced patterns in the sand with a stick. Esther's left arm was across the boy's shoulder. They both looked up at the same time, and I knew she saw me. Esther's eyes widened, she dropped her hand to her lap. I registered that the young man at the gate had stood aside. There was nothing between us now but a few short feet of dry, dusty earth and within it, everything.

Slowly Esther rose. She dusted her skirt and flicked a hand over her hair and across the front of her emerald green shirt. The boy rose too, his small hand reaching for hers, his eyes fixed on my face. I thought he knew who I was. She must have told him. She would have had to, I now realised with a shock, looking at his paler hand in her brown one. For a moment, the full extent of my responsibility caught my breath, stopping it in my throat, so that my feet stopped too.

An old woman poked her head out of a traditional mud hut built next to the brick house. She squinted

290

into the dying sun, uttered a throaty gasp and fled inside again. I could feel Joseph behind me. We stood like this, a fractured family in a setting sun, for a while. We might have stood like that for ever, but Esther knew what to do.

"You are here, Peter," she said. "You have come to visit us?" She shook her head slightly as soon as the words were out, as if she regretted them. She lowered her eyes and stood waiting for me to answer.

And finally, I knew what to say. I knew it because she had spoken, she had broken the spell and given me a place, and a role, and a purpose. I was a visitor. And I could be more.

"I would like to stay," I said. "I would like Godwin to know his father."

Esther smiled and looked down at the boy. I did not know then whether or not he understood me. He told me later that he did but that he did not dare answer. He was afraid I had made a mistake. He was afraid he had made a mistake. He was unsure what to make of this "military man, the pale visitor", as he called me.

The old lady came rushing out of her hut again on swollen feet. She muttered something at Esther, who lowered her head again, but I caught a hint of a smile.

"My mother is angry that I am treating you so badly. I have let you stand in the sun. She says I have dishonoured her. You must come and sit in the shade, and then we can talk."

"Does she know who I am?" I asked, feeling Esther's smile sneak onto my face. Godwin was staring harder now, his head turning from his flapping grandmother to his smiling mother to the pale stranger standing before him.

"I don't think so. But you are white and she is ashamed. She says she will see me later, so you cannot leave now, or I will be alone with her anger.

Joseph brought a white plastic chair and set it in the shade under the single tree in the compound. I suddenly remembered the mangoes. I handed them to the old lady. She laughed and gestured to the chair. Another man arrived. Esther introduced him as her brother Tobias. He also lived in this small compound in a second brick house, with his wife and four children. I sat in the chair, surrounded by mystified strangers. Esther brought Godwin to me.

"Godwin, shake hands with your father."

He stretched out his little hand and I took it in mine. And that was the start of our story.

I stayed in that compound for a few weeks, sleeping on a spare mattress in the one-room shed where Joseph collapsed each night. I drank palm wine with him, played with Godwin and Tobias' children, and sat in companionable silence with the old lady, who would pat my shoulder every so often and smile at me.

Eventually, we moved to a house by the sea. It's near the West Point Football Field. If you turn to the right while standing on our little beachside verandah, you face Sierra Leone. Straight ahead is the rest of the world. Our house is like a bridge that leads from the city to the ocean — from land to sea, from chaos to peace. From the narrow hall, you enter the main room, and here already you can see the water. You cross in a

292

few steps, going around the gaudy sofa, past Esther's sewing machine and Godwin's small desk, and then through the back door onto the verandah, where the sea's heartbeat drowns out the noise of the city.

On our first night, after Esther had put Godwin to bed, his skin still slick with the sweat of excitement, we sat in the main room, close together on the old sofa. I put my arm around Esther, tentatively. She did not pull away. It was the first time we had been truly alone since I arrived. As the waves hummed faintly in the background, I began to speak. I told Esther of Somalia, but my time there felt distant, as though it belonged to someone else. Strange how those few weeks already felt so unreal. I knew I sounded false, hesitant as I described those events, and yet they had defined my life. They just did not ring true. The words didn't fit. Maybe it will come.

I told Esther how my mother had decided to stay. I spoke of Tim, and here I cried. Then, I told her of Shaun Ridge, and his letter, and the story I had decided I was going to write.

But still I had not spoken of us. I stroked Esther's braided hair, and bent to kiss her stump, as I had before.

"Godwin does that. Every morning. He asks me if it pains, and then I say yes, and then he kisses it to make the pain go away." She spoke in a soft voice, as if the waves could overhear us.

"He is a good boy," I said. "You have raised him well."

"Thank you," she said. "They call him 'the bright boy'. It is not meant to be kind, but I think it is. He is my bright boy, and maybe he can be yours."

"It would be an honour," I said.

We fell into silence again. I would've liked to stay silent but this woman deserved more.

"I have never spoken the truth, Esther, because I have never known it. I'm not sure I know it now. I'm not sure I even believe in truth any more. I am tired of ideals. I am tired of absolutes."

I was speaking rapidly, the words tumbling out, rushing to give form to ideas that were eager to skip away unfettered.

"I remember, on the beach, I told you I could love you and love another. I thought that was so. It is not. And I am not that person anymore either."

Esther lowered her eyes. I lifted her chin and turned her face to mine. Her smile was bright, hopeful yet desperate not to appear too hopeful.

"I do not want to speak of love," I said. "I don't know what it means. I don't know what anything means now. All the words I have used have been wrong. I feel like I have been living in a different language, and I did not realise it until now. I need to learn again."

I paused. I had more to say, but I could not think of how. She took my hand and lifted it to her cheek. Then she put it down and placed her fingers over my lips. She did all this slowly.

"We have time to talk, Peter. We have time to learn, together, here in this house."

294

We sat in silence on that sagging couch until we fell asleep in each other's arms. Two people in a house on the sea, with a little boy dreaming to the sound of never-ending waves.

CHAPTER
TWENTY-TWO

PETER

My name is Peter Maguire. Today is August 10th, 2012. I am sitting on the edge of Africa, where the land meets the Atlantic Ocean. I am writing, so I shall say I am a writer. I am a father. I am a son. I am free.

The sea is hissing again, a reassuring sound that is soothing rather than sinister, and rain-swollen clouds are gathering above the horizon. Godwin and Esther will be home from school soon. My son, our son, will crash through the door from the street, I will hear the thud of his bag in the room behind me, and the squeak of the screen door, and shouts of "Father, Father, I am here".

He will run to me as I sit here on the verandah, but he will not hug me. We are not there yet. He will run across these sandy, wooden boards with his too-heavy new shoes, his face bright and wet above his canary-yellow shirt. And my son, my sun will be back.

He will tell me of his day, of his teacher, of his friends. I will stop typing. Esther will appear behind me, place a hand on my head as if to measure the intensity of the vibrations inside, as if trying to get a sense of today's turmoil. She will bring me coffee. I will take the NYC mug, and then Godwin and I will walk onto the beach, searching for shells, and sticks, and the detritus of the sea, to decorate the shelves I have placed along the verandah for this purpose. On one shelf, in pride of place, stands an undamaged sea urchin shell, lavender fading to green, achingly pretty and fragile. That one I found alone. I have varnished it. Its survival has become a totem.

On the day I found the shell, a few months after I arrived, I had run frantically onto the beach. It was raining with pellet-like drops spattering the sand. Thunder rumbled above the churning waves. I welcomed the climatic fury, turning my face up to the rain, wanting the sting of physical pain. I wanted to forget what I had just seen. I opened my eyes wide, as if the rain could wash the images away. I had come here to escape.

I had not been able to write for some days. Writer's block, I suppose, but that isn't quite right. I was not blocked as a writer, but as a man. I was trying to remember my captivity, that room with the monster's teeth outside Mogadishu. But the picture was already faded. My memories found hiding places, curling themselves up like cats on warm duvets. I dug deeper, finding nothing, grasping at the phrases I had doled out to the suited men in Nairobi. But how could I write about something I could not clearly remember? I tried a few sentences. They were flat, devoid of emotion, as though I was writing about something I had read about in the newspapers.

I sought inspiration on the Internet. The connection is patchy here, but after several tries it kicked in and suddenly my verandah sped out across the sea, into the world. I typed *Somalia* into Google News.

Somalia Theatre Bombing Kills Top Sports Officials was the first headline I read. A young woman had blown herself up in the newly opened National Theatre during a speech by the Somali prime minister to mark the first anniversary of the launch of a national television channel.

I read and read. Devoured every article on the attack. I felt drawn to the descriptions, hungry for detail. I found a video from inside the theatre on YouTube. It took ten minutes to load, stopping and starting, and endlessly buffering.

Finally, an image appeared. The prime minister, a small, slightly pudgy man with the look of an accountant, was speaking. Then, there was a sharp bang. Behind the prime minister, men in suits and sunglasses flinched away from the podium, heads down, hands up. The camera panned away. Blue and white plastic chairs had been overturned. Smoke and screams filled the small box on my screen. But then the camera moved to a smear of blood and empty sandals.

The video ended after just fifty seconds. I sought out more. Fear was awakening in me, and wanted to fully embrace it. I thought somehow that would unlock my own memories of horror and despair. I played the blast over and over again, jolting each time it boomed out from the computer. I relished the fearful anticipation.

298

I think it was on the third video I watched. It had been uploaded by a Somali news agency and eschewed the soft-stomached censorship we seem to favour on international media outlets. It makes sense — horror is only unbroadcastable horror if you have not seen it before. If you have lived it, and live it everyday, it is just news, not the stuff of nightmares.

Abdi was lying on his back, among the scattered chairs. He looked as though he was sleeping, as long as you did not focus on the chunk bitten from his chest by a greedy piece of shrapnel.

His face was untouched. His almond-shaped eyes stared sightlessly from beneath the arched eyebrows. His delicate lips were slightly open, as if he had been about to say something. His arms were undamaged, long fingers splayed on the ground, as if he was feeling the soil one last time. He was dressed in the uniform of the Somali National Army. Below the mess of flesh and bone, one foot was intact, knobbly toes in a red flip flop.

The camera panned away. I hit pause. I ran onto the beach, into the rain, towards the waves. On that beach, on that day, I decided it was too much. Of course, I had been moving towards this realisation for months. My decision to move to Monrovia was always a plaster on an open wound. It was not the solution, merely an attempt to live again.

But when I saw Abdi's shattered body, I decided this attempt to redefine myself through my accidental family was not going to work. I had never been truly convinced it would. It was something to do. A time-consuming task to give the illusion of purpose. With Abdi's death, the scales fell from my eyes. I wanted out.

I waded into the water. When it rose to my knees, I stopped. I remembered Abdi striding away from me at the AMISOM base, after we had been rescued. Had I cared enough then? If I had cared more, could I have persuaded him? How much of that young man's death was my responsibility? Was I too eager, as he said then, to return to my life. And for what? I had left it all behind to start again. No more.

As the waves crashed into me, sending fingers of cold creeping above my ribs, towards my neck, over my heart, I thought again of Guled, and his son, Ahmed, and a blood-red sunset over a technicolour road in the middle of nowhere.

I needed oblivion. It was my fault, and not my fault. I didn't have the energy to draw the line in the sand that would allow me to separate the story from me. I started wading out again. It seemed easier just to keep walking, to let my body alone experience this moment. I focused on my feet. I became the struggle against the waves. I welcomed the spray hitting my face, blinding my eyes and sending goosebumps along my arms. I could walk for ever.

Then, the softest part of my soft white man's foot scraped against something sharp, and as the man in me lost his footing, the boy in me lost his focus. I bent down and pushed my head under the furious waves, my hands scrabbling at the sand. I was dragged under. My ears filled with noise as my lungs emptied. In that moment, I could not go gracefully. My fingers closed over a shell and I started flailing, legs kicking, arms windmilling as I sought the surface. I was rolled and rocked by the covetous waves. They wanted me now, they had believed my promise to keep walking. I scraped the bottom, felt my knees graze the brittle sand and a sharp pain in my elbow. Angered by my U-turn, the sea spat me out, and I burst back into the world.

I was on my knees in the shallows. I had the sea urchin cradled in my hand. I knelt there for a long time, looking at the glassy sand as it wriggled and seethed under the spent waves, until I heard Godwin's voice calling me from the verandah. My son, my sun.

Esther stood in the shadows, her arm half raised to me, as if unsure whether to call me. I lifted myself from the sea and trudged up the sand, my feet sinking like deadweights into the ochre softness.

"It is the most beautiful shell I have ever seen," Godwin said, as I stood dripping before him, my hands outstretched. "You are lucky to have found it, Father."

I would not call it luck. Luck is an absolute. You either have it or you don't. It is too definitive. It implies we have no agency over our own destinies. But we do, up to a point. We do not deserve absolution, but neither are we totally innocent. If Abdi had chosen to let me help him, he might have been saved. But could he make that choice, given what had happened to Nadif, to his mother, to his father? Their choices, and their resulting fates, limited his world, hemmed him in by creating a web spun from character, chance and history. We are not as free as we think, but even the prisoner can choose when to eat, when to sleep, and, sometimes, when to die.

My mother called a week after Abdi's death. She is still in Mogadishu, still seeking peace in a place that did not know her before. In Mogadishu, she is Mama Nina. That is all. Not Nina the journalist. Not Nina the adultress. Not Nina the bereaved.

"You saw?" she asked as soon as I answered.

"Yes."

"There was nothing to be done. He came to us too late."

"He was dead at the theatre," I said. "I saw a video. He looked older, and harder, but he was still wearing the same sandals. I guess they provide their own shoes in the Somali army."

"I saw him, you know," she said. "In March. He came to the Medina hospital with a young woman. She had been hit by shrapnel when a car exploded beside a bus at K4. Abdi brought her to Robert, the Ugandan doctor here. He treated her. Afterwards, Robert said Abdi had saved her life. Her upper thigh had been pierced. She would have bled to death if he had not acted so fast. Robert patted him on the shoulder. Abdi seemed proud, he smiled. He had a beautiful smile, Peter. I had not seen that before."

I had nothing to say so I said nothing.

"I spoke to him too, just before he left. I asked if he was all right. A stupid question here, I know, but I don't remember how to talk to young men. I was never very good at it, as I'm sure you remember."

I did. She wasn't. But then, like all of us, she was always forced to recite lines from her own multi-authored script.

"He said he was well. He had joined the army, and had been trained for ten weeks by AMISOM. He was providing security around Villa Somalia and other government buildings. He was hoping to become part of the prime minister's personal security detail. I guess that happened."

"He got what he wanted then," I said, too bitterly.

"I think he did, Peter. For the first time, I think he did. What happened, happened. But he was living the life he had chosen. That is important."

My mother sounded calm. At ease. She had changed. She too had found what she wanted in Mogadishu. Or at least what she can now want, given the past.

I remained silent.

"And you? Are you living the life you want?" My mother's voice was soft now.

It had been years since we had asked each other such questions. I wanted to brush it off, to bury it under a glib, flip phrase, but I find glibness much harder now.

"I am living. I am learning, and I am writing. I don't know if that is what I want, Mum. How can I tell what I want when I am not sure who I am yet? I have been so many things to so many people. I have been your son. I have been a dream to a dead man, a lie to a live one. I have been a captive, and a free man. A journalist and a story. I am the nephew of a retired teacher in Colorado. I am a father to a boy I barely know. I live with a woman who believes in silence, and yet I work with words."

I paused, my heart racing. I was being sucked under by the waves again. My fingers were clenched so hard on the phone they were aching.

From across Africa, from the shores of another sea, my mother answered.

"You are a man, Peter. That is all." She paused. "I did not make life easy for you, but neither was it easy for me. We are all broken pieces of a mirror. A broken mirror's cracks are its own, but the images within are from elsewhere. Does the mirror choose what it reflects? I don't know, Peter. I don't know. We are what we are, and we must make do. That is the secret."

I heard her chuckle, or perhaps it was a strangled sob, and for a second, I could see her clearly, her light hair in the breeze, as it was when I took off from Mogadishu airport by the Indian Ocean.

"Do you love your child?" she asked.

"I am learning to."

"Then you are making a good start. Don't fight the questions, Peter. They will always be there. Try to answer them, and if you cannot, know that living in uncertainty is all there is. At least, for now. Maybe clarity comes with death. If it does, I will try to find a way to let you know."

I have not spoken to my mother since then. She sends the occasional email, and photographs for Godwin. One shows her sitting with Robert at a plastic table in front of the sea. There are two bottles of Coke on the table. This excited Godwin.

"Is it her birthday? Or his birthday?" he asked.

"No," I said. "Grown ups can drink as much Coke as they like. If they can pay for it."

His face lit up. Life was beautiful, and the future was brighter than ever, full of endless bottles of Coke on beaches in foreign countries with fascinating people.

I have also been in touch with Selena. I told her I had come to Monrovia. She sent me two photographs taken by Shaun. One shows a teenage boy, arms outstretched with joy, face beaming, celebrating Doe's coup. The boy looks like Godwin did when he heard of the limitless Coke. It is heartbreaking because of this. The second is from Sierra Leone, chosen for Esther, I'm sure. When Selena said Shaun had been to Freetown, I told her what had happened to Esther. The photograph she sent is one of Shaun's. He never witnessed what Sierra Leone became, and so he could still see the beauty. The photo shows the Cape Lighthouse in Freetown, silhouetted against a golden explosion of cloud and sun rays at the end of the day.

When I showed it to Esther, she held it daintily with her fingertips and looked for a long time.

"It is beautiful. I have never been to that place."

"We will go," I said on impulse, and suddenly, I meant it. It was the first time I had acknowledged the possibility of a future, since I had arrived.

Esther looked up and flashed her radiant smile, the one that didn't mean she was happy, or that she necessarily believed you.

"I would like that," she said.

Selena sent another photograph this week. She said she had found it while sorting through her attic. She and her husband are planning to move to New York to be closer to Maria, who gave up her passion to go to Afghanistan, and has now lost her bearings. I did speak to her after all, and I suppose I dissuaded her. In any case, I took action. It was my first intervention since leaving Somalia, since Abdi took my arm, and led me from the compound back to the world. With Maria, I was wary, afraid to say too much. I am still wary. Life has proved itself a malicious and vindictive adversary. I am still waiting for the other shoe to drop. But I acted.

This third photograph is of Shaun and my mother. On the back in faded blue ink, someone scribbled: *Nina Walters, Shaun Ridge, Monrovia, April 1980.* The quality is poor. This was a print man's photograph, I thought. Perhaps Don took it. Or some other hack.

My mother and father are sitting in a dim, candlelit restaurant. The picture is tightly framed, their upper bodies fill the shot. My mother faces the camera, but she is looking at Shaun, who is seated on her right. She is smiling at something he said, and her eyes are fixed on his face. His profile is animated, soft in the near-dark, his hands are empty, and one is reaching towards Nina. I wonder if he was about to stroke her hair, caress her face, or if his body was two steps ahead of his mind at that point. There is a complicity in the closeness of their heads, a mutual understanding in their bodies.

After the photograph arrived, I found my rucksack and removed the one album I took with me on this journey. I took out a photograph of Tim and I, playing in the waves on a summer holiday in Cork. I was about nine. My cousin Joe took the photo. My father was happy, happier than he had been for many years before. His voice rang out as we jumped over the waves, seaweed snaggling our legs.

"Higher, Peter! Jump for it. Thatta boy!"

I brought the photo out to my table on the verandah at the edge of the world. I put it beside the picture from Selena. And I called my son. Esther followed. I rose, and gestured to her to sit. Godwin perched on her lap.

"These are your grandfathers, Godwin," I said. "Tim and Shaun."

My bright boy picked up the photographs, holding them side by side.

"Who is the lady?"

"That is your grandmother. You have not met her yet, but you will, *inshallah*."

My boy looked confused. Esther raised her eyes from the photographs, and searched my face. Her smile, this time, was understanding.

"Your father is about to tell you a great story," she said. "It is the story of this family. It is the beginning of your story, of our story."

"And in this story," I continued, reaching out to grasp Esther's hand, "we will also meet Abdi, a young Somali man who saved my life. One day, we may go to Somalia so that you can see where he was from. There are many footsteps to follow, Godwin. We will have to start slow, and small."

Esther started to rise.

"No, please." I laid a hand on her good arm. "Please, listen. I want to tell you both."

"I am not leaving," she said. "I want you to tell the story while we walk on the beach. That way, the waves will hear it too."

We walked onto the sand, Godwin, Esther and me. And I started to tell my son about my fathers, and the woman who loved them, and the man who saved me. The waves listened, and caught my words in nets of spray, dragging them far out to sea.

Acknowledgements

I am deeply grateful to Lauren Parsons and Legend Press for taking a chance on this story. And special thanks to Lauren for her superb editing.

Thank you to Lucy Lamble and the team at the *Guardian* for supporting my trips and tales in East Africa, and for giving me a berth when I came back to London. And to all the editors and colleagues down the years who taught me what to ask, how to write and where to cut.

Thank you and cheers to the ladies of the Nairobi Book Club for making me laugh, pouring me wine, and always pushing me to keep at the book.

Eternal gratitude to my parents, sisters and brothers for their support, love, sheets and tea towels.

Thank you to all the people who helped me in Mogadishu, and to those who opened the doors of their lives to me in Somalia and elsewhere.

And finally, thank you to Lucy and Rachel: our gorgeous daughters and constant sources of light, hope, happiness and "hairy erics". And to David: a staunch believer, a patient listener, a gentle wielder of the red pen, and a shrewd observer. He is also, incidentally, a wonderful husband.

Thanks a million everyone.

THE LONG, HOT SUMMER

Kathleen MacMahon

The MacEntees are no ordinary family. Determined to be different from other people, they have carved out a place for themselves in Irish life by the sheer force of their own personalities. But when a horrifying act of violence befalls television star Alma, a chain of events is set in motion that will leave even the MacEntees struggling to make sense of who they are. As media storms rage about them and secrets rise to the surface, Deirdre, the flamboyant matriarch, is planning a birthday party for herself — and with it one final, shocking surprise . . .

A RISING MAN

Abir Mukherjee

Captain Sam Wyndham, a former Scotland Yard detective, is a new arrival to Calcutta. Desperately seeking a fresh start after his experiences during the Great War, he has been recruited to head up a new post in the police force. But with barely a moment to acclimatise to his new life, Wyndham is caught up in a murder investigation that will take him into the dark underbelly of the British Raj. A senior official has been murdered, and a note left in his mouth warns the British to quit India — or else. With rising political dissent and the stability of the Raj under threat, Wyndham and his colleagues embark upon an investigation that will take them from the luxurious parlours of wealthy British traders to the seedy opium dens of the city.